SPEECHES THAT CHANGED THE WORLD HISTORY

Famous PEOPLE'S Famous SPEECHES

Dr. Gagan Jain, *D.Litt.*

MG BOOKS
NEW DELHI (INDIA)

SPEECHES THAT CHANGED THE WORLD HISTORY

Famous PEOPLE'S Famous SPEECHES

Published by

MG BOOKS

An Imprint of

MAANU GRAPHICS

MAANU GRAPHICS
(PUBLISHERS OF GENERAL BOOKS)
5FF, Ganpati Bhawan, 21 Ansari Road,
Darya Ganj, New Delhi-110002
Ph: 65285220, 64138266
E-mail : maanugraphics@yahoo.com
mgbooks.maanu@yahoo.com

Printed at : Satyam Enterprises, Delhi

CONTENTS

FAMOUS PEOPLE'S FAMOUS SPEECHES

ADOLF HITLER

INTRODUCTION

ON April 20th, 1889 a child was born in the small town of Branau, Austria. The name of the child was Adolf Hitler. He was the son a Customs official Alois Hitler, and his third wife Klara.

Responsible for launching World War II under the leadership of National Socialist (Nazi) Party. Reich Chancellor In 1933 and Fuhrer in 1934, he climbed to power by ruthless execution of opponents. He was an arch enemy of England, USA, France and later on Russia. His defeat In World War 11 made him commit suicide. We give below excerpts from his speech delivered by him at Wilhelmshaven on 1st April 1939. It shows the working of his destructive mind and desire for revenge against political enemies.

Declaration of War on the US, Dec. 11th 1941

DEPUTIES, Men of the German Reichstag! A year of events of historical significance is drawing to an end. A year of great decisions lies ahead. In these serious times, I speak to you, deputies of the German Reichstag, as the representatives of the German nation. Beyond and above that, the whole German people should take note of this glance into the past, as well as of the coming decisions the present and future impose upon us.

After the renewed refusal of my peace offer in January 1940 by the then British Prime Minister and the clique which supported or dominated him, it became clear that this war - against all reasons of common sense and necessity - must be fought to its end. You know me, my old Party companions; you know I have always been an enemy of half measures or weak decisions.

If the Providence has so willed that the German people cannot be spared this fight, then I can only be grateful that it entrusted me with the leadership in this historic struggle which, for the next 500 or 1,000 years, will be described as decisive, not only for the history of Germany, but for the whole of Europe and indeed the whole world.

The German people and their soldiers are working and fighting today, not only for the present, but also for the coming, nay the most distant, generations. The Creator has imposed a historical revision on a unique scale upon us.

Shortly after the end of the campaign in Norway, the German Command was forced, first of all, to ensure the military security of the conquered areas. Since then the defences of the conquered countries have changed considerably. From Kirkenes to the Spanish Frontier there is a belt of great bases and fortifications; many airfields have been built, naval bases with protection for submarines, which are practically invulnerable from sea or air.

More than 1,500 new batteries have been planned and constructed. A network of roads and railways was constructed so that today communications from the Spanish Frontier to Petsano are independent of the sea. These installations in no way fall behind those of the Western Wall, and work continues incessantly on strengthening them. I am irrevocably determined to make the European Front unassailable by any enemy.

This defensive work was supplemented by offensive warfare. German surface and underwater naval Forces carried on their constant war of attrition against the British Merchant Navy and the ships in its service. The German Air Force supported these attacks by reconnaissance, by damaging enemy shipping, by numerous retaliatory raids which have given the English a better idea of the ' ever so charming ' war caused by their present Prime Minister.

In the middle of last year Germany was supported above all by Italy. For many months a great part of British power weighed heavily on the shoulders of Italy. Only because of their tremendous superiority in heavy tanks could the English create a temporary crisis in North Africa. On 24th March a small community of German-Italian units under Rommel's command began the counter-attack.

The German Africa Corps performed outstanding achievements though they were completely unaccustomed to the climate of this theatre of war. Just as once in Spain, now in North Africa Germans and Italians have taken up arms against the same enemy.

While with these bold measures the North African Front was again secured by the blood of German and Italian soldiers, the shadow of a terrible danger threatening Europe gathered overhead. Only in obedience of bitter necessity did I decide in my heart in 1939, to make the attempt, or at least, to create the prerequisites for a lasting peace in Europe by eliminating the causes of German-Russian tension.

This was psychologically difficult owing to the general attitude of the German people, and above all, of the party, towards Bolshevism. It was not difficult from a purely material point of view - because Germany was only intent on her economic interests in all the territories which England declared to be threatened by us and which she attacked with her promises of aid- for you will allow me to remind you that England, throughout the spring and late summer of 1939, offered its aid to numerous countries, declaring that it was our intention to invade those countries and thus deprive them of their liberty.

The German Reich and its Government were therefore able to affirm, with a clear conscience, that these allegations were false and had no bearing whatsoever on reality. Add to this the military realization that in the case of war, which British diplomacy was to force on the German people, a two front war would ensue and call for very great sacrifice.

When, on top of all this, the Baltic States and Rumania showed themselves prone to accept the British Pacts of assistance, and thus let it be seen that they, too, believed in such a threat, it was not only the right of the Reich Government, but its duty to fix the limits of German interests.

The countries in question, and above all, the Reich Government, could not but realize that the only factor, which could be a buttress against the East, was Germany. The moment they severed their connection with the German Reich, and entrusted their fate to the aid of that Power, which, in its proverbial selfishness has never rendered aid, but always requested it, they were lost. Yet the fate of these countries roused the sympathy of the German people. The winter struggle of the Finns forced on us mixed feelings of both bitterness and admiration. Admiration because we have a heart sensitive to sacrifice and heroism, being a nation of soldiers ourselves; bitterness, because with our eyes fixed on the menacing enemy in the West, and on the danger in the

East, we were not in a position to render any military assistance. As soon as it became evident that Soviet Russia decided it had the right to wipe out the nations living outside the limits of the German sphere of interest, as a result of that limitation of interests our subsequent relations were merely governed by utilitarian considerations, while both our reason and feelings were hostile.

With every month I became more convinced that the plans of the men in the Kremlin aimed at domination and annihilation of all Europe, I have had to disclose to the nation the full extent of the Russian military preparations. At a time when Germany had only a few divisions in the provinces bordering on Russia it would have been evident to a blind man that a concentration of power, of singular and historic, dimensions was taking place, and not in order to defend something which was threatened, but merely in order to attack an object it did not seem possible to defend. The lightening conclusion of the Western campaign, however, robbed the Moscow overlords of their hope of an early flagging of German power.

This did not alter their intentions - it merely led to a postponement of the date on which they intended to strike.

In the summer of 1941 they thought the time was ripe. A new Mongolian storm was now set to sweep over Europe. At the same time, however, Mr. Churchill spoke on the English aspect of the struggle with Germany. He saw fit, in a cowardly manner, to deny that in a secret session of House of Commons in 1940, that he had pointed out that the entry of Russia into the war would happen by 1941 at the very latest and was the most important factor, which would make a successful conclusion of the war possible.

This was also to enable England to take the offensive. In the spring of that year, Europe was to feel the full extent of the might of a world power, which seemed to dispose of inexhaustible human material and resources. Dark clouds began to gather on the European sky. For, my Deputies, what is Europe? There is no fitting geographical definition of our Continent, but only a national and cultural one.

Not the Urals form the frontier of our Continent, but the eternal line which divides the Eastern and Western conceptions of life. There was a time when Europe was that Greek Island into which Nordic tribes had penetrated in order to light a torch for the first time which from then onwards began slowly, but surely to brighten the world of man.

When these Greeks repulsed the invasion of the Persian conquerors they did not only defend their homeland, which was Greece, but that idea which we call Europe today. And then European concepts travelled from Hellas to Rome. The Greek spirit and culture, the Roman way of thinking and statesmanship, joined.

An empire was created which, to this day has not been equalled in its significance or creative power, let alone outdone. When, however the Roman legions were defending Rome against the African onslaught of Carthage and at last gained a victory, again it was not Rome they were fighting for, but the Europe of that time, which consisted of the Greek-Roman Empire. The next incursion against this homestead of European culture was carried out from the distant East. A terrible stream of barbarous, uncultured hordes sallied forth from the interior of Asia deep into the heart of the European Continent, burning, looting, murdering - a true scourge of the Lord. In the battle of the Catalonian fields Western Europe was formed. On the very ruins of Rome Western Europe was built, and its defence was a task, not only of the Romans, but also above all else of the Teutons.

In centuries to come the West, enlightened by Greek culture, built the Roman Empire and then expanded by the colonization of Teutons was able to call itself Europe. Whether it was the German Emperor who was repelling the attacks from the East on the Field of Lech or whether Africa was being pushed back from Spain in long fighting, it was also a struggle of Europe, coming into being, against a surrounding world alien in its very essence.

Once Rome had been given its due for the creative defence of this continent, Teutons took over the defence and the protection of a family of nations which might still differentiate and differ in their political structure and objective, but which nevertheless represented a cultural unity with blood ties. And it was from this Europe that a spiritual and cultural abundance went out, of which everyone must be aware who is willing to seek truth instead of denying it. Thus it was not England who brought culture to the Continent, but the offspring of Teutonic nationhood on the Continent who went as Anglo-Saxons and Normans to that Island made possible a development in a way surely unique. In just the same way, it was not America who discovered Europe, but the other way around.

And everything that America has not drawn from Europe may well appear worthy of admiration to a juda-ised, mixed race. Europe, on the other hand, sees in it a sign of cultural decay.

Deputies and Men of the German Reichstag, I had to make this survey, for the fight which, in the first months of this year, gradually began to become clear, and of which the German Reich is this time called to be the leader of, also far exceeds the interests of our nation and country.

Just as the Greeks once faced the Persians in war, and the Romans faced the Mongolians, the Spanish heroes defended not only Spain, but the whole of Europe against Africa, just so Germany is fighting today, not for herself, but for the entire Continent.

And it is fortunate that this realization is today so deep in the subconscious of most European nations that, whether by taking up their position openly or whether by a stream of volunteers, they are sharing in this struggle. When, on the 6th of April of this year, the German and Italian Armies took up their positions for the fight against Yugoslavia and Greece, it was the introduction to the great struggle in which we are still involved. The revolt in Belgrade, which led to the overthrow of the former Regent and his Government, was decisive for the future course of events in this part of Europe, for England was also a part to this putsch.

But the chief role was played by Soviet Russia. What I refused to Mr. Molotov on his visit to Berlin, Stalin now thought he could achieve by a revolutionary movement, even against our will. Without consideration for the agreements, which had been concluded, the intentions of the Bolsheviks in power grew still wider. The Pact of Friendship with the new revolutionary regime illuminated the closeness of the threatening danger like lightning.

The feats achieved by the German Armed Forces were given worthy recognition in the German Reichstag on the 4th of May. but what I was then unfortunately unable to express was the realization that we were progressing at tremendous speed toward a fight with a

State which was not yet intervening because it was not yet fully prepared, and because it was impossible to use the aerodromes and landing grounds at that time of year on account of the melting snow.

My deputies, when in 1940 I realized from communications in the English House of Commons and the observation of the Russian troop movements on our frontiers that there was the possibility of danger arising in the East of the Reich, I immediately gave orders to set up numerous new armoured motorized infantry divisions.

The logistics-for this were possible from the point of view both of material and personnel. I will give you, my Deputies, and indeed the whole German people, only one assurance: the more democracy needs more armaments, as is easily understandable, the harder National Socialist Germany works.

It was so in the past, it is no different today. Every year brings us increased, and above all, improved weapons. Hard decisions had to be made. In spite of my determination that under no circumstances to allow our opponent to make the first stab in our heart - in spite of that my decision was a very difficult one.

If democratic newspapers today declare that, had I known the strength of our Bolshevik opponents more accurately, I would have hesitated to attack, they understand the position just as little as they understand me.

I sought no war. On the contrary, I did everything to avoid it. But I would have been forgetful of my duty and responsibility if, in spite of realizing the inevitability of a fight by force of arms, I had failed to draw the only possible conclusions. In view of the mortal danger from Soviet Russia, not only to the German Reich, but also to all Europe, I decided, that if possible, a few days before the outbreak of this moral struggle, to give the signal to attack myself. Today, we have overwhelming and authentic proof that Russia intended to attack; we are also quite clear about the date on which the attack was to take place. In view of the great danger, the proportions of which we realise perhaps only today to the fullest extent, I can only thank God that He enlightened me at the proper time and that He gave me the strength to do what had to be done!

To this, not only millions of German soldiers owe their lives, but Europe its very existence. This much I may state today; had this wave of over 20,000 tanks, hundreds of divisions, tens of thousands of guns, accompanied by more than 10,000 aircraft, suddenly moved against the Reich, Europe would have been lost. Fate has destined a number of nations to forestall this attack, to ward it off with the sacrifice of their blood. Had Finland not decided immediately to take up arms for the second time, the leisurely bourgeois life of the other Nordic countries would soon have come to an end.

Had the German Reich not faced the enemy with her soldiers and arms, a flood would have swept over Europe, which once and for all would have finished the ridiculous British idea of maintaining the European balance of power in all its senselessness and stupid tradition. Had Slovaks, Hungarians, and Rumanians not taken over part of the protection of Europe, the Bolshevik hordes would have swept like Atilla's Huns over the Danubian countries, and at the cost of the Ionic Sea, Tartars and Mongols would have enforced today the revision of the Montreux Agreement. Had Italy, Spain and Croatia not sent their divisions, the establishment of a European defence Front would have been impossible, from which emanated the idea of a New Europe as propaganda to all other nations.

Sensing and realising this, volunteers have come from Northern and Western Europe, Norwegians, Danes, Dutchmen, Flemings, Belgians, even Frenchmen - volunteers who gave the struggle of the United Powers of the Axis the character of a European crusade - in the truest sense of the word. The time has not yet come to talk about the planning and the conduct of this campaign, but I believe that I may sketch in a few sentences about what has been achieved in this most gigantic of all struggles, in which memories of the various events might so easily fade because of the vastness of area and the great number of important events.

The attack began on 22nd of June; with considerable daring the frontier fortifications, which had been designed to resist any Russian advance against us, were passed over and on the 23rd Grodno fell. On the 24th Vilna and Kovno were taken after Brest-Litovsk had been occupied. On the 26th Duenaburg was in our hands and on 10th July, the first two great pincer battles of Bialystok and Minsk were concluded; 324,000 prisoners, 3,332 tanks and 1,809 guns fell to us.

Already, on 13th July, the Stalin Line had been broken through at all it's important points. On the 16th Smolensk fell after heavy fighting, and on the 19th German and Rumanian formations forced the crossing of the Dniester. On the 6th of August, the Battle of Smolensk was concluded in many pockets and again 310,000 Russians fell into German captivity, while 3,205 tanks and 3,120 guns were destroyed or captured.

Only three days later the fate of another Russian Army group was sealed and on 9th August another 103,000 Russians were taken prisoner in the Battle of Ouman; 317 tanks and 1,100 guns destroyed or captured. On 17th August Nicolaeff was taken, on the 21st, Kherson. On the same day the Battle of Gomel was concluded with 84,000 prisoners taken and 124 tanks, as well as 808 guns captured or destroyed. On the 21st August, the Russian positions between Lakes Peipus and Ilmen were broken through and on the 26th the bridgehead at Dniepropetrovsk fell into our hands.

On 28th August German troops marched into Reval and Boltisk Port after heavy fighting, while on the 30th the Finns took Viipuri. By conquering Schluesselburg on the 8th September, Leningrad was finally cut off, also from the South. On 6th September we succeeded in establishing bridgeheads on the Dnieper and on the 8th Poltava fell into our hands. On 9th September German formations stormed the citadel of Kiev and the occupation of Oesel was crowned by taking the Capital.

Only now have these great operations matured into the expected successes; on 27th September the Battle of Kiev was concluded; 665,000 prisoners began to move westwards, 884 tanks and 3,178 guns remained as booty in the pockets. As early as 2nd October the break-through battle on the Central Front began, while on 11th October the battle on the Sea of Azov was successfully concluded; again 107,000 prisoners, 212 tanks and 672 guns were counted.

On 16th October, German and Rumanian troops marched into Odessa following hard fighting. On 8th October the break-through on the Central Front was concluded with a new success, unique in history, when 663,000 prisoners were only part of its results; 1,242 tanks and 5,452 guns were either destroyed or captured. On 31st October, the conquest of Dagoo was concluded. On 24th October, the industrial centre of Kharkov was taken. On 28th October, the entrance of the Crimea was finally forced at great speed, and on 2nd November the capital Sinferopol was taken by storm. On 6th November we had pierced through the Crimea up to Kerch.

On 1st December, the total number of Soviet prisoners amounted to 3,806,865; the number of tanks destroyed or captured was 21,391, guns, 32,541 and aeroplanes, 17,322. During the same period 2,191 British planes were shot down. The Navy sank 4,170,611 g.r.t. of British shipping, the air force 2,346,080 g.r.t.; a total of 6,516,791 g.r.t. was thus destroyed.

All this had to be fought for by my staking health and life, and by efforts, which those at home can hardly imagine. Marching for an endless distance, tormented by heat and thirst, often held up by the mud of un-surfaced roads which would drive them almost to despair, exposed, from the Black Sea to the Arctic Sea, to the in-hospitability of a climate which from the blazing heat of the July and August days, dropped to the wintry storms of November and December, tortured by insects, suffering from dirt and vermin, freezing in the snow and ice, they have fought - the Germans and the Finns, Italians, Slovaks, Hungarians and Rumanians, the Croats, the volunteers from the North and West European countries, all in all the soldiers of the Eastern Front. The beginning of winter only will now check this movement; at the beginning of summer it will again no longer be possible to stop the movement. On this day I do not want to mention any individual section of the Armed Forces, I do not want to praise any particular command; they have all made a supreme effort. And yet, understanding and justice compel me to state one thing again and again; amongst our German soldiers the heaviest burden is born today, as in the past, by our matchless German infantry.

From 22nd June to 1st December the German Army lost in this heroic fight 158,773 killed, 563,082 wounded and 31,191 missing. The Air Force lost 3,231 killed, 8,453 wounded and 2,028 missing. The Navy lost 210 killed, 232 wounded and 115 missing. The total losses of the armed forces are thus 162,314 killed, 571,767 wounded and 33,334 missing.

That is to say, in killed and wounded slightly greater than the field of death at the Battle of the Somme, in missing a little less than half those missing at that time. But all were fathers and sons of our German people. And now permit me to define my attitude to that other world, which has its representative in that man, who while our soldiers are fighting in snow and ice, very tactfully likes to make his chats from the fireside, the man who is the main culprit of this war.

When in 1939 the conditions of our national interests in the then Polish State became more and more intolerable, I tried at first to eliminate those intolerable conditions by way of a peaceful settlement. For some time it seemed as though the Polish Government itself had seriously considered to agree to a sensible settlement.

I may add that in German proposals nothing was demanded that had not been German property in former times. On the contrary, we renounced very much of what, before the World War, had been German property. You will recall the dramatic development of that time, in which the sufferings of German nationals increased continuously. You, my deputies, are in the best position to gauge the extent of the blood sacrifice, if you compare it to the casualties of the present war.

The campaign in the East has so far cost the German armed forces about 160,000 killed; but in the midst of peace more than 62,000 Germans were killed during those months, some under the cruelest tortures. It could hardly be contested that the German Reich had had a right to object to such conditions on its Frontiers and to demand that they should case to exist and that it was entitled to think of its own safety; this could hardly be contested at a time when other countries were seeking elements of their safety even in foreign continents.

The problems, which had to be overcome, were of no territorial significance. Mainly they concerned Danzig and the union with the Reich of the torn-off province, East Prussia. More difficult were the cruel persecutions the Germans were exposed to, in Poland particularly. The other minorities, incidentally, had to suffer a fate hardly less bitter.

When in August the attitude of Poland - thanks to the carte blanche guarantee received from England - became still stiffer, the Government of the Reich found it necessary to submit, for the last time, a proposal on the basis of which we were willing to enter into negotiations with Poland - negotiations of which we fully and completely apprised the then British Ambassador. I may recall these proposals today: Proposal for the settlement of the problem of the Danzig Corridor and of the question of the German-Polish minorities. The situation between the German Reich and Poland has become so strained that any further incident may lead to a clash between the Armed Forces assembled on both sides. Any peaceful settlement must be so arranged that the events mainly responsible for the existing situation cannot occur again - a situation, which has caused a state of tension, not only in Eastern Europe, but also in other regions.

The cause of this situation lies in the impossible Frontiers laid down by the Versailles dictate and the inhuman treatment of the German minorities in Poland. I am now going to read the proposals in question. (Hitler then proceeded to read the first 12 points of these proposals.)'

Adolf HitlerAdolf HitlerAdolf HitlerAdolf Hitler

The same goes for the proposals for safeguarding the minorities. This is the offer of an agreement such as could not have been made in a more loyal and magnanimous form by any government other than the National Socialist Government of the German Reich. The Polish Government at that period refused even as much as to consider this proposal. The question then arises: how could such an unimportant State dare simply to refuse an offer of this nature and furthermore, not only indulge in further atrocities to its German inhabitants who had given that country the whole of its culture, but even order mobilization?

Perusal of documents of the Foreign Office in Warsaw

has now given us some surprising explanations. There was one who, with devilish lack of conscience, used all his influence to further the warlike intentions of Poland and to eliminate all possibilities of understanding.

The reports which the then Polish Ambassador in Washington, Count Potocki, sent to his Government are documents from which it may be seen with a terrifying clearness to what an extent one man alone and the forces driving him are responsible for the second World War.

The question next arises, how could this man fall into such fanatical enmity toward a country, which in the whole of its history has never done the least harm either to America or to him personally?

So far as Germany's attitude toward America is concerned, I have to state: One: Germany is perhaps the only great nation, which has never had a colony either in North or South America, or otherwise displayed there was any political activity, unless mention is made of the emigration of many millions of Germans and of their work, which, however, has only been to the benefit of the American Continent and of the U.S.A.,

Two: In the whole history of the coming into being and of the existence of the U.S.A. the German Reich has never adopted a politically unfriendly, let alone a hostile attitude, but on the contrary with the blood of many of its sons, it helped to defend the U.S.A.

The German Reich never took part in any war against the U.S.A. It itself had war imposed on it by the U.S.A. in 1917, and then for reasons which have been thoroughly revealed by an investigation committee set up by President Roosevelt himself. There are no other differences between the Germans and the American people, either territorial or political, which could possibly touch the interests let alone the existence of the U.S.A.

There was always a difference of Constitution, but that can't be a reason for hostilities so long as the one state does not try to interfere with the other. America is a Republic, a Democracy, and today is a Republic under strong authoritative leadership. The ocean lies between the two states. The divergences between Capitalist America and Bolshevik Russia, if such conceptions had any truth in them, would be much greater than between America led by a President and Germany led by a Fuhrer.

But it is a fact that the two conflicts between Germany and the U.S.A., were inspired by the same force and caused by two men in the U.S.A. – Wilson and Roosevelt.

History has already passed its verdict on Wilson, his name stands for one of the basest breaches of the given word, that led to the disruption not only among the so-called vanquished, but among the victors. This breach of his word alone made possible the dictate of Versailles. We know today that a group of interested financiers stood behind Wilson and made use of this paralytic professor because they hoped for increased business. The German people have had to pay for having believed this man with the collapse of their political and economic existence.

But why is there now another President of the U.S.A., who regards it as his only task to intensify anti-German feeling to the pitch of war? National Socialism came to power in Germany in the same years as Roosevelt was elected President. I understand only too well that a worldwide distance separates Roosevelt's ideas and my ideas.

Roosevelt comes from a rich family and belongs to the class whose path is smoothed in the Democracy. I am the only child of a small, poor family and had to fight my way by work and industry.

When the Great War came, Roosevelt occupied a position where he got to know only its pleasant consequences enjoyed by those who do business while others bleed. I was only one of those who carry out orders, as an ordinary soldier, and naturally returned from the war just as poor as I was in autumn of 1914. I shared the fate of millions, and Franklin Roosevelt only the fate of the so-called upper ten thousand.

After the war Roosevelt tried his hand at financial speculation; he made profits out of the inflation, out of the misery of others, while I, together with many hundreds of thousands more, lay in hospitals. When Roosevelt finally stepped on the political stage with all the advantages of his class, I was unknown and fought for the resurrection of my people.

When Roosevelt took his place at the head of the U.S.A., he was the candidate of a Capitalistic party which made use of him; when I became Chancellor of the German Reich, I was Fuehrer of the popular movement I had created. The powers behind Roosevelt were those powers I had fought at home. The Brains Trust were composed of people such as we had fought against in Germany as parasites and removed from public life.

Yet there is something in common between us. Roosevelt took over a State in a very poor economic condition, and I took over a Reich faced with complete ruin, also thanks to Democracy. In the U.S.A. there were 13 million unemployed, and in Germany 7,000,000 part-time workers. The finances of both States were in a bad way, and ordinary economic life could hardly be maintained. A development then started in the U.S.A. and in the German Reich, which will make it easy for posterity to pass a verdict on the correctness of the theories. While an unprecedented revival of economic life, culture and art took place in Germany under National Socialistic leadership within the space of a few years; President Roosevelt did not succeed in bringing about even the slightest improvements in his own country. And yet this work must have been much easier in the U.S.A. where there lived scarcely fifteen people on a square kilometre, as against 140 in Germany.

If such a country does not succeed in assuring economic prosperity, this must be a result either of the bad faith of its leaders in power, or of a total inefficiency on the part of the leading men. In scarcely five years, economic problems had been solved in Germany and unemployment had been overcome. During the same period, President Roosevelt had increased the State Debt of his country to an enormous extent, the decreased value of the dollar, had brought about a further disintegration of economic life, without diminishing the unemployment figures.

All this is not surprising if one bears in mind that the men he had called to support him, or rather, the men who had called him, belonged to the Jewish element, whose interests are all for disintegration and never for order. While speculation was being fought in National Socialist Germany, it thrived astoundingly under the Roosevelt regime.

Roosevelt's New Deal legislation was all-wrong, It was actually the biggest failure ever experienced by one man. There can be no doubt that a continuation of this economic policy would have undone this President in peace time, in spite of all his dialectical skill.

In a European State he would surely have come eventually before a State Court on a charge of deliberate waste of the national wealth; and he would have scarcely escaped at the hands of a civil court, on a charge of criminal business methods.

This fact was realized and fully appreciated also by many Americans including some of high standing. A threatening opposition was gathering over the head of this man. He guessed that the only salvation for him lay in diverting public attention from home to foreign policy. It is interesting to study in this connection the reports of the Polish Envoy in Washington, Potocki. He repeatedly points out that Roosevelt was fully aware of the danger threatening the card castle of his economic system with collapse, and that he was therefore urgently in need of a diversion in foreign policy.

He was strengthened in this resolve by the Jews surrounding him. Their Old Testament thirst for revenge saw in the U.S.A. an instrument for preparing a second "Purim" for the European nations, which were becoming increasingly anti-Semitic. The full diabolical meanness of Jewry rallied round this man, and he stretched out his hands.

Thus began the increasing efforts of the American President to create conflicts, to do everything to prevent conflicts from being peacefully solved. For years this man harboured one desire – that a conflict should break out somewhere in the world. The most convenient place would be in Europe, where American economy could be committed to the cause of one of the belligerents in such a way that a political interconnection of interests would arise calculated slowly to bring America nearer such a conflict.

This would thereby divert public interest from bankrupt economic policy at home towards foreign problem. His attitude to the German Reich in this spirit was particularly sharp. In 1937, Roosevelt made a number of speeches, including a particularly mean one pronounced in Chicago on 5th October 1937. Systematically he began to incite American public opinions against Germany. He threatened to establish a kind of Quarantine against the so-called Authoritarian States.

While making those increasingly spiteful and inflammatory speeches, President Roosevelt summoned the American Ambassadors to Washington to report to him. This event followed some further declarations of an insulting character; and ever since, the two countries have been connected with each other only through Charges d'Affairs.

From November 1938 onwards, his systematic efforts were directed towards sabotaging any possibility of an appeasement policy in Europe. In public, he was hypocritically pretending to be for peace; but at the same time he was threatening any country ready to pursue a policy of peaceful understanding with the freezing of assets, with economic reprisals, with demands for the repayment of loans, etc. Staggering information to this effort can be derived from the reports of Polish Ambassadors in Washington, London, Paris and Brussels.

In January, 1939, this man began to strengthen his campaign of incitement and threatened to take all possible Congressional measures against the Authoritarian States, with the exception of war, while alleging that other countries were trying to interfere in American affairs and insisting on the maintenance of the Monroe Doctrine, he himself began from March 1939 onwards, to meddle in European affairs which were no concern at all of the President of the U.S.A., since he does not understand those problems, and even if he did understand them and the historic background behind them, he would have just as little right to worry about the central European area as the German Reich has to judge conditions in a U.S. State and to take an attitude towards them.

But Mr. Roosevelt went even farther. In contradiction to all the tenets of international law, he declared that he would not recognize certain Governments which did not suit him, would not accept readjustments, would maintain Legations of States dissolved long before or actually set them up as legal Governments. He even went so far as to conclude agreements with such Envoys and thus to acquire a right simply to occupy foreign territories.

On 5th April 1939, came Roosevelt's famous appeal to

myself and the Duce. It was a clumsy combination of geographical and political ignorance and of the arrogance of the millionaire circles around him. It asked us to give undertakings to conclude non-aggression Pacts indiscriminately with any country, including mostly countries, which were not even free, since Mr. Roosevelt's allies had annexed them or changed them into Protectorates.

You will remember, my Deputies, that I then gave a polite and clear reply to this meddling gentleman. For some months at least, this stopped the flow of eloquence from this honest warmonger. But his place was taken by his honourable spouse. She declined to live with her sons in a world such as the one we have worked out. And quite right, for this is a world of labour and not of cheating and trafficking.

After a little rest, the husband of that woman came back on the scene and on the 4th November 1939, engineered the reversion of the Neutrality Law so as to suspend the ban on the export of arms, in favour of a one-sided delivery of arms to Germany's opponents. He then begins, somewhat as in Asia and in China, but by the roundabout way of economic infiltration to establish a community of interest destined to become operative at a later time.

In the same month, he recognizes, as a so-called Government in exile, a gang of Polish emigrants, whose only political foundation was a few million gold coins taken with them from Warsaw. On the 9th of April he goes on and he orders the blocking of Norwegian and Danish assets under the lying pretext of placing them beyond the German reach, although he knows perfectly well that the Danish Government in its financial administration is not in any way being interfered with, let alone controlled, by Germany.

To the various exiled Governments recognized by him, the Norwegian is now added. On the 15th May 1940, he recognizes the Dutch and Belgian émigré

Governments. This was followed by blocking Dutch and Belgian assets. His true mentality then comes clearly to light in a telegram of 15th June to the French Prime Minister, Reynaud. He advises him that the American government will double its help to France, provided that France continues the war against Germany. So as to give still greater expression to this, his wish for a continuation of the war, he issues a declaration that the American Government will not recognize the results of the conquest of territories – i.e., the restoration to Germany of lands, which had been stolen from her.

I don't need to assure you, Members of the Reichstag, that it is a matter of complete indifference to every German Government whether the President of the U.S.A. recognizes the frontiers of Europe or no, and that this indifference will likewise continue, in the future. I merely quote this to illustrate the methodical incitement, which has come from this man who speaks hypocritically of peace, but always urges to war.

But now he is seized with fear that if peace is brought about in Europe, his squandering of billions of money on armaments will be looked upon, since nobody will attack America, as plain fraud – and so he then must himself provoke this attack upon his country.

On the 17th July 1940, the American President orders the blocking of French assets with a view, as he puts it, to placing them beyond German reach, but really in order to transfer the French gold from Casablanca to America with the assistance of an American cruiser.

In July 1940 he tries by enlisting American citizens in the British Air Force and by training British airmen in the U.S.A. to pave ever better the way to war.

In August 1940, a military programme is jointly drawn up between the U.S.A. and Canada. To make the establishment of a Canadian-U.S. Defence Committee plausible – plausible at least to the biggest fools – he invents from time to time, crises, by means of which he pretends that America is being threatened with aggression.

This he wishes to impress upon the American people by suddenly returning on the 3rd April to Washington with all speed on account of the alleged danger of the situation. In September 1940 he draws still nearer to the war. He turns over to the British Fleet 50 destroyers of the American Navy in return for which, to be sure, he takes over several British bases in North and South America.

From all these actions, it may be clearly seen how, with all his hatred for Socialist Germany, he forms the resolution of taking over, as safely and securely as possible, the British Empire in the moment of its downfall. Since England is no longer in the position to pay cash for all the American deliveries, he imposes the Lease-Lend Law on the American people.

He thus receives powers to lend or lease support to countries, the defence of which may appear to him as vital in American's interests. Then, once more he takes a further step. As far back as the 9th December 1939, American naval forces in the security zone handed over the German ship Columbus to the British navy. Due to circumstances she had to be sunk. On the same day, U.S. forces cooperated to prevent the attempted escape of the German steamer Arauca.

On the 27th January 1940, a U.S. cruiser in contravention of International Law advised enemy naval forces of the movements of the German steamers, Arauca, La Plata and Mangoni.

On the 27th June 1940, he ordered, in complete contravention of International Law, a restriction of the freedom of movements of foreign ships in U.S. harbours.

In November, 1940, he ordered the German ships Reugeu, Niedervald and Rhein to be shadowed by American ships until these steamers were compelled to scuttle themselves so as not to fall into enemy hands.

On 30th April 1941, followed the opening up of the Red Sea to U.S. ships, so that they could carry supplies to the British armies in the Near East. Meanwhile, in March, the American authorities requisitioned all German ships. In the course of this German nationals were treated in a most inhuman manner, and in contravention of all notions of international law designated places of residence were assigned them, travelling restrictions imposed upon them, and so on.

Two German officers who had escaped from Canadian captivity, were – again contrary to all the dictates of international law – handcuffed and handed over to the Canadian authorities.

On the 24th March the same President who stands against every aggression, acclaimed Simovitch and his companions who gained their positions by aggression and by removing the lawful government of their country. Roosevelt had some months before sent Colonel Donovan, a completely unworthy creature, to the Balkans, to Sofia and Belgrade, to engineer a rising against Germany and Italy.

In April, he promised help to Yugoslavia and Greece under the Lend-Lease Act. At the end of April, this man recognized the Yugoslav and Greek émigré governments, and once more against international law, blocked Yugoslav and Greek assets.

From the middle of April onwards, the American watch over the Western Atlantic by U.S.A. patrols was extended, and reports were made to the British.

On the 26th April, Roosevelt transferred to the British 20 motor-torpedo-boats and at the same time, British war-ships were being repaired in U.S. ports.

On 5th May, the illegal arming and repairing of Norwegian ships for England took place.

On 4th June American troop transports arrived in Greenland, to build airdromes.

On 9th June, came the first British report that, on Roosevelt's orders, a U.S. warship had attacked a German u-boat with depth charges near Greenland.

On 4th June, German assets in the U.S.A. were illegally blocked. On the 7th June, Roosevelt demanded under mendacious pretexts, that German consuls should be withdrawn and German consulates closed. He also demanded the closing of the German Press Agency, Trans-ocean, the German Information Library and the German Reichsbank Central Office. On 6th and 7th July, American Forces occupied Iceland, which is within the German fighting zone, on the orders of Roosevelt. He intended, first of all, to force Germany to make war and to make the German U-boat warfare as ineffective as it was in 1915-16. At the same time he promised American help to the Soviet Union.

On 10th June, the Navy Minister, Knox, suddenly announced an American order to open fire on Axis warships.

On 4th September, the U.S. destroyer Greer, obeying orders, operated with British aircraft against German U-boats in the Atlantic. Five days later, a German U-boat noticed the U.S. destroyer acting as escort in a British convoy.
On 11th September Roosevelt finally made a speech in which he confirmed and repeated his order to fire on all Axis ships.

On 29th September, U.S. escort-vessels attacked a German U-boat with depth charges East of Greenland.

On 7th October, the U.S. destroyer Kearney acting as an escort vessel for Britain again attacked a German U-boat with depth charges. Finally, on 6th November, U.S. forces illegally seized the German steamer, Odenwald, and took it to an American port where the crew were taken prisoner. I will pass over the insulting attacks made by this so-called President against me. That he calls me a gangster is uninteresting. After all, this expression was not coined in Europe but in America, no doubt because such gangsters are lacking here. Apart from this, I cannot be insulted by Roosevelt for I consider him mad, just as Wilson was.

I don't need to mention what this man has done for years in the same way against Japan. First he incites war, then falsifies the causes, then odiously wraps himself in a cloak of Christian hypocrisy and slowly but surely leads mankind to war, not without calling God to witness the honesty of his attack - in the approved manner of an old Freemason.

I think you have all found it a relief that now, at last, one State has been the first to take the step of protest against his historically unique and shameless ill treatment of truth, and of right - which protest this man has desired and about which he cannot complain. The fact that the Japanese Government, which has been negotiating for years with this man, has at last become tired of being mocked by him, in such an unworthy way, fills us all, the German people, and I think, all other decent people in the world, with deep satisfaction. We have seen what the Jews have done to Soviet Russia. We have made the acquaintance of the Jewish Paradise on earth. Millions of German soldiers have been able to see this country where the international Jews have destroyed people and property. The President of the U.S.A. ought finally to understand - I say this only because of his limited intellect - that we know that the aim of this struggle is to destroy one State after another.

But the present German Reich has nothing more in common with the old Germany. And we, for our part, will now do what this provocateur has been trying to do so much for years. Not only because we are the ally of Japan, but also because Germany and Italy have enough insight and strength to comprehend that, in these historic times, the existence or non-existence of our nations, is being decided perhaps for ever.

We clearly see the intention of the rest of the world towards us. They reduced Democratic Germany to hunger. They would destroy our National Socialism. When Churchill and Roosevelt state that they want to build up a new social order, it is like a hairdresser with a baldhead recommending an ineffective hair-restorer. These men, who live in the most socially backward states, have misery and distress enough in their own countries to occupy themselves with the distribution of foodstuffs.

As for the German nation, it needs charity from neither Mr. Churchill nor from Mr. Roosevelt, let alone from Mr. Eden. It wants only its rights! It will secure for itself this right to life even if thousands of Churchill's and Roosevelt's conspire against it.

In the whole history of the German nation, of nearly 2,000 years, it has never been so united as today and, thanks to National Socialism it will remain united in the future. It probably has never seen so clearly, and rarely been so conscious of its honour.

As a consequence of the further extension of President Roosevelt's policy, which is aimed at unrestricted world domination and dictatorship the U.S.A. together with England have not hesitated from using any means to dispute the rights of the German, Italian and Japanese nations to the base of their natural existence.

The Governments of the U.S.A. and of England have therefore resisted, not only now but also for all time, every just understanding meant to bring about a better New Order in the world. Since the beginning of the war the American president, Roosevelt, has been guilty of a series of the worst crimes against international law; illegal seizure of ships and other property of German and Italian nationals, coupled with the threat to, and looting of, those who were deprived of their liberty by internment.

Roosevelt's ever increasing attacks finally went so far

that he ordered the American navy to attack everywhere ships under the German and Italian flags, and to sink them – this in gross violation of international law. American ministers boasted of having destroyed German submarines in this criminal way. German and Italian merchant ships were attacked by American cruisers, captured and their crews imprisoned.

With no attempt at an official denial there has now been revealed in America President Roosevelt's plan by which, at the latest in 1943, Germany and Italy were to be attacked in Europe by military means. In this way the sincere efforts of Germany and Italy to prevent an extension of the war and to maintain relations with the U.S.A. in spite of the unbearable provocations which have been carried on for years by President Roosevelt, have been frustrated. Germany and Italy have been finally compelled, in view of this, and in loyalty to the Tri-Partite act, to carry on the struggle against the U.S.A. and England jointly and side by side with Japan for the defence and thus for the maintenance of the liberty and independence of their nations and empires. The Three Powers have therefore concluded the following Agreement, which was signed in Berlin today:

"In their unshakable determination not to lay down arms until the joint war against the U.S.A. and England reaches a successful conclusion, the German, Italian, and Japanese governments have agreed on the following points:

Article 1. Germany, Italy and Japan will wage the common war forced upon them by the U.S.A. and England with all the means of power at their disposal, to a victorious conclusion.

Article II. Germany, Italy and Japan undertake not to conclude an armistice or peace with the U.S.A., or with England without complete mutual understanding.

Article III. Germany, Italy and Japan will continue the

closest cooperation even after the victorious conclusion of the war in order to bring about a just new order in the sense of the Tri-Partite Pact concluded by them on the 27th September 1940.

Article IV. This Agreement comes into force immediately after signature and remains in force as long as the Tri-Partite Pact of 27th September 1940. The Signatory Powers will confer in time before this period ends about the future form of the cooperation provided for in Article III of this agreement."
Deputies, Members of the German Reichstag:

Ever since my last peace proposal of July 1940 was rejected, we have realized that this struggle has to be fought out to its last implications. That the Anglo-Saxon-Jewish-Capitalist World finds itself now in one and the same Front with Bolshevism does not surprise us National Socialists: we have always found them in company.

We have concluded the struggle successfully inside Germany and have destroyed our adversaries after 16 years struggle for power. When 23 years ago, I decided to enter political life and to lift this nation out of its decline, I was a nameless, unknown soldier. Many among you know how difficult were the first few years of this struggle.

From the time when the Movement consisted of seven men, until we took over power in January 1933, the path was so miraculous that only Providence itself with its blessing could have made this possible.

Today I am at the head of the strongest Army in the world, the largest Air Force and of a proud Navy. Behind and around me stands the Party with which I became great and which has become great through me. The enemies I see before me are the same enemies as 20 years ago, but the path along which I look forward cannot be compared with that on which I look back. The German people recognizes the decisive hour of its existence, millions of soldiers do their duty, millions of German peasants and workers, women and girls, produce bread for the home country and arms for the Front. We are allied with strong peoples, who in the same need are faced with the same enemies. The American President and his Plutocratic clique have mocked us as the Have-nots – that is true, but the Have-nots will see to it that they are not robbed of the little they have.

You, my fellow party members, know my unalterable determination to carry a fight once begun to its successful conclusion. You know my determination in such a struggle to be deterred by nothing, to break every resistance, which must be broken. In September 1939 I assured you that neither force of arms nor time would overcome Germany. I will assure my enemies that neither force of arms nor time nor any internal doubts, can make us waver in the performance of our duty.

When we think of the sacrifices of our soldiers, any sacrifice made by the Home Front is completely unimportant. When we think of those who in past centuries have fallen for the Reich, then we realize the greatness of our duty. But anybody who tries to evade this duty has no claim to be regarded in our midst as a fellow German. Just as we were unmercifully hard in our struggle for power we shall be unmercifully hard in the struggle to maintain our nation. At a time when thousands of our best men are dying nobody must expect to live who tries to depreciate the sacrifices made at the Front. Immaterial under what camouflage he tries to disturb this German Front, to undermine the resistance of our people, to weaken the authority of the regime, to sabotage the achievements of the Home Front, he shall die for it!

But with the difference that this sacrifice brings the highest honour to the soldier at the Front, whereas the other dies dishonoured and disgraced.

Our enemies must not deceive themselves - in the 2,000 years of German history known to us, our people have never been more united than today. The Lord of the Universe has treated us so well in the past years that we bow in gratitude to a providence which has allowed us to be members of such a great nation. We thank Him that we also can be entered with honour into the everlasting book of German history!

DWIGHT D. EISENHOWER

INTRODUCTION

Born in Texas in 1890, brought up in Abilene, Kansas, Eisenhower was the third of seven sons. Stationed in Texas as a second lieutenant, he met Mamie Geneva Doud, whom he married in 1916.

In his early Army career, he excelled in staff assignments, serving under Generals John J. Pershing, Douglas MacArthur, and Walter Krueger. After Pearl Harbor, General George C. Marshall called him to Washington for a war plans assignment. He commanded the Allied Forces landing in North Africa in November 1942; on D-Day, 1944, he was Supreme Commander of the troops invading France. After the war, he became President of Columbia University, then took leave to assume supreme command over the new NATO forces being assembled in 1951. Republican emissaries to his headquarters near Paris persuaded him to run for President in 1952. He was president of U.S.A. from 1953 to 1961.

Farewell Address, January 17, 1961

MY fellow Americans:

This evening I come to you with a message of leave-taking and farewell, and to share a few final thoughts with you, my countrymen.Like every other citizen, I wish the new President, and all who will labor with him, Godspeed. I pray that the coming years will be blessed with peace and prosperity for all.

We now stand ten years past the midpoint of a century that has witnessed four major wars among great nations. Three of these involved our own country. Despite these holocausts America is today the strongest, the most influential and most productive nation in the world. Understandably proud of this pre-eminence, we yet realize that America's leadership and prestige depend, not merely upon our unmatched material progress, riches and military strength, but on how we use our power in the interests of world peace and human betterment.

Progress toward these noble goals is persistently threatened by the conflict now engulfing the world. It commands our whole attention, absorbs our very beings. We face a hostile ideology global in scope, atheistic in character, ruthless in purpose, and insidious in method. Unhappily the danger it poses promises to be of indefinite duration. To meet it successfully, there is called for, not so much the emotional and transitory sacrifices of crisis, but rather those which enable us to carry forward steadily, surely, and without complaint the burdens of a prolonged and complex struggle—with liberty the stake. Only thus shall we remain, despite every provocation, on our charted course toward permanent peace and human betterment. A vital element in keeping the peace is our military establishment. Our arms must be mighty, ready for instant action, so that no potential aggressor may be tempted to risk his own destruction. Our military organization today bears little relation to that known by any of my predecessors in peacetime, or indeed by the fighting men of World War II or Korea.

Until the latest of our world conflicts, the United States had no armaments industry. American makers of plowshares could, with time and as required, make swords as well. But now we can no longer risk emergency improvisation of national defense; we have been compelled to create a permanent armaments industry of vast proportions. Added to this, three and a half million men and women are directly engaged in the defense establishment. We annually spend on military security more than the net income of all United States corporations.

This conjunction of an immense military establishment and a large arms industry is new in the American experience. The total influence—economic, political, even spiritual—is felt in every city, every State house, every office of the Federal government. We recognize the imperative need for this development. Yet we must not fail to comprehend its grave implications. Our toil, resources and livelihood are all involved; so is the very structure of our society.

In the councils of government, we must guard against the acquisition of unwarranted influence, whether sought or unsought, by the military-industrial complex. The potential for the disastrous rise of misplaced power exists and will persist. We must never let the weight of this combination endanger our liberties or democratic processes. We should take nothing for granted. Only an alert and knowledgeable citizenry can compel the proper meshing of the huge industrial and military machinery of defense with our peaceful methods and goals, so that security and liberty may prosper together. Akin to, and largely responsible for the sweeping changes in our industrial-military posture, has been the technological revolution during recent decades. In this revolution, research has become central, it also becomes more formalized complex, and costly. A steadily increasing share is conducted for, by, or at the direction of, the Federal government.

Today, the solitary inventor, tinkering in his shop, has been overshadowed by task forces of scientists in laboratories and testing fields. In the same fashion, the free university, historically the fountainhead of free ideas and scientific discovery, has experienced a revolution in the conduct of research. Partly because of the huge costs involved, a government contract becomes virtually a substitute for intellectual curiosity. For every old blackboard there are now hundreds of new electronic computers.

The prospect of domination of the nation's scholars by Federal employment, project allocations, and the power of money is ever present—and is gravely to be regarded. Yet, in holding scientific research and discovery in respect, as we should, we must also be alert to the equal and opposite danger that public policy could itself become the captive of a scientific-technological elite. It is the task of statesmanship to mold, to balance, and to integrate these and other forces, new and old, within the principles of our democratic system-ever aiming toward the supreme goals of our free society.

Another factor in maintaining balance involves the element of time. As we peer into society's future, we—you and I, and our government—must avoid the impulse to live only for today, plundering for, for our own ease and convenience, the precious resources of tomorrow. We cannot mortgage the material assets of our grandchildren without asking the loss also of their political and spiritual heritage. We want democracy to survive for all generations to come, not to become the insolvent phantom of tomorrow.

Down the long lane of the history yet to be written America knows that this world of ours, ever growing smaller, must avoid becoming a community of dreadful fear and hate, and be, instead, a proud confederation of mutual trust and respect.

Dwight Eisenhower

FRANKLIN DELANO ROOSEVELT

INTRODUCTION

Franklin Delano Roosevelt was born in 1882 at Hyde Park, New York now a national historic site, he attended Harvard University and Columbia Law School.

On St. Patrick's Day, 1905, he married Eleanor Roosevelt. He was elected President in November 1932, to the first of four terms. In 1936 he was re-elected by a top-heavy margin. When the Japanese attacked Pearl Harbor on December 7, 1941, Roosevelt directed organization of the Nation's manpower and resources for global war. As the war drew to a close, Roosevelt's health deteriorated, and on April 12, 1945, while at Warm Springs, Georgia, he died of a cerebral hemorrhage.

Pearl Harbor Speech, December 8, 1941

TO the Congress of the United States

Yesterday, Dec. 7, 1941 - a date which will live in infamy - the United States of America was suddenly and deliberately attacked by naval and air forces of the Empire of Japan.

The United States was at peace with that nation and, at the solicitation of Japan, was still in conversation with the government and its emperor looking toward the maintenance of peace in the Pacific.

Indeed, one hour after Japanese air squadrons had commenced bombing in Oahu, the Japanese ambassador to the United States and his colleagues delivered to the Secretary of State a formal reply to a recent American message. While this reply stated that it seemed useless to continue the existing diplomatic negotiations, it contained no threat or hint of war or armed attack.

It will be recorded that the distance of Hawaii from Japan makes it obvious that the attack was deliberately planned many days or even weeks ago. During the intervening time, the Japanese government has deliberately sought to deceive the United States by false statements and expressions of hope for continued peace.

The attack yesterday on the Hawaiian islands has caused severe damage to American naval and military forces. Very many American lives have been lost. In addition, American ships have been reported torpedoed on the high seas between San Francisco and Honolulu.

Yesterday, the Japanese government also launched an attack against Malaya.

Last night, Japanese forces attacked Hong Kong.

Last night, Japanese forces attacked Guam.

Last night, Japanese forces attacked the Philippine Islands.

Last night, the Japanese attacked Wake Island.

This morning, the Japanese attacked Midway Island.

Japan has, therefore, undertaken a surprise offensive extending throughout the Pacific area. The facts of yesterday speak for themselves. The people of the United States have already formed their opinions and well understand the implications to the very life and safety of our nation.

As commander in chief of the Army and Navy, I have directed that all measures be taken for our defense.

Always will we remember the character of the onslaught against us.

No matter how long it may take us to overcome this premeditated invasion, the American people in their righteous might will win through to absolute victory.

I believe I interpret the will of the Congress and of the people when I assert that we will not only defend ourselves to the uttermost, but will make very certain that this form of treachery shall never endanger us again.

Hostilities exist. There is no blinking at the fact that our people, our territory and our interests are in grave danger.

With confidence in our armed forces - with the unbounding determination of our people - we will gain the inevitable triumph - so help us God.

I ask that the Congress declare that since the unprovoked and dastardly attack by Japan on Sunday,

Dec. 7, a state of war has existed between the United States and the Japanese empire.
Franklin Roosevelt

State of the Union, 1945

IN considering the state of the Union, the war and the peace that is to follow are naturally uppermost in the minds of all of us.

This war must be waged—it is being waged—with the greatest and most persistent intensity. Everything we are and have is at stake. Everything we are and have will be given. American men, fighting far from home, have already won victories which the world will never forget.

We have no question of the ultimate victory. We have no question of the cost. Our losses will be heavy.

We and our allies will go on fighting together to ultimate total victory.

We have seen a year marked, on the whole, by substantial progress toward victory, even though the year ended with a set-back for our arms, when the Germans launched a ferocious counterattack into Luxemburg and Belgium with the obvious objective of cutting our line in the center.

Our men have fought with indescribable and unforgettable gallantry under most difficult conditions, and our German enemies have sustained considerable losses while failing to obtain their objectives.

The high tide of this German effort was reached 2 days after Christmas. Since then we have reassumed the offensive, rescued the isolated garrison at Bastogne, and forced a German withdrawal along the whole line of the salient. The speed with which we recovered from this savage attack was largely possible because we have one supreme commander in complete control of all the Allied armies in France. General Eisenhower has faced this period of trial with admirable calm and resolution and with steadily increasing success. He has my complete confidence.

Further desperate attempts may well be made to break our lines, to slow our progress. We must never make the mistake of assuming that the Germans are beaten until the last Nazi has surrendered.

And I would express another most serious warning against the poisonous effects of enemy propaganda.

The wedge that the Germans attempted to drive in western Europe was less dangerous in actual terms of winning the war than the wedges which they are continually attempting to drive between ourselves and our allies.

Every little rumor which is intended to weaken our faith in our allies is like an actual enemy agent in our midst—seeking to sabotage our war effort. There are, here and there, evil and baseless rumors against the Russians—rumors against the British—rumors against our own American commanders in the field.

When you examine these rumors closely, you will observe that every one of them bears the same trademark—"Made in Germany."

We must resist this divisive propaganda—we must destroy it— with the same strength and the same determination that our fighting men are displaying as they resist and destroy the panzer divisions.

In Europe, we shall resume the attack and—despite temporary setbacks here or there—we shall continue the attack relentlessly until Germany is completely defeated.

It is appropriate at this time to review the basic strategy which has guided us through 3 years of war, and which will lead, eventually, to total victory.

The tremendous effort of the first years of this war was directed toward the concentration of men and supplies in the various theaters of action at the points where they could hurt our enemies most.

It was an effort—in the language of the military men—of deployment of our forces. Many battles—essential battles—were fought; many victories—vital victories—were won. But these battles and these victories were fought and won to hold back the attacking enemy, and to put us in positions from which we and our allies could deliver the final, decisive blows.

In the beginning our most important military task was to prevent our enemies—the strongest and most violently aggressive powers that ever have threatened civilization—from winning decisive victories. But even while we were conducting defensive, delaying actions, we were looking forward to the time when we could wrest the initiative from our enemies and place our superior resources of men and materials into direct competition with them.

It was plain then that the defeat of either enemy would require the massing of overwhelming forces—ground, sea, and air—in positions from which we and our allies could strike directly against the enemy homelands and destroy the Nazi and Japanese war machines.

In the case of Japan, we had to await the completion of extensive preliminary operations—operations designed to establish secure supply lines through the Japanese outer-zone defenses. This called for overwhelming sea power and air power—supported by ground forces strategically employed against isolated outpost garrisons.

Always—from the very day we were attacked—it was right militarily as well as morally to reject the arguments of those shortsighted people who would have had us throw Britain and Russia to the Nazi wolves and concentrate against the Japanese. Such people urged that we fight a purely defensive war against Japan while allowing the domination of all the rest of the world by nazi-ism and fascism.

In the European theater the necessary bases for the massing of ground and airpower against Germany were already available in Great Britain. In the Mediterranean area we could begin ground operations against major elements of the German Army as rapidly as we could put troops in the field, first in north Africa and then in Italy.

Therefore, our decision was made to concentrate the bulk of our ground and air forces against Germany until her utter defeat. That decision was based on all these factors; and it was also based on the realization that, of our two enemies, Germany would be more able to digest quickly her conquests, the more able quickly to convert the manpower and resources of her conquered territory into a war potential.

We had in Europe two active and indomitable allies—Britain and the Soviet Union—and there were also the heroic resistance movements in the occupied countries, constantly engaging and harassing the Germans.

We cannot forget how Britain held the line, alone, in 1940 and 1941; and at the same time, despite ferocious bombardment from the air, built up a tremendous armaments industry which enabled her to take the offensive at El Alamein in 1942.

We cannot forget the heroic defense of Moscow and Leningrad and Stalingrad, or the tremendous Russian offensives of 1943 and 1944 which destroyed formidable German armies.

Nor can we forget how, for more than 7 long years, the Chinese people have been sustaining the barbarous attacks of the Japanese and containing large enemy forces on the vast areas of the Asiatic mainland.

In the future we must never forget the lesson that we have learned— that we must have friends who will work with us in peace as they have fought at our side in war.

As a result of the combined effort of the Allied forces, great military victories were achieved in 1944: The liberation of France, Belgium, Greece, and parts of the Netherlands, Norway, Poland, Yugoslavia, and Czechoslovakia; the surrender of Rumania and Bulgaria; the invasion of Germany itself and Hungary; the steady march through the Pacific islands to the Philippines, Guam and Saipan; and the beginnings of a mighty air offensive against the Japanese islands.

Now, as this Seventy-ninth Congress meets, we have reached the most critical phase of the war.

The greatest victory of the last year was, of course, the successful breach on June 6, 1944, of the German "impregnable" sea wall of Europe and the victorious sweep of the Allied forces through France and Belgium and Luxemburg—almost to the Rhine itself.

The cross-channel invasion of the Allied armies was the greatest amphibious operation in the history of the world. It overshadowed all other operations in this or any other war in its immensity. Its success is a tribute to the fighting courage of the soldiers who stormed the beaches—to the sailors and merchant seamen who put the soldiers ashore and kept them supplied—and to the military and naval leaders who achieved a real miracle of planning and execution. And it is also a tribute to the ability of two nations, Britain and America, to plan together, and work together, and fight together in perfect cooperation and perfect harmony.

This cross-channel invasion was followed in August by a second great amphibious operation, landing troops in Southern France. In this, the same cooperation and the same harmony existed between the American, French, and other Allied forces based in north Africa and Italy.

The success of the two invasions is a tribute also to the ability of many men and women to maintain silence, when a few careless words would have imperiled the lives of hundreds of thousands, and would have jeopardized the whole vast undertakings.

These two great operations were made possible by success in the Battle of the Atlantic.

Without this success over German submarines, we could not have built up our invasion forces or air forces in Great Britain, nor could we have kept a steady stream of supplies flowing to them after they had landed in France.

The Nazis, however, may succeed in improving their submarines and their crews. They have recently increased their U-boat activity. The battle of the Atlantic—like all campaigns in this war—demands eternal vigilance. But the British, Canadian, and other Allied Navies, together with our own, are constantly on the alert.

The tremendous operations in Western Europe have overshadowed in the public mind the less spectacular but vitally important Italian front. Its place in the strategic conduct of the war in Europe has been obscured, and—by some people unfortunately—underrated.

It is important that any misconception on that score be corrected—now.

What the Allied forces in Italy are doing is a well-considered part in our strategy in Europe, now aimed at only one objective—the total defeat of the Germans. These valiant forces in Italy are continuing to keep a substantial portion of the German Army under constant pressure—including some 20 first-line German divisions and the necessary supply and transport and replacement troops—all of which our enemies need so badly elsewhere.

Over very difficult terrain and through adverse weather conditions, our Fifth Army and the British Eighth Army—reinforced by units from other United Nations, including a brave and well-equipped unit of the Brazilian Army—have, in the past year, pushed north through bloody Cassino and the Anzio beachhead, and through Rome until now they occupy heights overlooking the valley of the Po.

The greatest tribute which can be paid to the courage

and fighting ability of these splendid soldiers in Italy is to point out that although their strength is about equal to that of the Germans they oppose, the Allies have been continuously on the offensive.

That pressure, that offensive, by our troops in Italy will continue.

The American people—and every soldier now fighting in the Apennines—should remember that the Italian front has not lost any of the importance which it had in the days when it was the only Allied front in Europe.

In the Pacific during the past year, we have conducted the fastest-moving offensive in the history of modern warfare. We have driven the enemy back more than 3,000 miles across the Central Pacific.

A year ago, our conquest of Tarawa was a little more than a month old.

A year ago, we were preparing for our invasion of Kwajalein, the second of our great strides across the Central Pacific to the Philippines.

A year ago, General MacArthur was still fighting in New Guinea almost 1,500 miles from his present position in the Philippine Islands.

We now have firmly established bases in the Mariana Islands, from which our Superfortresses bomb Tokyo itself—and will continue to blast Japan in ever-increasing numbers.

Japanese forces in the Philippines have been cut in two. There is still hard fighting ahead—costly fighting. But the liberation of the Philippines will mean that Japan has been largely cut off from her conquests in the East Indies.

The landing of our troops on Leyte was the largest

amphibious operation thus far conducted in the Pacific.

Moreover, these landings drew the Japanese Fleet into the first great sea battle which Japan has risked in almost 2 years. Not since the night engagements around Guadalcanal in November-December 1942, had our Navy been able to come to grips with major units of the Japanese Fleet. We had brushed against their fleet in the first battle of the Philippine Sea in June 1944, but not until last October were we able really to engage a major portion of the Japanese Navy in actual combat. The naval engagement which raged for 3 days was the heaviest blow ever struck against Japanese sea power.

As a result of that battle, much of what is left of the Japanese Fleet has been driven behind the screen of islands that separates the Yellow Sea, the China Sea, and the Sea of Japan from the Pacific.

Our Navy looks forward to any opportunity which the lords of the Japanese Navy will give us to fight them again.

The people of this Nation have a right to be proud of the courage and fighting ability of the men in the armed forces—on all fronts. They also have a right to be proud of American leadership which has guided their sons into battle.

The history of the generalship of this war has been a history of teamwork and cooperation, of skill and daring. Let me give you one example out of last year's operations in the Pacific.

Last September Admiral Halsey led American naval task forces into Philippine waters and north to the East China Sea, and struck heavy blows at Japanese air and sea power.

At that time it was our plan to approach the Philippines

by further stages, taking islands which we may call A, C, and E. However, Admiral Halsey reported that a direct attack on Leyte appeared feasible. When General MacArthur received the reports from Admiral Halsey's task forces, he also concluded that it might be possible to attack the Japanese in the Philippines directly—by passing islands, A, C, and E.

Admiral Nimitz thereupon offered to make available to General MacArthur several divisions which had been scheduled to take the intermediate objectives. These discussions, conducted at great distances, all took place in one day.

General MacArthur immediately informed the Joint Chiefs of Staff here in Washington that he was prepared to initiate plans for an attack on Leyte in October. Approval of the change in plan was given on the same day.

Thus, within the space of 24 hours, a major change of plans was accomplished which involved Army and Navy forces from two different theaters of operations—a change which hastened the liberation of the Philippines and the final day of victory—a change which saved lives which would have been expended in the capture of islands which are now neutralized far behind our lines.

Our over-all strategy has not neglected the important task of rendering all possible aid to China. Despite almost insuperable difficulties, we increased this aid during 1944. At present our aid to China must be accomplished by air transport—there is no other way. By the end of 1944, the Air Transport Command was carrying into China a tonnage of supplies three times as great as that delivered a year ago, and much more, each month, than the Burma Road ever delivered at its peak.

Despite the loss of important bases in China, the tonnage delivered by air transport has enabled General Chennault's Fourteenth Air Force, which includes many Chinese flyers, to wage an effective and aggressive campaign against the Japanese. In 1944 aircraft of the Fourteenth Air Force flew more than 35,000 sorties against the Japanese and sank enormous tonnage of enemy shipping, greatly diminishing the usefulness of the China Sea lanes.

British, Dominion, and Chinese forces together with our own have not only held the line in Burma against determined Japanese attacks but have gained bases of considerable importance to the supply line into China.

The Burma campaigns have involved incredible hardship, and have demanded exceptional fortitude and determination. The officers and men who have served with so much devotion in these far distant jungles and mountains deserve high honor from their countrymen.

In all of the far-flung operations of our own armed forces—on land, and sea and in the air—the final job, the toughest job, has been performed by the average, easy-going, hard-fighting young American, who carries the weight of battle on his own shoulders.

It is to him that we and all future generations of Americans must pay grateful tribute.

But—it is of small satisfaction to him to know that monuments will be raised to him in the future. He wants, he needs, and he is entitled to insist upon, our full and active support—now.

Although unprecedented production figures have made

possible our victories, we shall have to increase our goals even more in certain items.

Peak deliveries of supplies were made to the War Department in December 1943. Due in part to cutbacks, we have not produced as much since then. Deliveries of Army supplies were down by 15 percent by July 1944, before the upward trend was once more resumed.

Because of increased demands from overseas, the Army Service Forces in the month of October 1944, had to increase its estimate of required production by 10 percent. But in November, 1 month later, the requirements for 1945 had to be increased another 10 percent, sending the production goal well above anything we have yet attained. Our armed forces in combat have steadily increased their expenditure of medium and heavy artillery ammunition. As we continue the decisive phases of this war, the munitions that we expend will mount day by day.

In October 1944, while some were saying the war in Europe was over, the Army was shipping more men to Europe than in any previous month of the war.

One of the most urgent immediate requirements of the armed forces is more nurses. Last April the Army requirement for nurses was set at 50,000. Actual strength in nurses was then 40,000. Since that time the Army has tried to raise the additional 10,000. Active recruiting has been carried on, but the net gain in 8 months has been only 2,000. There are now 42,000 nurses in the Army.

Recent estimates have increased the total number needed to 60,000. That means that 18,000 more nurses must be obtained for the Army alone and the Navy now requires 2,000 additional nurses.

The present shortage of Army nurses is reflected in undue strain on the existing force. More than a thousand nurses are now hospitalized, and part of this is due to overwork. The shortage is also indicated by the fact that 11 Army hospital units have been sent overseas without their complement of nurses. At Army hospitals in the United States there is only 1 nurse to 26 beds, instead of the recommended 1 to 15 beds.

It is tragic that the gallant women who have volunteered for service as nurses should be so overworked. It is tragic that our wounded men should ever want for the best possible nursing care.

The inability to get the needed nurses for the Army is not due to any shortage of nurses; 280,000 registered nurses are now practicing in this country. It has been estimated by the War Manpower Commission that 27,000 additional nurses could be made available to the armed forces without interfering too seriously with the needs of the civilian population for nurses.

Since volunteering has not produced the number of nurses required, I urge that the Selective Service Act be amended to provide for the induction of nurses into the armed forces. The need is too pressing to await the outcome of further efforts at recruiting.

The care and treatment given to our wounded and sick soldiers have been the best known to medical science. Those standards must be maintained at all costs. We cannot tolerate a lowering of them by failure to provide adequate nursing for the brave men who stand desperately in need of it.

In the continuing progress of this war we have constant need for new types of weapons, for we cannot afford to fight the war of today or tomorrow with the weapons of yesterday. For example, the American Army now has developed a new tank with a gun more powerful than any yet mounted on a fast-moving vehicle. The Army will need many thousands of these new tanks in 1945.

Almost every month finds some new development in electronics which must be put into production in order to maintain our technical superiority—and in order to save lives. We have to work every day to keep ahead of the enemy in radar. On D-day, in France, with our superior new equipment, we located and then put out of operation every warning set which the Germans had along the French coast.

If we do not keep constantly ahead of our enemies in the development of new weapons, we pay for our backwardness with the life's blood of our sons.

The only way to meet these increased needs for new weapons and more of them is for every American engaged in war work to stay on his war job—for additional American civilians, men and women, not engaged in essential work, to go out and get a war job. Workers who are released because their production is cut back should get another job where production is being increased. This is no time to quit or change to less essential jobs.

There is an old and true saying that the Lord hates a quitter. And this Nation must pay for all those who leave their essential jobs—or all those who lay down on their essential jobs for nonessential reasons. And—again—that payment must be made with the life's blood of our sons.

Many critical production programs with sharply rising needs are now seriously hampered by manpower shortages. The most important Army needs are artillery ammunition, cotton duck, bombs, tires, tanks, heavy trucks, and even B-29's. In each of these vital programs, present production is behind requirements.

Navy production of bombardment ammunition is hampered by manpower shortages; so is production for its huge rocket program. Labor shortages have also delayed its cruiser and carrier programs, and production of certain types of aircraft.

There is critical need for more repair workers and repair parts; this lack delays the return of damaged fighting ships to their places in the fleet, and prevents ships now in the fighting line from getting needed overhauling.

The pool of young men under 26 classified as I-A is almost depleted. Increased replacements for the armed forces will take men now deferred who are at work in war industry. The armed forces must have an assurance of a steady flow of young men for replacements. Meeting this paramount need will be difficult, and will also make it progressively more difficult to attain the 1945 production goals.

Last year, after much consideration, I recommended that the Congress adopt a national service act as the most efficient and democratic way of insuring full production for our war requirements. This recommendation was not adopted.

I now again call upon the Congress to enact this measure for the total mobilization of all our human resources for the prosecution of the war. I urge that this be done at the earliest possible moment.

It is not too late in the war. In fact, bitter experience has shown that in this kind of mechanized warfare where new weapons are constantly being created by our enemies and by ourselves, the closer we come to the end of the war, the more pressing becomes the need for sustained war production with which to deliver the final blow to the enemy.

There are three basic arguments for a national service law:

First, it would assure that we have the right numbers of workers in the right places at the right times.

Second, it would provide supreme proof to all our fighting men that we are giving them what they are entitled to, which is nothing less than our total effort.

And, third, it would be the final, unequivocal answer to the hopes of the Nazis and the Japanese that we may become half-hearted about this war and that they can get from us a negotiated peace.

National service legislation would make it possible to put ourselves in a position to assure certain and speedy action in meeting our manpower needs.

It would be used only to the extent absolutely required by military necessities. In fact, experience in Great Britain and in other nations at war indicates that use of the compulsory powers of national service is necessary only in rare instances.

This proposed legislation would provide against loss of retirement and seniority rights and benefits. It would not mean reduction in wages.

In adopting such legislation, it is not necessary to discard the voluntary and cooperative processes which have prevailed up to this time. This cooperation has already produced great results. The contribution of our workers to the war effort has been beyond measure.

We must build on the foundations that have already been laid and supplement the measures now in operation, in order to guarantee the production that may be necessary in the critical period that lies ahead.

At the present time we are using the inadequate tools at hand to do the best we can by such expedients as manpower ceilings, and the use of priority and other powers, to induce men and women to shift from nonessential to essential war jobs.

I am in receipt of a joint letter from the Secretary of War and the Secretary of the Navy, dated January 3, 1945, which says:

"With the experience of 3 years of war and after the most thorough consideration, we are convinced that it is now necessary to carry out the statement made by the Congress in the joint resolutions declaring that a state of war existed with Japan and Germany: That 'to bring the conflict to a successful conclusion, all of the resources of the country are hereby pledged by the Congress of the United States.'

"In our considered judgment, which is supported by General Marshall and Admiral King, this requires total mobilization of our manpower by the passage of a national war service law. The armed forces need this legislation to hasten the day of final victory, and to keep to a minimum the cost in lives.

"National war service, the recognition by law of the duty of every citizen to do his or her part in winning the war, will give complete assurance that the need for war equipment will be filled. In the coming year we must increase the output of many weapons and supplies on short notice. Otherwise we shall not keep our production abreast of the swiftly changing needs of war. At the same time it will be necessary to draw progressively many men now engaged in war production to serve with the armed forces, and their places in war production must be filled promptly. These developments will require the addition of hundreds of thousands to those already working in war industry. We do not believe that these needs can be met effectively under present methods.

"The record made by management and labor in war industry has been a notable testimony to the resourcefulness and power of America. The needs are so great, nevertheless, that in many instances we have been forced to recall soldiers and sailors from military duty to do work of a civilian character in war production, because of the urgency of the need for equipment and because of inability to recruit civilian labor."

Pending action by the Congress on the broader aspects of national service, I recommend that the Congress immediately enact legislation which will be effective in using the services of the 4,000,000 men now classified as IV-F in whatever capacity is best for the war effort.

In the field of foreign policy, we propose to stand together with the United Nations not for the war alone but for the victory for which the war is fought.

It is not only a common danger which unites us but a common hope. Ours is an association not of governments but of peoples—and the peoples' hope is peace. Here, as in England; in England, as in Russia; in Russia, as in China; in France, and through the continent of Europe, and throughout the world; wherever men love freedom, the hope and purpose of the people are for peace—a peace that is durable and secure.

It will not be easy to create this peoples' peace. We delude ourselves if we believe that the surrender of the armies of our enemies will make the peace we long for. The unconditional surrender of the armies of our enemies is the first and necessary step—but the first step only.

We have seen already, in areas liberated from the Nazi and the Fascist tyranny, what problems peace will bring. And we delude ourselves if we attempt to believe wishfully that all these problems can be solved overnight.

The firm foundation can be built—and it will be built. But the continuance and assurance of a living peace must, in the long run, be the work of the people themselves.

We ourselves, like all peoples who have gone through the difficult processes of liberation and adjustment, know of our own experience how great the difficulties can be. We know that they are not difficulties peculiar to any continent or any nation. Our own Revolutionary War left behind it, in the words of one American historian, "an eddy of lawlessness and disregard of human life." There were separatist movements of one kind or another in Vermont, Pennsylvania, Virginia, Tennessee, Kentucky, and Maine. There were insurrections, open or threatened, in Massachusetts and New Hampshire. These difficulties we worked out for ourselves as the peoples of the liberated areas of Europe, faced with complex problems of adjustment, will work out their difficulties for themselves.

Peace can be made and kept only by the united determination of free and peace-loving peoples who are willing to work together—willing to help one another—

willing to respect and tolerate and try to understand one another's opinions and feelings.

The nearer we come to vanquishing our enemies the more we inevitably become conscious of differences among the victors.

We must not let those differences divide us and blind us to our more important common and continuing interests in winning the war and building the peace.

International cooperation on which enduring peace must be based is not a one-way street.

Nations like individuals do not always see alike or think alike, and international cooperation and progress are not helped by any nation assuming that it has a monopoly of wisdom or of virtue.

In the future world the misuse of power, as implied in the term "power politics," must not be a controlling factor in international relations. That is the heart of the principles to which we have subscribed. We cannot deny that power is a factor in world politics any more than we can deny its existence as a factor in national politics. But in a democratic world, as in a democratic nation, power must be linked with responsibility, and obliged to defend and justify itself within the framework of the general good.

Perfectionism, no less than isolationism or imperialir politics, may obstruct the paths to international peace. Let us not forget that the retreat to isolationism a quarter of a-century ago was started not by a direct attack against international cooperation but against the alleged imperfections of the peace.

In our disillusionment after the last war we preferred international anarchy to international cooperation with nations which did not see and think exactly as we did. We gave up the hope of gradually achieving a better peace because we had not the courage to fulfill our responsibilities in an admittedly imperfect world.

We must not let that happen again, or we shall follow the same tragic road again—the road to a third world war.

We can fulfill our responsibilities for maintaining the security of our own country only by exercising our power and our influence to achieve the principles in which we believe and for which we have fought.

In August 1941 Prime Minister Churchill and I agreed to the principles of the Atlantic Charter, these being later incorporated into the Declaration by United Nations of January 1, 1942. At that time certain isolationists protested vigorously against our right to proclaim the principles—and against the very principles themselves. Today, many of the same people are protesting against the possibility of violation of the same principles.

It is true that the statement of principles in the Atlantic Charter does not provide rules of easy application to each and every one of this war-torn world's tangled situations. But it is a good and a useful thing—it is an essential thing—to have principles toward which we can aim.

And we shall not hesitate to use our influence—and to use it now— to secure so far as is humanly possible the fulfillment of the principles of the Atlantic Charter. We have not shrunk from the military responsibilities brought on by this war. We cannot and will not shrink from the political responsibilities which follow in the wake of battle.

I do not wish to give the impression that all mistakes can be avoided and that many disappointments are not inevitable in the making of peace. But we must not this time lose the hope of establishing an international order which will be capable of maintaining peace and realizing through the years more perfect justice between nations.

To do this we must be on our guard not to exploit and exaggerate the differences between us and our allies, particularly with reference to the peoples who have been liberated from Fascist tyranny. That is not the way to secure a better settlement of those differences or to secure international machinery which can rectify mistakes which may be made.

I should not be frank if I did not admit concern about many situations—the Greek and Polish for example. But those situations are not as easy or as simple to deal with as some spokesmen, whose sincerity I do not question, would have us believe. We have obligations, not necessarily legal, to the exiled governments, to the underground leaders, and to our major allies who came much nearer the shadows than we did.

We and our allies have declared that it is our purpose to respect the right of all peoples to choose the form of government under which they will live and to see sovereign rights and self-government restored to those who have been forcibly deprived of them. But with internal dissension, with many citizens of liberated countries still prisoners of war or forced to labor in Germany, it is difficult to guess the kind of self-government the people really want.

During the interim period, until conditions permit a genuine expression of the people's will, we and our allies have a duty, which we cannot ignore, to use our influence to the end that no temporary or provisional authorities in the liberated countries block the eventual exercise of the peoples' right freely to choose the government and institutions under which, as freemen, they are to live.

It is only too easy for all of us to rationalize what we want to believe, and to consider those leaders we like responsible and those we dislike irresponsible. And our task is not helped by stubborn partisanship, however understandable on the part of opposed internal factions.

It is our purpose to help the peace-loving peoples of Europe to live together as good neighbors, to recognize their common interests and not to nurse their traditional grievances against one another.

But we must not permit the many specific and immediate problems of adjustment connected with the liberation of Europe to delay the establishment of permanent machinery for the maintenance of peace. Under the threat of a common danger, the United Nations joined together in war to preserve their independence and their freedom. They must now join together to make secure the independence and freedom of all peace-loving states, so that never again shall tyranny be able to divide and conquer.

International peace and well-being, like national peace and well-being, require constant alertness, continuing cooperation, and organized effort.

International peace and well-being, like national peace and well-being, can be secured only through institutions capable of life and growth.

Many of the problems of the peace are upon us even now while the conclusion of the war is still before us.

The atmosphere of friendship and mutual understanding and determination to find a common ground of common understanding, which surrounded the conversations at Dumbarton Oaks, gives us reason to hope that future discussions will succeed in developing the democratic and fully integrated world security system toward which these preparatory conversations were directed.

We and the other United Nations are going forward, with vigor and resolution, in our efforts to create such a system by providing for it strong and flexible institutions of joint and cooperative action.

The aroused conscience of humanity will not permit failure in this supreme endeavor.

We believe that the extraordinary advances in the means of intercommunication between peoples over the past generation offer a practical method of advancing the mutual understanding upon which peace and the institutions of peace must rest, and it is our policy and purpose to use these great technological achievements for the common advantage of the world.

We support the greatest possible freedom of trade and commerce.

We Americans have always believed in freedom of opportunity, and equality of opportunity remains one of the principal objectives of our national life. What we believe in for individuals, we believe in also for nations. We are opposed to restrictions, whether by public act or private arrangement, which distort and impair commerce, transit and trade.

We have house cleaning of our own to do in this regard. But it is our hope, not only in the interest of our own prosperity but in the interest of the prosperity of the world, that trade and commerce and access to materials and markets may be freer after this war than ever before in the history of the world.

One of the most heartening events of the year in the international field has been the renaissance of the French people and the return of the French nation to the ranks of the United Nations. Far from having been crushed by the terror of Nazi domination, the French people have emerged with stronger faith than ever in the destiny of their country and in the soundness of the democratic ideals to which the French nation has traditionally contributed so greatly.

During her liberation, France has given proof of her unceasing determination to fight the Germans, continuing the heroic efforts of the resistance groups under the occupation and of all those Frenchmen throughout the world who refused to surrender after the disaster of 1940.

Today, French armies are again on the German frontier, and are again fighting shoulder to shoulder with our sons.

Since our landings in Africa, we have placed in French hands all the arms and material of war which our resources and the military situation permitted. And I am glad to say that we are now about to equip large new French forces with the most modern weapons for combat duty.

In addition to the contribution which France can make to our common victory, her liberation likewise means that her great influence will again be available in meeting the problems of peace.

We fully recognize France's vital interest in a lasting solution of the German problem and the contribution which she can make in achieving international security. Her formal adherence to the declaration by United Nations a few days ago and the proposal at the Dumbarton Oaks discussions, whereby France would receive one of the five permanent seats in the proposed Security Council, demonstrate the extent to which France has resumed her proper position of strength and leadership.

I am clear in my own mind that, as an essential factor in the maintenance of peace in the future, we must have universal military training after this war, and I shall send a special message to the Congress on this subject.

An enduring peace cannot be achieved without a strong America— strong in the social and economic sense as well as in the military sense.

In the state of the Union message last year I set forth what I considered to be an American economic bill of rights.

I said then, and I say now, that these economic truths represent a second bill of rights under which a new basis of security and prosperity can be established for all—regardless of station, race or creed.

Of these rights the most fundamental, and one on which the fulfillment of the others in large degree depends, is the "right to a useful and remunerative job in the industries or shops or farms or mines of the Nation." In turn, others of the economic rights of American citizenship, such as the right to a decent home, to a good education, to good medical care, to social security, to reasonable farm income, will, if fulfilled, make major contributions to achieving adequate levels of employment.

The Federal Government must see to it that these rights become realities—with the help of States, municipalities, business, labor, and agriculture.

We have had full employment during the war. We have had it because the Government has been ready to buy all the materials of war which the country could produce—and this has amounted to approximately half our present productive capacity.

After the war we must maintain full employment with Government performing its peacetime functions. This means that we must achieve a level of demand and purchasing power by private consumers— farmers, businessmen, workers, professional men, housewives— which is sufficiently high to replace wartime Government demands; and it means also that we must greatly increase our export trade above the pre-war level.

Our policy is, of course, to rely as much as possible on private enterprise to provide jobs. But the American people will not accept mass unemployment or mere makeshift work. There will be need for the work of everyone willing and able to work—and that means close to 60,000,000 jobs.

Full employment means not only jobs—but productive jobs. Americans do not regard jobs that pay substandard wages as productive jobs.

We must make sure that private enterprise works as it is supposed to work—on the basis of initiative and vigorous competition, without the stifling presence of monopolies and cartels.

During the war we have guaranteed investment in enterprise essential to the war effort. We should also take appropriate measures in peacetime to secure opportunities for new small enterprises and for productive business expansion for which finance would otherwise be unavailable.

This necessary expansion of our peacetime productive capacity will require new facilities, new plants, and new equipment.

It will require large outlays of money which should be raised through normal investment channels. But while private capital should finance this expansion program, the Government should recognize its responsibility for sharing part of any special or abnormal risk of loss attached to such financing.

Our full-employment program requires the extensive development of our natural resources and other useful public works. The undeveloped resources of this continent are still vast. Our river-watershed projects will add new and fertile territories to the United States. The Tennessee Valley Authority, which was constructed at a cost of $750,000,000—the cost of waging this war for less than 4 days—was a bargain. We have similar opportunities in our other great river basins. By harnessing the resources of these river basins, as we have in the Tennessee Valley, we shall provide the same kind of stimulus to enterprise as was provided by the Louisiana Purchase and the new discoveries in the West during the nineteenth century.

If we are to avail ourselves fully of the benefits of civil aviation, and if we are to use the automobiles we can produce, it will be necessary to construct thousands of airports and to overhaul our entire national highway system.

The provision of a decent home for every family is a national necessity, if this country is to be worthy of its greatness—and that task will itself create great employment opportunities. Most of our cities need extensive rebuilding. Much of our farm plant is in a state of disrepair. To make a frontal attack on the problems of housing and urban reconstruction will require thoroughgoing cooperation between industry and labor, and the Federal, State, and local governments.

An expanded social-security program, and adequate health and education programs, must play essential roles in a program designed to support individual productivity and mass purchasing power. I shall communicate further with the Congress on these subjects at a later date.

The millions of productive jobs that a program of this nature could bring are jobs in private enterprise. They are jobs based on the expanded demand for the output of our economy for consumption and investment. Through a program of this character we can maintain a national income high enough to provide for an orderly retirement of the public debt along with reasonable tax reduction.

Our present tax system geared primarily to war requirements must be revised for peacetime so as to encourage private demand.

While no general revision of the tax structure can be made until the war ends on all fronts, the Congress should be prepared to provide tax modifications at the end of the war in Europe, designed to encourage capital to invest in new enterprises and to provide jobs. As an integral part of this program to maintain high employment, we must, after the war is over, reduce or eliminate taxes which bear too heavily on consumption.

The war will leave deep disturbances in the world economy, in our national economy, in many communities, in many families, and in many individuals. It will require determined effort and responsible action of all of us to find our way back to peacetime, and to help others to find their way back to peacetime—a peacetime that holds the values of the past and the promise of the future.

If we attack our problems with determination we shall succeed. And we must succeed. For freedom and peace cannot exist without security.

During the past year the American people, in a national election, reasserted their democratic faith.

In the course of that campaign various references were made to "strife" between this administration and the Congress, with the implication, if not the direct assertion, that this administration and the Congress could never work together harmoniously in the service of the Nation.

It cannot be denied that there have been disagreements between the legislative and executive branches—as there have been disagreements during the past century and a half.

I think we all realize too that there are some people in this Capital City whose task is in large part to stir up dissension, and to magnify normal healthy disagreements so that they appear to be irreconcilable conflicts.

But—I think that the over-all record in this respect is eloquent: The Government of the United States of America—all branches of it—has a good record of achievement in this war.

The Congress, the Executive, and the Judiciary have worked together for the common good.

I myself want to tell you, the Members of the Senate and of the House of Representatives, how happy I am in our relationships and friendships. I have not yet had the pleasure of meeting some of the new Members in each House, but I hope that opportunity will offer itself in the near future.

We have a great many problems ahead of us and we must approach them with realism and courage.

This new year of 1945 can be the greatest year of achievement in human history.

Nineteen forty-five can see the final ending of the Nazi-Fascist reign of terror in Europe.

Nineteen forty-five can see the closing in of the forces of retribution about the center of the malignant power of imperialistic Japan.

Most important of all—1945 can and must see the substantial beginning of the organization of world peace. This organization must be the fulfillment of the promise for which men have fought and died in this war. It must be the justification of all the sacrifices that have been made—of all the dreadful misery that this world has endured.

We Americans of today, together with our allies, are making history—and I hope it will be better history than ever has been made before.

We pray that we may be worthy of the unlimited opportunities that God has given us.

Franklin Roosevelt

GEORGE W. BUSH

INTRODUCTION

President Bush was born on 6th July, 1946, in New Haven, Connecticut, and grew up in Midland and Houston, Texas.

He is the 43rd President of the United States. He was sworn into office on January 20, 2001, reelected on November 2, 2004, and sworn in for a second term on January 20, 2005. Prior to his Presidency, President Bush served for 6 years as the 46th Governor of the State of Texas, where he earned a reputation for bipartisanship and as a compassionate conservative who shaped public policy based on the principles of limited government, personal responsibility, strong families, and local control.

Attack on Iraq speech
Washington D.C. - Jan. 16th 1991

JUST two hours ago, Allied air forces began an attack on military targets in Iraq and Kuwait. These attacks continue as I speak. Ground forces are not engaged. This conflict started Aug. 2, when the dictator of Iraq invaded a small and helpless neighbour. Kuwait, a member of the Arab League and a member of the United Nations, was crushed, its people brutalized. Five months ago, Saddam Hussein started this cruel war against Kuwait; tonight, the battle has been joined.

This military action, taken in accord with United Nations resolutions and with the consent of the United States Congress, follows months of constant and virtually endless diplomatic activity on the part of the United Nations, the United States and many, many other countries.

Arab leaders sought what became known as an Arab solution, only to conclude that Saddam Hussein was unwilling to leave Kuwait. Others travelled to Baghdad in a variety of efforts to restore peace and justice. Our Secretary of State, James Baker, held an historic meeting in Geneva, only to be totally rebuffed.

This past weekend, in a last-ditch effort, the Secretary General of the United Nations went to the Middle East with peace in his heart - his second such mission. And he came back from Baghdad with no progress at all in getting Saddam Hussein to withdraw from Kuwait. Now, the 28 countries with forces in the Gulf area have exhausted all reasonable efforts to reach a peaceful resolution, and have no choice but to drive

Saddam from Kuwait by force. We will not fail.

As I report to you, air attacks are under way against military targets in Iraq. We are determined to knock out Saddam Hussein's nuclear bomb potential. We will also destroy his chemical weapons facilities. Much of Saddam's artillery and tanks will be destroyed. Our operations are designed to best protect the lives of all the coalition forces by targeting Saddam's vast military arsenal.

Initial reports from General Schwartzkopf are that our operations are proceeding according to plan. Our objectives are clear: Saddam Hussein's forces will leave Kuwait. The legitimate government of Kuwait will be restored to its rightful place, and Kuwait will once again be free. Iraq will eventually comply with all relevant United Nations resolutions, and then, when peace is restored, it is our hope that Iraq will live as a peaceful and cooperative member of the family of nations, thus enhancing the security and stability of the Gulf.

Some may ask, why act now? Why not wait? The answer is clear. The world could wait no longer. Sanctions, though having some effect, showed no signs of accomplishing their objective. Sanctions were tried for well over five months, and we and our allies concluded that sanctions alone would not force Saddam from Kuwait.

While the world waited, Saddam Hussein systematically raped, pillaged, and plundered a tiny nation no threat to his own. He subjected the people of Kuwait to unspeakable atrocities, and among those, maimed and murdered innocent children.

While the world waited, Saddam sought to add to the chemical weapons arsenal he now possesses an infinitely more dangerous weapon of mass destruction—a nuclear weapon. And while the world waited, while the world talked peace and withdrawal, Saddam Hussein dug in and moved massive forces into Kuwait.

While the world waited, while Saddam stalled, more damage was being done to the fragile economies of the Third World, emerging democracies of Eastern Europe, to the entire world, including to our own economy. The United States, together with the United Nations, exhausted every means at our disposal to bring this crisis to a peaceful end. However, Saddam clearly felt that by stalling and threatening and defying the United Nations, he could weaken the forces arrayed against him. While the world waited, Saddam Hussein met every overture of peace with open contempt.

While the world prayed for peace, Saddam prepared for war. I had hoped that when the United States Congress, in historic debate, took its resolute action, Saddam would realize he could not prevail, and would move out of Kuwait in accord with the United Nations resolutions. He did not do that. Instead, he remained intransigent, certain that time was on his side. Saddam was warned over and over again to comply with the will of the United Nations: Leave Kuwait or be driven out. Saddam has arrogantly rejected all warnings. Instead, he tried to make this a dispute between Iraq and the United States of America.

Well, he failed. Tonight 28 nations - countries from five continents, Europe and Asia, Africa and the Arab League - have forces in the Gulf area standing shoulder-to-shoulder against Saddam Hussein. These countries had hoped the use of force could be avoided. Regrettably, we now believe that only force will make him leave.

Prior to ordering our forces into battle, I instructed our military commanders to take every necessary step to prevail, as quickly as possible, and with the greatest degree of protection possible for American and Allied service men and women..

I've told the American people before that this will not be another Vietnam, and I repeat this here tonight. Our troops will have the best possible support in the entire world, and they will not be asked to fight with one hand tied behind their back. I'm hopeful that this fighting will not go on for long, and that casualties will be held to an absolute minimum.

This is an historic moment. We have in this past year made great progress in ending the long era of conflict and cold war. We have before us the opportunity to forge for ourselves and for future generations a new world order, a world where the rule of law, not the law of the jungle, governs the conduct of nations. When we are successful, and we will be, we have a real chance at this new world order, an order in which a credible United Nations can use its peace-keeping role to fulfil the promise and vision of the U.N.'s founders. We have no argument with the people of Iraq. Indeed, for the innocents caught in this conflict, I pray for their safety.

Our goal is not the conquest of Iraq. It is the liberation of Kuwait. It is my hope that somehow the Iraqi people can, even now, convince their dictator that he must lay down his arms, leave Kuwait, and let Iraq itself rejoin the family of peace-loving nations.

Thomas Paine wrote many years ago: "These are the times that try men's souls." Those well-known words are so very true today. But even as planes of the multinational forces attack Iraq, I prefer to think of peace, not war. I am convinced not only that we will prevail, but that out of the horror of combat will come the recognition that no nation can stand against a world united. No nation will be permitted to brutally assault its neighbour.

No President can easily commit our sons and daughters to war. They are the nation's finest. Ours is an all-volunteer force, magnificently trained, highly motivated. The troops know why they're there. And listen to what they say, because they've said it better than any President or Prime Minister ever could.

Listen to 'Hollywood' Huddleston, Marine lance corporal. He says:"Let's free these people so we can go home and be free again." And he's right. The terrible crimes and tortures committed by Saddam's henchmen against the innocent people of Kuwait are an affront to mankind and a challenge to the freedom of all.

Listen to one of our great officers out there, Marine Lieutenant-General Walter Boomer: "There are things worth fighting for. A world in which brutality and lawlessness are allowed to go unchecked isn't the kind of world we're going to want to live in."

Listen to Master Sergeant J.P. Kendall of the 82nd Airborne: "We're here for more than just the price of a gallon of gas. What we're doing is going to chart the future of the world for the next hundred years. It's better to deal with this guy now than five years from now." And finally, we should all sit up and listen to Jackie Jones, an Army Lieutenant, when she says, "If we let him get away with this, who knows what's going to be next."

I've called upon Hollywood and Walter and J.P. and Jackie, and all their courageous comrades-in-arms, to do what must be done. Tonight, America and the world are deeply grateful to them and to their families. And let me say to everyone listening or watching tonight: When the troops we've sent in finish their work, I'm determined to bring them home as soon as possible. Tonight, as our forces fight, they and their families are in our prayers. May God bless each and every one of them, and the coalition forces at our side in the Gulf, and may He continue to bless our nation, the United States of America.

GEORGE WASHINGTON

INTRODUCTION

George Washington was born in 1732 into a Virginia planter family, he learned the morals, manners, and body of knowledge requisite for an 18th century Virginia gentleman.

He was Commander of American forces and First President of the USA.

Fought in the campaign of French and Indian War (1754-1763); In 1787 he presided over the constitutional convention and became President, and in due course became a member of the Federalist Party.

Washington enjoyed less than three years of retirement at Mount Vernon, for he died of a throat infection December 14, 1799. For months the Nation mourned him.

Prevents the Revolt of his Officers (1783)

GENTLEMEN:

By an anonymous summons, an attempt has been made to convene you together; how inconsistent with the rules of propriety, how unmilitary, and how subversive of all order and discipline, let the good sense of the army decide...

Thus much, gentlemen, I have thought it incumbent on me to observe to you, to show upon what principles I opposed the irregular and hasty meeting which was proposed to have been held on Tuesday last - and not because I wanted a disposition to give you every opportunity consistent with your own honor, and the dignity of the army, to make known your grievances. If my conduct heretofore has not evinced to you that I have been a faithful friend to the army, my declaration of it at this time would be equally unavailing and improper. But as I was among the first who embarked in the cause of our common country. As I have never left your side one moment, but when called from you on public duty. As I have been the constant companion and witness of your distresses, and not among the last to feel and acknowledge your merits. As I have ever considered my own military reputation as inseparably connected with that of the army. As my heart has ever expanded with joy, when I have heard its praises, and my indignation has arisen, when the mouth of detraction has been opened against it, it can scarcely be supposed, at this late stage of the war, that I am indifferent to its interests.

But how are they to be promoted? The way is plain,

says the anonymous addresser. If war continues, remove into the unsettled country, there establish yourselves, and leave an ungrateful country to defend itself. But who are they to defend? Our wives, our children, our farms, and other property which we leave behind us. Or, in this state of hostile separation, are we to take the two first (the latter cannot be removed) to perish in a wilderness, with hunger, cold, and nakedness? If peace takes place, never sheathe your swords, says he, until you have obtained full and ample justice; this dreadful alternative, of either deserting our country in the extremest hour of her distress or turning our arms against it (which is the apparent object, unless Congress can be compelled into instant compliance), has something so shocking in it that humanity revolts at the idea. My God! What can this writer have in view, by recommending such measures? Can he be a friend to the army? Can he be a friend to this country? Rather, is he not an insidious foe? Some emissary, perhaps, from New York, plotting the ruin of both, by sowing the seeds of discord and separation between the civil and military powers of the continent? And what a compliment does he pay to our understandings when he recommends measures in either alternative, impracticable in their nature?

I cannot, in justice to my own belief, and what I have great reason to conceive is the intention of Congress, conclude this address, without giving it as my decided opinion, that that honorable body entertain exalted sentiments of the services of the army; and, from a full conviction of its merits and sufferings, will do it complete justice. That their endeavors to discover and establish funds for this purpose have been unwearied, and will not cease till they have succeeded, I have not a doubt. But, like all other large bodies, where there is a variety of different interests to reconcile, their deliberations are slow. Why, then, should we distrust them? And, in consequence of that distrust, adopt measures which may cast a shade over that glory which has been so justly acquired; and tarnish the reputation of an army which is celebrated through all Europe, for its fortitude and patriotism? And for what is this done? To bring the object we seek nearer? No! most certainly, in my opinion, it will cast it at a greater distance.

For myself (and I take no merit in giving the assurance, being induced to it from principles of gratitude, veracity, and justice), a grateful sense of the confidence you have ever placed in me, a recollection of the cheerful assistance and prompt obedience I have experienced from you, under every vicissitude of fortune, and the sincere affection I feel for an army I have so long had the honor to command will oblige me to declare, in this public and solemn manner, that, in the attainment of complete justice for all your toils and dangers, and in the gratification of every wish, so far as may be done consistently with the great duty I owe my country and those powers we are bound to respect, you may freely command my services to the utmost of my abilities.

While I give you these assurances, and pledge myself in the most unequivocal manner to exert whatever ability I am possessed of in your favor, let me entreat you, gentlemen, on your part, not to take any measures which, viewed in the calm light of reason, will lessen the dignity and sully the glory you have hitherto maintained; let me request you to rely on the plighted faith of your country, and place a full confidence in the purity of the intentions of Congress; that, previous to your dissolution as an army, they will cause all your accounts to be fairly liquidated, as directed in their resolutions, which were published to you two days ago, and that they will adopt the most effectual measures in their power to render ample justice to you, for your faithful and meritorious services. And let me conjure you, in the name of our common country, as you value your own sacred honor, as you respect the rights of humanity, and as you regard the military and national character of America, to express your utmost horror and detestation of the man who wishes, under any specious pretenses, to overturn the liberties of our country, and who wickedly attempts to open the floodgates of civil discord and deluge our rising empire in blood.

By thus determining and thus acting, you will pursue the plain and direct road to the attainment of your wishes. You will defeat the insidious designs of our enemies, who are compelled to resort from open force to secret artifice. You will give one more distinguished proof of unexampled patriotism and patient virtue, rising superior to the pressure of the most complicated sufferings. And you will, by the dignity of your conduct, afford occasion for posterity to say, when speaking of the glorious example you have exhibited to mankind, "Had this day been wanting, the world had never seen the last stage of perfection to which human nature is capable of attaining."

George Washington - March 15, 1783

Second Inaugural Address
In the City of Philadelphia
Monday, March 4, 1793

FELLOW CITIZENS:

I am again called upon by the voice of my country to execute the functions of its Chief Magistrate. When the occasion proper for it shall arrive, I shall endeavor to express the high sense I entertain of this distinguished honor, and of the confidence which has been reposed in me by the people of united America. Previous to the execution of any official act of the President the Constitution requires an oath of office.

This oath I am now about to take, and in your presence: That if it shall be found during my administration of the Government I have in any instance violated willingly or knowingly the injunctions thereof, I may (besides incurring constitutional punishment) be subject to the upbraidings of all who are now witnesses of the present solemn ceremony.

INDIRA GANDHI

INTRODUCTION

Indira Nehru Gandhi was born on November 19, 1917 and would be the only child of Jawaharlal and Kamala Nehru.

In 1938, Indira finally joined the Indian National Congress Party, something she always longed to do. Soon afterwards in 1942, she married journalist Feroze Gandhi to whom she eventually bore two sons. Soon after the couple was married, they were sent to prison on charges of subversion by the British.

Her first and only imprisonment lasted from September 11, 1942 until May 13, 1943 at the Naini Central Jail in Allahabad. She was assassinated by her own guards on October 31, 1984.

Martin Luther King Famous Speech
New Delhi, India: January 24, 1969

THIS is a poignant moment for all of us. We remember vividly your last visit to our country. We had hoped that on this occasion, Dr. King and you would be standing side by side on this platform. That was not to be. He is not with us but we feel his spirit. We admired Dr. King. We felt his loss as our own. The tragedy rekindled memories of the great martyrs of all time who gave their lives so that men might live and grow. We thought of the great men in your own country who fell to the assassin's bullet and of Mahatma Gandhi's martyrdom here in this city, this very month, twenty-one years ago. Such events remain as wounds in the human consciousness, reminding us of battles, yet to be fought and tasks still to be accomplished. We should not mourn for men of high ideals. Rather we should rejoice that we had the privilege of having had them with us, to inspire us by their radiant personalities. So today we are gathered not to offer you grief, but to salute a man who achieved so much in so short a time. It is befitting, Madam, that you whom he called the "courage by my side", you who gave him strength and encouragement in his historic mission, should be with us to receive this award.

You and your husband both had foreseen that death might come to him violently. It was perhaps inherent in the situation. Dr. King chose death for the theme of a sermon, remarking that he would like to be remembered as a drum major for justice, for peace and for righteousness. When you were once asked what you would do if your husband were assassinated, you were courage personified, replying that you might weep but the work would go on. Your face of sorrow, so beautiful in its dignity coupled with infinite compassion, will forever be engraved in our hearts.

Mahatma Gandhi also had foreseen his end and had prepared himself for it. Just as training for violence included learning to kill, the training for non-violence, he said, included learning how to die. The true badge of the satyagrahi is to be unafraid.

As if he too had envisaged the martyrdoms of Mahatma Gandhi and Martin Luther King, Rabindranath Tagore once sang:

In anger we slew him,

With love let us embrace him now,

For in death he lives again amongst us,

The mighty conqueror of death.

This award, Madam, is the highest tribute our nation can bestow on work for understanding and brotherhood among men. It is named after a man who himself was a peace-maker and who all his life laboured passionately for freedom, justice and peace in India and throughout the world. Dr. Martin Luther King's struggle was for these same values. He paid for his ideals with his blood, forging a new bond among the brave and the conscientious of all races and all nations.

Dr. King's dream embraced the poor and the oppressed of all lands. His work ennobled us. He spoke of the right of man to survive and recognized three threats to the survival of man—racial injustice, poverty and war. He realised that even under the lamp of affluence which was held aloft by science, lay the shadow of poverty, compelling two-thirds of the peoples of the world to exist in hunger and want. He proclaimed that mankind could be saved from war only if we cared enough for peace to sacrifice for it.

Dr. Martin Luther King drew his inspiration from Christ, and his method of action from Mahatma Gandhi. Only through truth can untruth be vanquished. Only through love can hatred be quenched. This is the path of the Buddha and of Christ, and in our own times, that of Mahatma Gandhi and of Martin Luther King.

They believed in the equality of all men. No more false doctrine has been spread than that of the superiority of one race over another. It is ironical that there should still be people in this world who judge men not by their moral worth and intellectual merit but by the pigment of their skin or other physical characteristics.

Some governments still rest on the theory of racist superiority—such as the governments of South Africa and the lawless regime in Rhodesia. Unregenerate groups in other countries consider one colour superior to another. Our own battle is not yet over. Caste and other prejudices still survive, but most of us are ashamed of them and recognise them as evils to be combated. We are trying hard to eradicate them.

While there is bondage anywhere, we ourselves cannot be fully free. While there is oppression anywhere, we ourselves cannot soar high. Martin Luther King was convinced that one day the misguided people who believed in racial superiority would realise the error of their ways. His dream was that white and black, brown and yellow would live and grow together as flowers in a garden with their faces turned towards the sun. As you yourself said, "All of us who believe in what Martin Luther King stood for, must see to it that his spirit never dies". That spirit can never die. There may be setbacks in our fight for the equality of all men. There may be moments of gloom. But victory must and will be ours. Let us not rest until the equality of all races and religions becomes a living fact. That is the most effective and lasting tribute that we can pay to Dr. King.

JAWAHARLAL NEHRU

INTRODUCTION

Jawaharlal Nehru was born in 14th November, 1889. His father Motilal Nehru being a reputed barrister. He spent two years studying Law in London & returned home in 1912 as a barrister. When India became Independent in 1947, he was asked to take over as the Prime Minister, which he did in 1951 when India became a republic. The great pillar of India's struggle for her freedom passed away on 27th May 1964, while in office. The whole country submerged into an ocean of grief & paid their last homage through prayers. After cremation his ashes were spread in the holy water of the Ganges. Jawaharlal Nehru's legacy of a democratic, federal, and secular India continues to survive in spite of attempts by later leaders to establish either an autocratic or a theocratic state.

On the Granting of Indian Independence, August 14, 1947

LONG YEARS AGO we made a tryst with destiny, and now the time comes when we shall redeem our pledge, not wholly or in full measure, but very substantially. At the stroke of the midnight hour, when the world sleeps, India will awake to life and freedom. A moment comes, which comes but rarely in history, when we step out from the old to the new, when an age ends, and when the soul of a nation, long supressed, finds utterance. It is fitting that at this solemn moment we take the pledge of dedication to the service of Inida and her people and to the still larger cause of humanity.

At the dawn of history India started on her unending quest, and trackless centuries are filled with her striving and the grandeur of her success and her failures. Through good and ill fortune alike she has never lost sight of that quest or forgotten the ideals which gave her strength. We end today a period of ill fortune and India discovers herself again. The achievement we celebrate today is but a step, an opening of opportunity, to the greater triumphs and achievements that await us. Are we brave enough and wise enough to grasp this opportunity and accept the challenge of the future?

Freedom and power bring responsibility. The responsibility rests upon this Assembly, a sovereign body representing the sovereign people of India. Before the birth of freedom we have endured all the pains of labour and our hearts are heavy with the memory of this sorrow. Some of those pains continue even now.

Nevertheless, the past is over and it is the future that beckons to us now.

That future is not one of ease or resting but of incessant striving so that we may fulfil the pledges we have so often taken and the one we shall take today. The service of India means the service of the millions who suffer. It means the ending of poverty and ignorance and disease and inequality of opportunity. The ambition of the greatest man of our generation has been to wipe every tear from every eye. That may be beyond us, but as long as there are tears and suffering, so long our work will not be over.

And so we have to labour and to work, and work hard, to give reality to our dreams. Those dreams are for India, but they are also for the world, for all the nations and peoples are too closely knit together today for any one of them to imagine that it can live apart Peace has been said to be indivisible; so is freedom, so is prosperity now, and so also is disaster in this One World that can no longer be split into isolated fragments.

To the people of India, whose representatives we are, we make an appeal to join us with faith and confidence in this great adventure. This is no time for petty and destructive criticism, no time for ill-will or blaming others. We have to build the noble mansion of free India where all her children may dwell.

The appointed day has come-the day appointed by destiny-and India stands forth again, after long slumber and struggle, awake, vital, free and independent. The past clings on to us still in some measure and we have to do much before we redeem the pledges we have so often taken. Yet the turning-point is past, and history begins anew for us, the history which we shall live and act and others will write about.

It is a fateful moment for us in India, for all Asia and for the world. A new star rises, the star of freedom in the East, a new hope comes into being, a vision long cherished materializes. May the star never set and that hope never be betrayed!

We rejoice in that freedom, even though clouds surround us, and many of our people are sorrowstricken and difficult problems encompass us. But freedom brings responsibilities and burdens and we have to face them in the spirit of a free and disciplined people.

On this day our first thoughts go to the architect of this freedom, the Father of our Nation [Gandhi], who, embodying the old spirit of India, held aloft the torch of freedom and lighted up the darkness that surrounded us. We have often been unworthy followers of his and have strayed from his message, but not only we but succeeding generations will remember this message and bear the imprint in their hearts of this great son of India, magnificent in his faith and strength and courage and humility. We shall never allow that torch of freedom to be blown out, however high the wind or stormy the tempest.

Our next thoughts must be of the unknown volunteers and soldiers of freedom who, without praise or reward, have served India even unto death.

We think also of our brothers and sisters who have been cut off from us by political boundaries and who unhappily cannot share at present in the freedom

that has come. They are of us and will remain of us whatever may happen, and we shall be sharers in their good [or] ill fortune alike.

The future beckons to us. Whither do we go and what shall be our endeavour? To bring freedom and opportunity to the common man, to the peasants and workers of India; to fight and end poverty and ignorance and disease; to build up a prosperous, democratic and progressive nation, and to create social, economic and political institutions which will ensure justice and fullness of life to every man and woman.

We have hard work ahead. There is no resting for any one of us till we redeem our pledge in full, till we make all the people of India what destiny intended them to be. We are citizens of a great country on the verge of bold advance, and we have to live up to that high standard. All of us, to whatever religion we may belong, are equally the children of India with equal rights, privileges and obligations. We cannot encourage communalism or narrow-mindedness, for no nation can be great whose people are narrow in thought or in action.

To the nations and peoples of the world we send greetings and pledge ourselves to cooperate with them in furthering peace, freedom and democracy.

And to India, our much-loved motherland, the ancient, the eternal and the ever-new, we pay our reverent homage and we bind ourselves afresh to her service.

JAI HIND.

At United Nations General Assembly, New York, October 3, 1960

I have listened attentively and with respect to many of the speeches made here, and sometimes I have felt as if I was being buffeted by the icy winds of the cold war. Coming from a warm country, I have shivered occasionally at these cold blasts.

Speaking here in this assembly chamber, an old memory comes back to me. In the fateful summer of 1938. I was a visitor at a meeting of the League of Nations in Geneva. Hitler was advancing then and holding out threats of war. There was mobilization in many parts of Europe, and the tramp of armed men was being heard. Even so, the League of Nations appeared to be unconcerned and discussed all manner of subjects, except the most vital subject of the day. The war had not started then. A year later it descended upon the world with all its thunder and destructive fury. After many years of carnage, the war ended, and a new age - the atomic age - was ushered in by the terrible experience of Hiroshima and Nagasaki.

Fresh from these horrors, the minds of men turned to thoughts of peace and there was a passionate desire to put an end to war itself. The United Nations took birth on a note of high idealism embodied in the noble wording of the Charter. But there was also a realization of the state of the postwar world as it was. Therefore, provision was made in the structure of the organization to balance certain conflicting urges. There were permanent members of the Security Council and there was provision for unanimity amongst the great powers. All this was not very logical. But it represented certain realities of the world as it was, and because of this, we accepted them.

During these past fifteen years, the United Nations has often been criticized for its structure and for some of its activities. These criticisms have had some Justification behind them. But, looking at the broad picture, I think we can definitely say that the United Nations has amply justified its existence and repeatedly prevented the recurrent crises from developing into war. It has played a great role, and it is a little difficult now to think of this troubled world without the U.N. If it had defects, they lay in the world situation Itself which inevitably it mirrored. If there had been no United Nations today, our first task would be to create something of that kind. I should like, therefore, to pay my tribute to the work of the United Nations as a whole, even though I might criticize some aspect of it from time to time.

In the context of things as they are today, the great nations, the United States of America and the Soviet Union, hold the key to war and peace. Their is a great responsibility. But every country, big or small, is concerned in this matter of peace and war, and, therefore, every country must shoulder its responsibility and work to this end. In order to deal with these big Issues effectively, we have to take big and impersonal views. It is only the United Nations as a whole that can ultimately solve these problems. Therefore, while all efforts towards disarmament must be welcomed, the United Nations should be closely associated with such efforts.

The question of disarmament has been considered at various levels. There is the question of general disarmament, and of the ending of test explosions of nuclear and thermonuclear weapons. So far as test explosions are concerned, considerable progress has been made in the discussions of the committee which has been meeting in Geneva. Indeed, it would appear that an agreement has been reached on many basic issues and only a little more effort is needed to complete this agreement. I suggest that a final agreement on this subject should be reached as early as possible. This is not, strictly speaking, disarmament. but undoubtedly any such agreement will bring a large measure of relief to the world. Disarmament must include the prohibition of the manufacture, storage and use of weapons of mass destruction, as well as the progressive limitation of conventional weapons.

It is admitted that disarmament should take place in such ,stages as to maintain broadly the balance of armed power. It is only on this basis that success can be achieved and this pervading sense of fear countered. It must also be clearly understood that disarmament and a machinery for control must go together, and neither of these can be taken up singly.

A proposal has been made that the question of disarmament should be referred to a committee of experts. In fact, experts have been considering this matter during the past years, and we have had the advantage of their views. A reference to a committee of experts should not lead to a postponement of the major issue. Any such delay may well be disastrous. Possibly, while the major issues are being considered by the United Nations Commission or other committees, a reference of any special aspect might be made to the experts. What is important is that the United Nations, at the present juncture, should ensure that there is adequate machinery for promoting disarmament and that this machinery should function continuously.

The fear of surprise attacks or accidental happenings leading to dangerous developments is undoubtedly present in the existing situation. The best way to deal with this fear is to reduce the national tension and create an atmosphere which will make it very difficult for any surprise attack to take place. In addition, such other steps as may be considered necessary for prevention of surprise attacks should be taken. If there is an agreement on the stoppage of nuclear tests and use of carriers, immediately danger from surprise attacks will be greatly lessened.

In the preamble of the constitution of UNESCO it is stated that war begins in the minds of men. That is essentially true; and ultimately it is necessary to bring about the change in our minds and to remove fears and apprehensions, hatreds and suspicions. Disarmament is a part of this process, for it will create an atmosphere of cooperation. But it is only a step towards our objective, a part of the larger efforts to rid the world of war and the causes of war.

In the present context, however, disarmament assumes a very special importance for us, overriding all other issues. For many years past, there have been talks on disarmament and some progress has undoubtedly been made in so far as the plans and proposals are concerned. Still we find that the race of armaments continues, as also the efforts to invent ever more powerful engines of destruction. If even a small part of these efforts was directed to the search for peace, probably the problem of disarmament would have been solved by this time.

Apart from the moral imperative of peace, every practical consideration leads us to that conclusion. For, as everyone knows, the choice today in this nuclear age is one of utter annihilation and destruction of civilization or of some way to have peaceful coexistence between nations. There is no middle way. If war Is an abomination and an ultimate crime which has to be avoided, we must fashion our minds and policies accordingly. There may be risks, but the greatest risk is to allow the present dangerous drift to continue. In order to achieve peace we have to develop a climate of peace and tolerance and to avoid speech and action which tend to increase fear and hatred.

It may not be possible to reach full disarmament in one step, though every step should be conditioned to that end. Much ground has already been covered in the discussions on disarmament. But the sands of time run out, and we dare not play about with this issue or delay its consideration. This, indeed, is the main duty of the United Nations today and if it fails in this, the United Nations falls in its main purpose.

We live in an age of great revolutionary changes brought about by the advance of science and technology. Therein lies the hope for the world and also the danger of sudden death. Because of these advances, the time we have for controlling the forces of destruction is strictly limited. If within the next three or four years, effective disarmament is not agreed to and implemented, then all the goodwill in the world will not be able to stop the drift to certain disaster.

I do believe that the vast majority of the people in every country wants us to labour for peace and to succeed. Whether we are big or small, we have to face big issues vital to the future of humanity. Everything else is of lesser importance than this major question. I am absolutely convinced that we shall never settle this question by war or by a mental approach which envisages war and prepares for it.

I am equally convinced that if we aim at right ends, right means must be employed. Good will not emerge out of evil methods. That was the lesson which our great leader Gandhi taught us, and though we in India have failed in many ways in following his advice, something of his message still clings to our minds and hearts. In ages long past a great son of India, the Buddha, said that the only real victory was one in which all were equally victorious and there was defeat for no one. In the world today that is the only practical victory. Any other way will lead to disaster.

It is, therefore, this real victory of peace in which all are winners that I would like this great Assembly to keep before its mind and to endeavour to achieve.

Speech at the Anit-Nuclear Arms Convention, New Delhi, June 16, 1962

WHAT do we, who are gathered here in this Convention, represent? Some of us have talked about nonviolence. Do we all believe fully in nonviolence, taking it to its utmost conclusions? I suppose not. We are not all pacifists. The word "Gandhian" is being used more and more frequently nowadays, and by frequent use it has lost all meaning, so that the most violent of men call themselves Gandhian. We all of us had the privilege of serving Gandhi, but I think it would be a little presumptuous on my part, for instance, to call myself a Gandhian. I am powerfully influenced by what he said, by what he taught us. But he was too big a man

— let us recognise It. We live in his glory, In the glory of his name. We in India, take the name of the Buddha and Gandhi and think we have done our duty. We assume vicariously, to some, extent, the virtues of the Buddha and Gandhi, just as to some extent in the West fierce and brutal wars were fought in the name of Christ.

The tremendous problem which faces the world today is one of survival; one of not being gradually reduced to the level of beasts; one of the increase of eivilisation, of moral values. It does not require any argument for all of us to know that a nuclear war not only means the end, the destruction of humanity, but that it is something infinitely degrading to our sense of values. Nobody, surely, can like being liquidated or having any part in this widespread destruction. But, nevertheless, large numbers of people are prepared to put up with this eventuality because presumably they think that something worse may take place unless they are ready for a nuclear war. They are afraid of defeat by another country, and, therefore, resign themselves to an arms race and the possibility of a nuclear war. Or else, they satisfy themselves by saying that nobody wants a nuclear war, but that they must have nuclear bombs as deterrents to prevent the other party from using them. This is curious logicand meanwhile we go nearer to the final explosion. It is all these bombs that are being made and collected, and all these tests, that are gradually bringing the probability of an explosion nearer. And time is limited, if you don't put an end to it soon enough, it may later on be beyond the capacity of human beings or nations to stop the rot.

At the present moment we have four powers, essentially two of them and two others, who have nuclear arms

and who have already collected vast numbers of them. If and when we decide on complete disarmament, it will be a terrible problem as to what we shall do with these bombs that we have collected. How shall we dispose of them without injury to somebody? You cannot throw them into the sea; the sea will be contaminated. I do not know what one can do with them, but that is a matter for the scientists. Anyhow, there is this vast collection of arms with us and the time is limited, and it is really a question of a race between the good sense of humanity and the fear between man and man.

Fear, I think, is a terrible thing. Fear and cowardice are the most degrading things anybody or any nation can have. They make one brutal. That is, why, when people talk about nonviolence in theory, speaking for myself, I completely agree. But I am horrified at the idea of the coward and the weak and the persons who are afraid of living under the shade of nonviolence. Of course, Gandhi's nonviolence was of the brave and he said so: "I would rather that you take out the sword you have in your heart and use it." There is nothing in this to do with fear. It is his idea of nonviolence. But, I am afraid the nonviolence of many people in this country and I say so quite frankly is nonviolence of the timid and the afraid and the fearful and from that nothing good can come. Nothing good can come from people who are afraid, who are cowards, and from their kind of nonviolence.

So the difficulty arises that when you ask masses of human beings to follow a policy, they must be trained up to it, as Gandhi indeed tried to train up and succeeded in a large measure in a limited field. But they must morally, spiritually call it what you like realise the significance of their action. If not, then they fall between two stools. They are neither here nor there and only fearfully look ahead to what might happen. That is a bad thing. Therein lies the difficulty, I think, of applying nonviolence in large numbers: that it should not make them cowards. If they are really nonviolent, well and good, let's go ahead; and I am quite sure if we went ahead in courage, nonviolence would win, not cowardice. In India, especially, we have the habit of talking in the highest terms but not acting up to them, our actions not coming anywhere near the ideals we profess.

I am very proud of India and of the many things that India has given to humanity. I think those are things of the greatest value to humanity and I do believe humanity will yet profit by them. But I know my people to some extent, liking them enormously, and I know their failings too, and I do not want to make them profess one thing and do something entirely opposite. That is hypocrisy and cowardice, and a grave danger. I am convinced of the virtue of nonviolence and of its power. But I am not sure that people in this country, or for that matter people of any other country, at the present moment are capable of carrying their burden of nonviolenceand if they fail, they fail utterly.

I am absolutely convinced that if any country adopted unilateral disarmament through strength, nobody would be able to injure it and it will win in the end. But what is the good of my saying so when I feel that those who adopt nonviolence do not do so through strength, but in fact are fearful of the consequences of their action and indulge In violence of all types? Vinobaji, a man of the present day in the great tradition of India, has said in his message to the Convention that he is less afraid of nuclear bombs than of the dagger and the

sword. What does it mean? Is he not stressing the evil in our hearts which comes out with everything that we do?

It is true that nuclear bombs have increased the danger tremendously, leading to a crisis in human affairs where either humanity survives or it does not. And this crisis can only be resolved, I think, finally not by some nuclear tests being stopped, but by something deeper, by the minds and hearts of men and the spirit of man rising to somewhat higher levels. I believe that humanity will rise; it is my firm faith, because there is no other way. Otherwise it might perish. We talk about nuclear bombs, but these are parts of a larger thingabolishing war, putting an end to war, absolutely. Before war goes we must have full disarmament. All these things are connected, each leading to the next step. Or we talk of the final step all the time. We never take any step at all. Therefore, for the present, we should concentrate on the stoppage of nuclear tests, though I shall be very happy to subscribe to the banning of the whole manufacture for all our desire to put an end to it will not lead us far, because nuclear bombs in an advanced scientific age, in a country which is advanced in science and technology, can be manufactured with ease. Can you put an end to all the nuclear bombs today? And, even so, if human beings want to make them later, they will make them. They will make them in a year or two. They are advanced enough and maybe technology will advance still further and make it easier to manufacture these bombs. I remember a very eminent nuclear physicist telling me once that one of these days you will manufacture nuclear bombs in your backgardens or in a small laboratory. Well, that may be a slight exaggeration.

But the fact Is nuclear bombs are all the time planted in our minds and hearts and unless we can get rid of them there, how can we be certain?

SO, in the ultimate analysis, war must be abolished. War will not be abolished till there is a change in human beings. That is a big question which I do not feel I am competent enough to answer. But there is no alternative left. So we must have disarmament. We must have a world without war, it is said. But a present step, an urgent step, is to Put an end to nuclear tests. The horror of It seems to me amazing, that a thing like this could be continued even purely on grounds of decency, if not anything else. Then also continuing nuclear tests brings the possibility of war nearer. It may create an atmosphere of an arms race. of fear and of the possibility of the accidents happening.

One other thing I should like to suggest, not as solution, but as a step towards lessening of tensions; and that is, having areas, atomfree areas, in Asia, In Africa, in Europe, which are recognised to have no nuclear weapons and which will not be used for nuclear weapons. All this cannot mean much, because the ultimate thing is having no war. full disarmament. But all these are steps which help. Today, the worst thing is the terrible tension and the fear behind it. Imagine thousands of aircraft with nuclear bombs always being in the air day and night. Imagine also those thousands of aircraft being piloted by brave young men. Any one of them may lose his nerve and do something which may lead to a war. It is horrible thought and still on goes this mad race.

Every little step that we take towards the goal is a good one, and although I do not know what effect this Convention may have on other countries, in India at

any rate, I hope it will draw away the attention of our people these problems, because we are a curious mixture exceedingly mild people who occasionally turn violent and misbehave. An average Indian will deliberately avoid stepping on a little insect; he will go round it. But that same average Indian may not be so to human beings. So I hope that this Convention bring some education and throw some light on the problems to our own people, because after all we are small men, grappling with enormous problems, grappling with the future of humanity. And small as we are, we can do something if we work together, if we understand problem and do our little towards its solution.

JIMMY CARTER

INTRODUCTION

Jimmy Carter (James Earl Carter, Jr.), 39th president of the United States, was born October 1, 1924, Georgia. On July 7, 1946, he married Rosalynn Smith of Plains. The Carters have three sons, one daughter, eight grandsons, and three granddaughters. In 1962 he won election to the Georgia Senate. He became Georgia's 76th governor on January 12, 1971. He was the Democratic National Committee campaign chairman for the 1974 congressional and gubernatorial elections.

He won the presidential election and was elected president on November 2, 1976. Jimmy Carter served as president from January 20, 1977 to January 20, 1981.

Inaugural address
Thursday, January 20, 1977

FOR myself and for our Nation, I want to thank my predecessor for all he has done to heal our land.

In this outward and physical ceremony we attest once again to the inner and spiritual strength of our Nation. As my high school teacher, Miss Julia Coleman, used to say: "We must adjust to changing times and still hold to unchanging principles."

Here before me is the Bible used in the inauguration of our first President, in 1789, and I have just taken the oath of office on the Bible my mother gave me a few years ago, opened to a timeless admonition from the ancient prophet Micah: "He hath showed thee, O man, what is good; and what doth the Lord require of thee, but to do justly, and to love mercy, and to walk humbly with thy God."

This inauguration ceremony marks a new beginning, a new dedication within our Government, and a new spirit among us all. A President may sense and proclaim that new spirit, but only a people can provide it.

Two centuries ago our Nation's birth was a milestone in the long quest for freedom, but the bold and brilliant dream which excited the founders of this Nation still awaits its consummation. I have no new dream to set forth today, but rather urge a fresh faith in the old dream.

Ours was the first society openly to define itself in terms of both spirituality and of human liberty. It is that unique self-definition which has given us an that unique self-definition which has given us an exceptional appeal, but it also imposes on us a special obligation, to take on those moral duties which, when assumed, seem invariably to be in our own best interests.

You have given me a great responsibility—to stay close to you, to be worthy of you, and to exemplify what you are. Let us create together a new national spirit of unity and trust. Your strength can compensate for my weakness, and your wisdom can help to minimize my mistakes.

Let us learn together and laugh together and work together and pray together, confident that in the end we will triumph together in the right.

The American dream endures. We must once again have full faith in our country—and in one another. I believe America can be better. We can be even stronger than before.

Let our recent mistakes bring a resurgent commitment to the basic principles of our Nation, for we know that if we despise our own government we have no future. We recall in special times when we have stood briefly, but magnificently, united. In those times no prize was beyond our grasp.

But we cannot dwell upon remembered glory. We cannot afford to drift. We reject the prospect of failure or mediocrity or an inferior quality of life for any person. Our Government must at the same time be both competent and compassionate.

We have already found a high degree of personal liberty, and we are now struggling to enhance equality of opportunity. Our commitment to human rights must be absolute, our laws fair, our natural beauty preserved; the powerful must not persecute the weak, and human dignity must be enhanced.

We have learned that "more" is not necessarily "better,"

that even our great Nation has its recognized limits, and that we can neither answer all questions nor solve all problems. We cannot afford to do everything, nor can we afford to lack boldness as we meet the future. So, together, in a spirit of individual sacrifice for the common good, we must simply do our best.

Our Nation can be strong abroad only if it is strong at home. And we know that the best way to enhance freedom in other lands is to demonstrate here that our democratic system is worthy of emulation.

To be true to ourselves, we must be true to others. We will not behave in foreign places so as to violate our rules and standards here at home, for we know that the trust which our Nation earns is essential to our strength.

The world itself is now dominated by a new spirit. Peoples more numerous and more politically aware are craving and now demanding their place in the sun—not just for the benefit of their own physical condition, but for basic human rights.

The passion for freedom is on the rise. Tapping this new spirit, there can be no nobler nor more ambitious task for America to undertake on this day of a new beginning than to help shape a just and peaceful world that is truly humane.

We are a strong nation, and we will maintain strength so sufficient that it need not be proven in combat—a quiet strength based not merely on the size of an arsenal, but on the nobility of ideas.

We will be ever vigilant and never vulnerable, and we will fight our wars against poverty, ignorance, and injustice—for those are the enemies against which our forces can be honorably marshaled.

We are a purely idealistic Nation, but let no one confuse our idealism with weakness.

Because we are free we can never be indifferent to the fate of freedom elsewhere. Our moral sense dictates a clearcut preference for these societies which share with us an abiding respect for individual human rights. We do not seek to intimidate, but it is clear that a world which others can dominate with impunity would be inhospitable to decency and a threat to the well-being of all people.

The world is still engaged in a massive armaments race designed to ensure continuing equivalent strength among potential adversaries. We pledge perseverance and wisdom in our efforts to limit the world's armaments to those necessary for each nation's own domestic safety. And we will move this year a step toward ultimate goal—the elimination of all nuclear weapons from this Earth. We urge all other people to join us, for success can mean life instead of death.

Within us, the people of the United States, there is evident a serious and purposeful rekindling of confidence. And I join in the hope that when my time as your President has ended, people might say this about our Nation: that we had remembered the words of Micah and renewed our search for humility, mercy, and justice; that we had torn down the barriers that separated those of different race and region and religion, and where there had been mistrust, built unity, with a respect for diversity; that we had found productive work for those able to perform it; that we had strengthened the American family, which is the basis of our society; that we had ensured respect for the law, and equal treatment under the law, for the weak and the powerful, for the rich and the poor; and that we had enabled our people to be proud of their own Government once again.

I would hope that the nations of the world might say that we had built a lasting peace, built not on weapons of war but on international policies which reflect our own most precious values.

These are not just my goals, and they will not be my accomplishments, but the affirmation of our Nation's continuing moral strength and our belief in an undiminished, ever-expanding American dream.

Jimmy Carter

JOHN F. KENNEDY

INTRODUCTION

U. S. statesman and 35th President (1961-1963) received education at Harward and London. He was born in Brookline, Massachusetts, on May 29, 1917.

He married Jacqueline Bouvier on September 12, 1953. He was a great Intellectual when he wrote "Profiles In Courte" which won him a Pulitzer Prize (1956). Elected Democrat Representative (1947) and Senator (1952) for Massachussetts and youngest President In 1960. He displayed firmness and moderation in foreign policy. He Induced Russia to withdraw its missiles from Cuba and advised a partial nuclear test ban treaty in 1963. On November 22, 1963, he was assassinated by Lee Harvey Oswald while being driven in an open car.

Ask Not What Your Country Can Do For You speech
Inaugural Address - January 20th 1961

VICE PRESIDENT JOHNSON, Mr. Speaker, Mr. Chief Justice, President Eisenhower, Vice President Nixon, President Truman, reverend clergy, fellow citizens, we observe today not a victory of party, but a celebration of freedom - symbolizing an end, as well as a beginning - signifying renewal, as well as change. For I have sworn before you and Almighty God the same solemn oath our forebears prescribed nearly a century and three quarters ago.

The world is very different now. For man holds in his mortal hands the power to abolish all forms of human poverty and all forms of human life. And yet the same revolutionary beliefs for which our forebears fought are still at issue around the globe - the belief that the rights of man come not from the generosity of the state, but from the hand of God.

We dare not forget today that we are the heirs of that first revolution. Let the word go forth from this time and place, to friend and foe alike, that the torch has been passed to a new generation of Americans - born in this century, tempered by war, disciplined by a hard and bitter peace, proud of our ancient heritage - and unwilling to witness or permit the slow undoing of those human rights to which this Nation has always been committed, and to which we are committed today at home and around the world.

Let every nation know, whether it wishes us well or ill, that we shall pay any price, bear any burden, meet any hardship, support any friend, oppose any foe, in order to assure the survival and the success of liberty. This much we pledge - and more.

To those old allies whose cultural and spiritual origins we share, we pledge the loyalty of faithful friends. United, there is little we cannot do in a host of cooperative ventures. Divided, there is little we can do - for we dare not meet a powerful challenge at odds and split asunder.

To those new States whom we welcome to the ranks of the free, we pledge our word that one form of colonial control shall not have passed away merely to be replaced by a far more iron tyranny. We shall not always expect to find them supporting our view. But we shall always hope to find them strongly supporting their own freedom - and to remember that, in the past, those who foolishly sought power by riding the back of the tiger ended up inside.

To those peoples in the huts and villages across the globe struggling to break the bonds of mass misery, we pledge our best efforts to help them help themselves, for whatever period is required - not because the Communists may be doing it, not because we seek their votes, but because it is right. If a free society cannot help the many who are poor, it cannot save the few who are rich.

To our sister republics south of our border, we offer a special pledge - to convert our good words into good deeds - in a new alliance for progress - to assist free men and free governments in casting off the chains of poverty. But this peaceful revolution of hope cannot become the prey of hostile powers. Let all our neighbours know that we shall join with them to oppose aggression or subversion anywhere in the Americas. And let every other power know that this Hemisphere intends to remain the master of its own house.

To that world assembly of sovereign states, the United

Nations, our last best hope in an age where the instruments of war have far outpaced the instruments of peace, we renew our pledge of support - to prevent it from becoming merely a forum for invective - to strengthen its shield of the new and the weak - and to enlarge the area in which its writ may run.

Finally, to those nations who would make themselves our adversary, we offer not a pledge but a request: that both sides begin anew the quest for peace, before the dark powers of destruction unleashed by science engulf all humanity in planned or accidental self-destruction.

We dare not tempt them with weakness. For only when our arms are sufficient beyond doubt can we be certain beyond doubt that they will never be employed.

But neither can two great and powerful groups of nations take comfort from our present course - both sides overburdened by the cost of modern weapons, both rightly alarmed by the steady spread of the deadly atom, yet both racing to alter that uncertain balance of terror that stays the hand of mankind's final war.

So let us begin anew - remembering on both sides that civility is not a sign of weakness, and sincerity is always subject to proof. Let us never negotiate out of fear. But let us never fear to negotiate.

Let both sides explore what problems unite us instead of belabouring those problems which divide us.

Let both sides, for the first time, formulate serious and precise proposals for the inspection and control of arms - and bring the absolute power to destroy other nations under the absolute control of all nations.

Let both sides seek to invoke the wonders of science instead of its terrors. Together let us explore the stars, conquer the deserts, eradicate disease, tap the ocean depths, and encourage the arts and commerce.

Let both sides unite to heed in all corners of the earth

the command of Isaiah - to "undo the heavy burdens - . and to let the oppressed go free."

And if a beachhead of cooperation may push back the jungle of suspicion, let both sides join in creating a new endeavour, not a new balance of power, but a new world of law, where the strong are just and the weak secure and the peace preserved.

All this will not be finished in the first 100 days. Nor will it be finished in the first 1,000 days, nor in the life of this Administration, nor even perhaps in our lifetime on this planet. But let us begin.

In your hands, my fellow citizens, more than in mine, will rest the final success or failure of our course. Since this country was founded, each generation of Americans has been summoned to give testimony to its national loyalty. The graves of young Americans who answered the call to service surround the globe.

Now the trumpet summons us again - not as a call to bear arms, though arms we need; not as a call to battle, though embattled we are - but a call to bear the burden of a long twilight struggle, year in and year out, "rejoicing in hope, patient in tribulation" - a struggle against the common enemies of man: tyranny, poverty, disease, and war itself.

Can we forge against these enemies a grand and global alliance, North and South, East and West, that can assure a more fruitful life for all mankind? Will you join in that historic effort?

In the long history of the world, only a few generations have been granted the role of defending freedom in its hour of maximum danger. I do not shank from this responsibility - I welcome it. I do not believe that any of us would exchange places with any other people or any other generation. The energy, the faith, the devotion which we bring to this endeavour will light our country and all who serve it — and the glow from that fire can truly light the world.

And so, my fellow Americans: ask not what your country can do for you - ask what you can do for your country.

My fellow citizens of the world: ask not what America will do for you, but what together we can do for the freedom of man.

Finally, whether you are citizens of America or citizens of the world, ask of us the same high standards of strength and sacrifice which we ask of you. With a good conscience our only sure reward, with history the final judge of our deeds, let us go forth to lead the land we love, asking His blessing and His help, but knowing that here on earth God's work must truly be our own.

Cuban Missile Crisis Speech
October 22nd 1962

GOOD EVENING, my fellow citizens: - This Government, as promised, has maintained the closest surveillance of the Soviet military build-up on the island of Cuba. Within the past week, unmistakable evidence has established the fact that a series of offensive Missile sites is now in preparation on that imprisoned island. The purpose of these bases can be none other than to provide a nuclear strike capability against the Western Hemisphere.

Upon receiving the first preliminary hard information of this nature last Tuesday morning at 9 a.m., I directed that our surveillance be stepped up. And having now confirmed and completed our evaluation of the evidence and our decision on a course of action, this Government feels obliged to report this new crisis to you in fullest detail.

The characteristics of these new missile sites indicate two distinct types of installations. Several of them include medium range ballistic missiles, capable of carrying a nuclear warhead for a distance of more than 1000 nautical miles. Each of these missiles, in short, is capable of striking Washington, D.C., the Panama Canal, Cape Canaveral, Mexico City, or any other city in the south-eastern part of the United States, in Central America, or in the Caribbean area.

Additional sites not yet completed appear to be designed for intermediate range ballistic missiles capable of travelling more than twice as far-and thus capable of striking most of the major cities in the Western Hemisphere, ranging as far north as Hudson Bay, Canada, and as far south as Lima, Peru. In addition, jet bombers, capable of carrying nuclear weapons, are now being un-crated and assembled in Cuba, while the necessary air bases are being prepared.

This urgent transformation of Cuba into an important strategic base- by the presence of these large, long-range, and clearly offensive weapons of sudden mass destruction constitutes an explicit threat to the peace and security of all the Americas, in flagrant and deliberate defiance of the Rio Pact of 1947, the traditions of this Nation and hemisphere, the joint resolution of the 87th Congress, the Charter of the United Nations, and my own public warnings to the Soviets on September 4 and 13. This action also contradicts the repeated assurances of Soviet spokesmen, both publicly and privately delivered, that the arms build-up in Cuba would retain its original defensive character, and that the Soviet Union had no need or desire to station strategic missiles on the territory of any other nation.

The size of this undertaking makes clear that it has been planned for some months. Yet only last month, after I had made clear the distinction between any introduction of ground-to- ground missiles and the existence of defensive anti-aircraft missiles, the Soviet

Government publicly stated on September 11th that, and I quote, "the armaments and military equipment sent to Cuba are designed exclusively for defensive purposes," that, and I quote the Soviet Government, "there is no need for the Soviet Government to shift its weapons... for a retaliatory blow to any other country, for instance Cuba," and that, and I quote their government, "the Soviet Union has so powerful rockets to carry these nuclear warheads that there is no need to search for sites for them beyond the boundaries of the Soviet Union." That statement was false. Only last Thursday, as evidence of this rapid offensive build-up was already in my hand, Soviet Foreign Minister Gromyko told me in my office that he was instructed to make it clear once again, as he said his government had already done, that Soviet assistance to Cuba, and I quote, "pursued solely for the purpose of contributing to the defence capabilities of Cuba," that, and I quote him, "training by Soviet specialists of Cuban nationals in handling defensive armaments was by no means offensive, and if it were otherwise," Mr. Gromyko went on, "the Soviet Government would never become involved in rendering such assistance." That statement also was false.

Neither the United States of America nor the world community of nations can tolerate deliberate deception and offensive threats on the part of any nation, large or small. We no longer live in a world where only the actual firing of weapons represents an efficient challenge to a nation's security to constitute maximum peril. Nuclear weapons are so destructive and ballistic missiles are so swift, that any substantially increased possibility of their use or any sudden change in their deployment may well be regarded as a definite threat to peace.

For many years, both the Soviet Union and the United States, recognizing this fact, have deployed strategic nuclear weapons with great care, never upsetting the precarious status quo which insured that these weapons would not be used in the absence of some vital challenge. Our own strategic missiles have never been transferred to the territory of any other nation under a cloak of secrecy and deception; and our history - unlike that of the Soviets since the end of World War II - demonstrates that we have no desire to dominate or conquer any other nation or impose our system upon its people. Nevertheless, American citizens have become adjusted to living daily on the bull's-eye of Soviet missiles located inside the U.S.S.R. or in submarines.

In that sense, missiles in Cuba add to an already clear and present danger - although it should be noted the nations of Latin America have never previously been subjected to a potential nuclear threat. But this secret, swift, and extraordinary build-up of Communist missiles-in an area well known to have a special and historical relationship to the United States and the nations of the Western Hemisphere, in violation of Soviet assurances, and in defiance of American and hemispheric policy - this sudden, clandestine decision to station strategic weapons for the first time outside of Soviet soil - is a deliberately provocative and unjustified change in the status quo which cannot be accepted by this country, if our courage and our commitments are ever to be trusted again by either friend or foe.

The 1930's taught us a clear lesson: aggressive conduct, if allowed to go unchecked and unchallenged, ultimately leads to war. This nation is opposed to war. We are also true to our word. Our unswerving objective, therefore, must be to prevent the use of these missiles against this or any other country, and to secure their withdrawal or elimination from the Western Hemisphere.

Our policy has been one of patience and restraint, as befits a peaceful and powerful nation, which leads a worldwide alliance. We have been determined not to be diverted from our central concerns by mere irritants and fanatics. But now further action is required - and it is under way; and these actions may only be the beginning. We will not prematurely or unnecessarily risk the costs of worldwide nuclear war in which even the fruits of victory would be ashes in our mouth - but neither will we shrink from that risk at any time it must be faced.

Acting, therefore, in the defence of our own security and of the entire Western Hemisphere, and under the authority end trusted to me by the Constitution as endorsed by the resolution of the Congress, I have directed that the following initial steps be taken immediately:

First: To halt this offensive build-up, a strict quarantine on all offensive military in equipment under shipment to Cuba is being initiated. All ships of any kind bound for Cuba from whatever nation or port will, if found to contain cargoes of offensive weapons, be turned back. This quarantine will be extended, if needed, to other types of cargo and carriers. We are not at this time, however, denying the necessities of life as the Soviets attempted to do in their Berlin blockade of I948 -

Second: I have directed the continued and increased close surveillance of Cuba and its military build-up. The foreign ministers of the OAS, in their communiqué of October 6th, rejected secrecy on such matters in this hemisphere. Should these offensive military preparations continue, thus increasing the threat to the hemisphere, further action will be justified. I have directed the Armed Forces to prepare for any eventualities; and I trust that in the interest of both the Cuban people and the Soviet technicians at the sites, the hazards to all concerned of continuing this threat will be recognized.

Third: It shall be the policy of this Nation to regard any

nuclear missile launched from Cuba against any nation in the Western Hemisphere as an attack by the Soviet Union on the United States, requiring a full retaliatory response upon the Soviet Union.

Fourth: As a necessary military precaution., I have reinforced our base at Guantanamo, evacuated today the dependents of our personnel there, and ordered additional military units to be on a standby alert basis.

Fifth: We are calling tonight for an immediate meeting of the Organ of Consultation under the Organization of American States, to consider this threat to hemispheric security and to invoke articles 6 and 8 of the Rio Treaty in support of all necessary action. The United Nations Charter allows for regional security arrangements - and the nations of this hemisphere decided long ago against the military presence of outside powers. Our other allies around the world have also been alerted.

Sixth: Under the Charter of the United Nations, we are asking tonight that an emergency meeting of the Security Council be convoked without delay to take action against this latest Soviet threat to world peace. Our resolution will call for the prompt dismantling and withdrawal of all offensive weapons in Cuba, under the supervision of U.N. observers, before the quarantine can be lifted.

Seventh and finally: I call upon Chairman Khrushchev to halt and eliminate this clandestine, reckless, and provocative threat to world peace and to stable relations between our two nations. I call upon him further to abandon this course of world domination, and to join in an historic effort to end the perilous arms race and to transform the history of man. He has an opportunity now to move the world back from the abyss of destruction - by returning to his government's own words that it had no need to station missiles outside its own territory, and withdrawing these weapons from

Cuba - by refraining from any action which will widen or deepen the present crisis - and then by participating in a search for peaceful and permanent solutions.

This Nation is prepared to present its case against the Soviet threat to peace, and our own proposals for a peaceful world, at any time and in any forum - in the OAS, in the United Nations, or in any other meeting that could be useful - without limiting our freedom of action. We have in the past made strenuous efforts to limit the spread of nuclear weapons. We have proposed the elimination of all arms and military bases in a fair and effective disarmament treaty. We are prepared to discuss new proposals for the removal of tensions on both sides - including the possibilities of a genuinely independent Cuba, free to determine its own destiny. We have no wish to war with the Soviet Union - for we are a peaceful people who desire to live in peace with all other peoples. But it is difficult to settle or even discuss these problems in an atmosphere of intimidation. That is why this latest Soviet threat - or any oilier threat which is made either independently or in response to our actions this week - must and will be met with determination. Any hostile move anywhere in the world against the safety and freedom of peoples to whom we are committed - including in particular the brave people of West Berlin - will be met by whatever action is needed.

Finally, I want to say a few words to the captive people of Cuba, to whom this speech is being directly carried by special radio facilities. I speak to you as a friend, as one who knows of your deep attachment to your fatherland, as one who shares your aspirations for liberty and justice for all. And I have watched and the American people have watched with deep sorrow how your nationalist revolution was betrayed - and how your fatherland fell under foreign domination. Now your leaders are no longer Cuban leaders inspired by Cuban ideals.

They are puppets and agents of an international conspiracy which has turned Cuba against your friends and neighbours in the Americas - and turned it into the first Latin American country to become a target for nuclear war - the first Latin American country to have these weapons on its soil.

These new weapons are not in your interest. They contribute nothing to your peace and well-being. They can only undermine it. But this country has no wish to cause you to suffer or to impose any system upon you. We know that your lives and land are being used as pawns by those who deny your freedom.

Many times in the past, the Cuban people have risen to throw out tyrants who destroyed their liberty. And I have no doubt that most Cubans today look forward to the time when they will be truly from foreign domination, free to choose their own leaders, free to select their own system, free to own their own land, free to speak and write and worship without fear or degradation. And then shall Cuba be welcomed back to the society of free nations and to the association of nations of this hemisphere.

My fellow citizens: let no one doubt that this is a difficult and dangerous effort on which we have set out. No one can foresee precisely what course it will take or what costs or casualties will be incurred. Many months of sacrifice and self-discipline lie ahead - months in which both our patience and our will be tested - months in which many threats and denunciations will keep us aware of our dangers. But the greatest danger of all would be to do nothing.

The path we have chosen for the present is full of hazards, as all paths are - but it is the one most consistent with our character and courage as a nation and our commitments around the world. The cost of freedom is always high - but Americans have always paid it. And one path we shall never choose, and that is the path of surrender or submission. Our goal is not the victory of might, but the vindication of right-not peace at the expense of freedom, but both peace and freedom, here in this hemisphere, and, we hope, around the world. God willing, that goal will be achieved.

The Berlin Address speech
June 26, 1963

I am proud to come to this city as the guest of your distinguished Mayor, who has symbolized throughout the world the fighting spirit of West Berlin. And I am proud to visit the Federal Republic with your distinguished Chancellor who for so many years has committed Germany to democracy and freedom and progress, and to come here in the company of my fellow American, General Clay, who has been in this city during its great moments of crisis and will come again if ever needed.

Two thousand years ago the proudest boast was "civis Romanus sum." Today, in the world of freedom, the proudest boast is "Ich bin ein Berliner." I appreciate my interpreter translating my German!

There are many people in the world who really don't understand, or say they don't, what is the great issue between the free world and the Communist world. Let them come to Berlin. There are some who say that communism is the wave of the future. Let them come to Berlin. And there are some who say in Europe and elsewhere we can work with the Communists. Let them come to Berlin. And there are even a few who say that it is true that communism is an evil system, but it permits us to make economic progress. Lass' sie nach Berlin kommen. Let them come to Berlin.

Freedom has many difficulties and democracy is not perfect, but we have never had to put a wall up to keep our people in, to prevent them from leaving us. I want to say, on behalf of my countrymen, who live many miles away on the other side of the Atlantic, who are far distant from you, that they take the greatest pride that they have been able to share with you, even from a distance, the story of the last 18 years. I know of no town, no city, that has been besieged for 18 years that still lives with the vitality and the force, and the hope and the determination of the city of West Berlin. While the wall is the most obvious and vivid demonstration of the failures of the Communist system, for all the world to see, we take no satisfaction in it, for it is, as your Mayor has said, an offence not only against history but an offence against humanity, separating families, dividing husbands and wives and brothers and sisters, and dividing a people who wish to be joined together.

What is true of this city is true of Germany—real, lasting peace in Europe can never be assured as long as one German out of four is denied the elementary right of free men, and that is to make a free choice. In 18 years of peace and good faith, this generation of Germans has earned the right to be free, including the right to unite their families and their nation in lasting peace, with good will to all people. You live in a defended island of freedom, but your life is part of the main. So let me ask you as I close, to lift your eyes beyond the dangers of today, to the hopes of tomorrow, beyond the freedom merely of this city of Berlin, or your country of Germany, to the advance of freedom everywhere, beyond the wall to the day of peace with justice, beyond yourselves and ourselves to all mankind.

Freedom is indivisible, and when one man is enslaved, all are not free. When all are free, then we can look forward to that day when this city will be joined as one and this country and this great Continent of Europe in a peaceful and hopeful globe. When that day finally comes, as it will, the people of West Berlin can take sober satisfaction in the fact that they were in the front lines for almost two decades.

All free men, wherever they may live, are citizens of Berlin, and, therefore, as a free man, I take pride in the words "Ich bin ein Berliner."

MARTIN LUTHER KING

INTRODUCTION

Michael Luther King, Jr. was born in January 15, 1929, but later had his name changed to Martin.

In 1954, Martin Luther King accepted the pastorale of the Dexter Avenue Baptist Church in Montgomery, Alabama.

At the age of thirty-five, Martin Luther King, Jr., was the youngest man to have received the Nobel Peace Prize. When notified of his selection, he announced that he would turn over the prize money of $54,123 to the furtherance of the civil rights movement.

He fought aginst the racism and it ultimately saw the whites and blacks at par. Today the American society is dominated by the blacks. He died on April 4, 1968.

Birth of a New Nation speech
April 7th 1957

I want to preach this morning from the subject, "The Birth of a New Nation." And I would like to use as a basis for our thinking together a story that has long since been stencilled on the mental sheets of succeeding generations. It is the story of the Exodus, the story of the flight of the Hebrew people from the bondage of Egypt, through the wilderness, and finally to the Promised Land. It's a beautiful story. I had the privilege the other night of seeing the story in movie terms in New York City, entitled "The Ten Commandments," and I came to see it in all of its beauty - the struggle of Moses, the struggle of his devoted followers as they sought to get out of Egypt. And they finally moved on to the wilderness and toward the Promised Land. This is something of the story of every people struggling for freedom. It is the first story of man's explicit quest for freedom. And it demonstrates the stages that seem to inevitably follow the quest for freedom.

Prior to March the sixth, 1957, there existed a country known as the Gold Coast. This country was a colony of the British Empire. This country was situated in that vast continent known as Africa. I'm sure you know a great deal about Africa, that continent with some two hundred million people and it extends and covers a great deal of territory. There are many familiar names associated with Africa that you would probably remember, and there are some countries in Africa that many people never realize. For instance, Egypt is in

Africa. And there is that vast area of North Africa with Egypt and Ethiopia, with Tunisia and Algeria and Morocco and Libya. Then you might move to South Africa and you think of that extensive territory known as the Union of South Africa. There is that capital city Johannesburg that you read so much about these days. Then there is central Africa with places like Rhodesia and the Belgian Congo. And then there is East Africa with places like Kenya and Tanganyika, and places like Uganda and other very powerful countries right there. And then you move over to West Africa, where you find the French West Africa and Nigeria, and Liberia and Sierra Leone and places like that. And it is in this spot, in this section of Africa, that we find the Gold Coast, there in West Africa.

You also know that for years and for centuries, Africa has been one of the most exploited continents in the history of the world. It's been the "Dark Continent." It's been the continent that has suffered all of the pain and the affliction that could be mustered up by other nations. And it is that continent which has experienced slavery, which has experienced all of the lowest standards that we can think about, and its been brought into being by the exploitation inflicted upon it by other nations.

And this country, the Gold Coast, was a part of this extensive continent known as Africa. It's a little country there in West Africa about ninety-one thousand miles in area, with a population of about five million people, a little more than four and a half million. And it stands there with its capital city, Accra. For years the Gold Coast was exploited and dominated and trampled over. The first European settlers came in there about 1444, the Portuguese, and they started legitimate trade with the people in the Gold Coast. They started dealing with them with their gold, and in turn they gave them guns and ammunition and gunpowder and that type of thing. Well, pretty soon America was discovered a few years later in the fourteen hundreds, and then the British West Indies. And all of these growing discoveries brought about the slave trade. You remember it started in America in 1619.

And there was a big scramble for power in Africa. With the growth of the slave trade, there came into Africa, into the Gold Coast in particular, not only the Portuguese but also the Swedes and the Danes and the Dutch and the British. And all of these nations competed with each other to win the power of the Gold Coast so that they could exploit these people for commercial reasons and sell them into slavery.

Finally, in 1850, Britain won out, and she gained possession of the total territorial expansion of the Gold Coast. From 1850 to 1957, March sixth, the Gold Coast was a colony of the British Empire. And as a colony she suffered all of the injustices, all of the exploitation, all of the humiliation that comes as a result of colonialism. But like all slavery, like all domination, like all exploitation, it came to the point that the people got tired of it.

And that seems to be the long story of history. There seems to be a throbbing desire, there seems to be an internal desire for freedom within the soul of every man. And it's there - it might not break forth in the beginning, but eventually it breaks out Men realize that freedom is something basic, and to rob a man of his freedom is to take from him the essential basis of his manhood. To take from him his freedom is to rob him of something of God's image. To paraphrase the words of Shakespeare's Othello: Who steals my purse steals trash; 'tis something, nothing; twas mine, 'tis his, has been the slave of thousands; but he who filches from me my freedom robs me of that which not enriches him, but makes me poor indeed.

There is something in the soul that cries out for freedom. There is something deep down within the very soul of man that reaches out for Canaan. Men cannot be satisfied with Egypt. They tried to adjust to it for awhile. Many men have vested interests in Egypt, and they are slow to leave. Egypt makes it profitable to them; some people profit by Egypt. The vast majority, the masses of people never profit by Egypt, and they are never content with it. And eventually they rise up and begin to cry out for Canaan's land.

And so these people got tired. It had a long history. As far back as 1844, the chiefs themselves of the Gold Coast rose up and came together and revolted against the British Empire and the other powers that were in existence at that time dominating the Gold Coast. They revolted, saying that they wanted to govern themselves. But these powers clamped down on them, and the British said that we will not let you go.

About 1909, a young man was born on the twelfth of September. History didn't know at that time what that young man had in his mind. His mother and father, illiterate, not a part of the powerful tribal life of Africa, not chiefs at all, but humble people. And that boy grew up. He went to school at Achimota for a while in Africa, and then he finished there with honours and decided to work his way to America. And he landed to America one day with about fifty dollars in his pocket in terms of pounds, getting ready to get an education. And he went down to Pennsylvania, to Lincoln University. He started studying there, and he started reading the great insights of the philosophers, he started reading the great insights of the ages. And he finished there and took his theological degree there and preached awhile around Philadelphia and other areas as he was in the country. And went over to the University of Pennsylvania and took up a masters there in philosophy and sociology. All the years that he stood in America, he was poor, he had to work hard. He says in his autobiography how he worked as a bellhop in hotels, as a dishwasher, and during the summer how he worked as a waiter trying to struggle through school.

"I want to go back home. I want to go back to West Africa, the land of my people, my native land There is some work to be done there." He got a ship and went to London and stopped for a while by London School of Economy and picked up another degree there. Then while in London, he started thinking about Pan-Africanism and the problem of how to free his people from colonialism. For as he said, he always realized that colonialism was made for domination and for exploitation. It was made to keep a certain group down and exploit that group economically for the advantage of another. He studied and thought about all of this, and one day he decided to go back to Africa.

He got to Africa and he was immediately elected the executive secretary of the United Party of the Gold Coast. And he worked hard, and he started getting a following. And the people in this party, the old, the people who had had their hands on the plow for a long time, thought he was pushing a little too fast, and they got a little jealous of his influence. and so finally he had to break from the United Party of the Gold Coast, and in 1949 he organized the Convention People's Party. It was this party that started out working for the independence of the Gold Coast. He started out in a humble way, urging his people to unite for freedom and urging the officials of the British Empire to give them freedom. They were slow to respond, but the masses of people were with him, and they had united to become the most powerful and influential party that had ever been organized in that section of Africa.

He started writing. And his companions with him, and many of them started writing so much that the officials got afraid, and they put them in jail. And Nkrumah himself was finally placed in jail for several years because he was a seditious man, he was an agitator. He was imprisoned on the basis of sedition, and he was placed there to stay in prison for many years. But he had inspired some people outside of prison. They got together just a few months after he'd been in prison and elected him the prime minister while he was in prison. For awhile the British officials tried to keep him there, and Gbedemah says - one of his close associates, the Minister of Finance, Mr. Gbedemah - said that that night the people were getting ready to go down to the jail and get him out. But Gbedemah said, "This isn't the way; we can't do it like this. Violence will break out and we will defeat our purpose." But the British Empire saw that they had better let him out. And in a few hours Kwame Nkrumah was out of jail, the prime minister of the Gold Coast. He was placed there for fifteen years but he only served eight or nine months, and now he comes out the Prime Minister of the Gold Coast.

And this was the struggling that had been going on for years. It was now coming to the point that this little nation was moving toward its independence. Then came the continual agitation, the continual resistance, so that the British Empire saw that it could no longer rule the Gold Coast. And they agreed that on the sixth of March, 1957, they would release this nation. This nation would no longer be a colony of the British Empire, that this nation would be a sovereign nation within the British Commonwealth. All of this was because of the persistent protest, the continual agitation on the part of Prime Minister Kwame Nkrumah and the other leaders who worked along with him and the masses of people who were willing to follow.

So that day finally came. It was a great day. The week ahead was a great week. They had been preparing for this day for many years, and now it was here. People coming in from all over the world. They had started getting in by the second of March. Seventy nations represented to come to say to this new nation: "We greet you, and we give you our moral support. We hope for you God's guidance as you move now into the realm of independence." From America itself more than a hundred persons: the press, the diplomatic guests, and the prime minister's guests. And oh, it was a beautiful experience to see some of the leading persons on the scene of civil rights in America on hand to say, "Greetings to you," as this new nation was born. Look over, to my right is Adam Powell, to my left is Charles Diggs, to my right again is Ralph Bunche. To the other side is Her Majesty's First Minister of Jamaica, Manning, Ambassador Jones of Liberia. All of these people from America, Mordecai Johnson, Horace Mann Bond, all of these people just going over to say, "We want to greet you and we want you to know that you have our moral support as you grow." Then you look out and see the vice-president of the United States, you see A. Philip Randolph, you see all of the people who have stood in the forefront of the struggle for civil rights over the years, coming over to Africa to say, "We bid you Godspeed." This was a great day not only for Nkrumah, but for the whole of the Gold Coast.

Then came Tuesday, [March] the fifth, many events leading up to it. That night we walked into the closing of Parliament - the closing of the old Parliament, the old Parliament, which was presided over by the British Empire. The old Parliament which designated colonialism and imperialism. Now that Parliament is closing. That was a great sight and a great picture and a great scene. We sat there that night, just about five hundred able to get in there. People, thousands and thousands of people waiting outside, just about five hundred in there, and we were fortunate enough to be sitting there at that moment as guests of the prime minister. At that hour we noticed Prime Minister Nkrumah walking in with all of his ministers, with his justices of the Supreme Court of the Gold Coast, and with all of the people of the Convention People's Party, the leaders of that party. Nkrumah came up to make his closing speech to the old Gold Coast. There was something old now passing away.

The thing that impressed me more than anything else that night was the fact that when Nkrumah walked in, and his other ministers who had been in prison with him, they didn't come in with the crowns and all of the garments of kings, but they walked in with prison caps and the coats that they had lived with for all of the months that they had been in prison. Nkrumah stood up and made his closing speech to Parliament with the little cap that he wore in prison for several months and the coat that he wore in prison for several months, and all of his ministers round about him. That was a great hour. An old Parliament passing away.

And then at twelve o'clock that night we walked out. As we walked out we noticed all over the polo grounds almost a half-a-million people. They had waited for this hour and this moment for years. As we walked out of the door and looked at that beautiful building, we looked up to the top of it and there was a little flag that had been flowing around the sky for many years. It was the Union Jack flag of the Gold Coast, the British flag, you see. But at twelve o'clock that night we saw a little flag coming down, and another flag went up. The old Union Jack flag came down, and the new flag of Ghana went up. This was a new nation now, a new nation being born.

And when Prime Minister Nkrumah stood up before his people out in the polo ground and said, "We are no longer a British colony. We are a free, sovereign people," all over that vast throng of people we could see tears. And I stood there thinking about so many things. Before I knew it, I started weeping. I was crying for joy. And I knew about all of the struggles, and all of the pain, and all of the agony that these people had gone through for this moment.

After Nkrumah had made that final speech, it was about twelve-thirty now. And we walked away. And we could hear little children six years old and old people eighty and ninety years old walking the streets of Accra crying, "Freedom! Freedom!" They couldn't say it in the sense that we'd say it - many of them don't speak

English too well - but they had their accents and it could ring out, "Free-doom!" They were crying it in a sense that they had never heard it before, and I could hear that old Negro spiritual once more crying out:

Free at last! Free at last!

Great God Almighty, I'm free at last!

They were experiencing that in their very souls. And everywhere we turned, we could hear it ringing out from the housetops. We could hear it from every corner, every nook and crook of the community: "Freedom! Freedom!" This was the birth of a new nation. This was the breaking aloose from Egypt.

Wednesday morning the official opening of Parliament was held. There again we were able to get on the inside. There Nkrumah made his new speech. And now the prime minister of the Gold Coast with no superior, with all of the power that MacMillan of England has, with all of the power that Nehru of India has - now a free nation, now the prime minister of a sovereign nation. The Duchess of Kent walked in, the Duchess of Kent, who represented the Queen of England, no longer had authority now. She was just a passing visitor now. The night before, she was the official leader and spokesman for the Queen, thereby the power behind the throne of the Gold Coast. But now it's Ghana. It's a new nation now, and she's just an official visitor like M. L. King and Ralph Bunche and Coretta King and everybody else, because this is a new nation. A new Ghana has come into being.

And now Nkrumah stands the leader of that great nation. And when he drives out, the people standing around the streets of the city after Parliament is open, cry out: "All hail, Nkrumah!" The name of Nkrumah crowning around the whole city, everybody crying this name, because they knew he had suffered for them, he had sacrificed for them, he'd gone to jail for them. This was the birth of a new nation. This nation was now out of Egypt and had crossed the Red Sea.

Now it will confront its wilderness. Like any breaking loose from Egypt, there is a wilderness ahead. There is a problem of adjustment. Nkrumah realizes that. There is always this wilderness standing before him. For instance, it's a one-crop country, cocoa mainly. Sixty percent of the cocoa of the world comes from the Gold Coast, or from Ghana. And, in order to make the economic system more stable, it will be necessary to industrialize. Cocoa is too fluctuating to base a whole economy on that, so there is the necessity of industrializing. Nkrumah said to me that one of the first things that he will do is to work toward industrialization. And also he plans to work toward the whole problem of increasing the cultural standards of the community. Still ninety percent of the people are illiterate, and it is necessary to lift the whole cultural standard of the community in order to make it possible to stand up in the free world.

Yes, there is a wilderness ahead, though it is my hope that even people from America will go to Africa as immigrants, right there to the Gold Coast, and lend their technical assistance, for there is great need and there are rich opportunities there. Right now is the time that American Negroes can lend their technical assistance to a growing new nation. I was very happy to see already people who have moved in and making good. The son of the late president of Bennett College, Dr. Jones, is there, who started an insurance company and making good, going to the top. A doctor from Brooklyn, New York, had just come in that week and his wife is also a dentist, and they are living there now, going in there and working, and the people love them. There will be hundreds and thousands of people, I'm sure, going over to make for the growth of this new nation. And Nkrumah made it very clear to me that he would welcome any persons coming there as immigrants and to live there. Now don't think that because they have five million people the nation can't grow, that that's a small nation to be overlooked. Never forget the fact that when America was born in 1776, when it received its independence from the British Empire, there were fewer, less than four million people in America, and today it's more than a hundred and sixty million. So never underestimate a people because it's small now. America was smaller than Ghana when it was born.

There is a great day ahead. The future is on its side. It's going now through the wilderness, but the Promised Land is ahead.

And I want to take just a few more minutes as I close to say three or four things that this reminds us of and things that it says to us - things that we must never forget as we ourselves find ourselves breaking loose from an evil Egypt, trying to move through the wilderness toward the promised land of cultural integration. Ghana has something to say to us. It says to us first that the oppressor never voluntarily gives freedom to the oppressed. You have to work for it. And if Nkrumah and the people of the Gold Coast had not stood up persistently, revolting against the system, it would still be a colony of the British Empire. Freedom is never given to anybody, for the oppressor has you in domination because he plans to keep you there, and he never voluntarily gives it up. And that is where the strong resistance comes. Privileged classes never give up their privileges without strong resistance.

So don't go out this morning with any illusions. Don't go back into your homes and around Montgomery thinking that the Montgomery City Commission and that all of the forces in the leadership of the South will eventually work out this thing for Negroes, it's going to work out; it's going to roll in on the wheels of inevitability. If we wait for it to work itself out, it will never be worked out. Freedom only comes through persistent revolt, through persistent agitation, through persistently rising up against the system of evil. The bus protest is just the beginning. Buses are integrated in Montgomery, but that is just the beginning. And don't sit down and do nothing now because the buses are integrated, because, if you stop now, we will be in the dungeons of segregation and discrimination for another hundred years, and our children and our children's children will suffer all of the bondage that we have lived under for years. It never comes voluntarily. We've got to keep on keeping on in order to gain freedom. It never comes like that. It would be fortunate if the people in power had sense enough to go on and give up, but they don't do it like that. It is not done voluntarily, but it is done through the pressure that comes about from people who are oppressed.

If there had not been a Gandhi in India with all of his noble followers, India would have never been free. If there had not been an Nkrumah and his followers in Ghana, Ghana would still be a British colony. If there had not been abolitionists in America, both Negro and white, we might still stand today in the dungeons of slavery. And then because there have been, in every period, there are always those people in every period of human history who don't mind getting their necks cut off, who don't mind being persecuted and discriminated and kicked about, because they know that freedom is never given out, but it comes through the persistent and the continual agitation and revolt on the part of those who are caught in the system. Ghana teaches us that.

It says to us another thing. It reminds us of the fact that a nation or a people can break aloose from oppression without violence. Nkrumah says in the first two pages of his autobiography, which was published on the sixth of March - a great book which you ought to read - he said that he had studied the social systems of social philosophers and he started studying the life of Gandhi and his techniques. And he said that in the beginning he could not see how they could ever get loose from colonialism without armed revolt, without armies and ammunition, rising up. Then he says after he continued to study Gandhi and continued to study this technique, he came to see that the only way was through non-violent positive action. And he called his program "positive action." And it's a beautiful thing, isn't it? That here is a nation that is now free, and it is free without rising up with arms and with ammunition. It is free through non-violent means. Because of that the British Empire will not have the bitterness for Ghana that she has for China, so to speak. Because of that, when the British Empire leaves Ghana, she leaves with a different attitude than she would have left with if she had been driven out by armies. We've got to revolt in such a way that after revolt is over we can live with people as their brothers and their sisters. Our aim must never be to defeat them or humiliate them.

On the night of the State Ball, standing up talking with some people, Mordecai Johnson called my attention to the fact that Prime Minister Kwame Nkrumah was there dancing with the Duchess of Kent. And I said, "Isn't this something? Here is the once-serf, the once-slave, now dancing with the lord on an equal plane." And that is done because there is no bitterness. These two nations will be able to live together and work together because the breaking loose was through non-violence and not through violence.

The aftermath of non-violence is the creation of the beloved community. The aftermath of non-violence is redemption. The aftermath of non-violence is reconciliation. The aftermath of violence however, are emptiness and bitterness. This is the thing I'm concerned about. Let us fight passionately and unrelentingly for the goals of justice and peace, but let's be sure that our hands are clean in this struggle. Let us never fight with falsehood and violence and hate and malice, but always fight with love, so that, when the day comes that the walls of segregation have completely crumbled in Montgomery. that we will be able to live with people as their brothers and sisters.

Oh, my friends, our aim must be not to defeat Mr. Engelhardt, not to defeat Mr. Sellers and Mr. Gayle and Mr. Parks. Our aim must be to defeat the evil that's in them. But our aim must be to win the friendship of Mr. Gayle and Mr. Sellers and Mr. Engelhardt. We must come to the point of seeing that our ultimate aim is to live with all men as brothers and sisters under God and not be their enemies or anything that goes with that type of relationship. And this is one thing that Ghana teaches us: that you can break loose from evil through non-violence, through a lack of bitterness. Nkrumah says in his book: "When I came out of prison, I was not bitter toward Britain. I came out merely with the determination to free my people from the colonialism and imperialism that had been inflicted upon them by the British. But I came out with no bitterness." And, because of that, this world will be a better place in which to live.

There's another thing that Ghana reminds us. I'm coming to the conclusion now. Ghana reminds us that freedom never comes on a silver platter. It's never easy. Ghana reminds us that whenever you break out of Egypt, you better get ready for stiff backs. You better get ready for some homes to be bombed. You better get ready for some churches to be bombed. You better get ready for a lot of nasty things to be said about you, because you're getting out of Egypt, and, whenever you break loose from Egypt, the initial response of the Egyptian is bitterness. It never comes with ease. It comes only through the hardness and persistence of life. Ghana reminds us of that. You better get ready to go to prison. When I looked out and saw the prime minister there with his prison cap on that night, that reminded me of that fact, that freedom never comes easy. It comes through hard labour and it comes through toil. It comes through hours of despair and disappointment.

That's the way it goes. There is no crown without a cross. I wish we could get to Easter without going to

Good Friday, but history tells us that we got to go by Good Friday before we can get to Easter. That's the long story of freedom, isn't it? Before you get to Canaan, you've got a Red Sea to confront. You have a hardened heart of a pharaoh to confront. You have the prodigious hilltops of evil in the wilderness to confront. And, even when you get up to the Promised Land, you have giants in the land. The beautiful thing about it is that there are a few people who've been over in the land. They have spied enough to say, "Even though the giants are there we can possess the land, because we got the internal fibre to stand up amid anything that we have to face."

The road to freedom is a difficult, hard road. It always makes for temporary setbacks. And those people who tell you today that there is more tension in Montgomery than there has ever been are telling you right. Whenever you get out of Egypt, you always confront a little tension, you always confront a little temporary setback. If you didn't confront that you'd never get out. You must remember that the tensionless period that we like to think of was the period when the Negro was complacently adjusted to segregation, discrimination, insult, and exploitation. And the period of tension is the period when the Negro has decided to rise up and break loose from that. And this is the peace that we are seeking: not an old negative obnoxious peace which is merely the absence of tension, but a positive, lasting peace, which is the presence of brotherhood and justice. And it is never brought about without this temporary period of tension. The road to freedom is difficult.

But finally Ghana tells us that the forces of the universe are on the side of justice. That's what it tells us, now. You can interpret Ghana any kind of way you want to, but Ghana tells me that the forces of the universe are on the side of justice. That night when I saw that old flag coming down and the new flag coming up, I saw something else. That wasn't just an Ephemeral, evanescent event appearing on the stage of history, but it was an event with eternal meaning, for it symbolizes something. That thing symbolized to me that an old order is passing away and a new order is coming into being. An old order of colonialism, of segregation, of discrimination is passing away now, and a new order of justice and freedom and goodwill is being born. That's what it said: that somehow the forces of justice stand on the side of the universe, and that you can't ultimately trample over God's children and profit by it.

I want to come back to Montgomery now, but I must stop by London for a moment, for London reminds me of something. I never will forget the day we went into London. The next day we started moving around this great city, the only city in the world that is almost as large as New York City. Over eight million people in London, about eight million, three hundred thousand; New York about eight million, five hundred thousand. London larger in area than New York, though. Standing in London is an amazing picture. And I never will forget the experience I had, the thoughts that came to my mind. We went to Buckingham Palace, and I looked there at all of Britain, at all of the pomp and circumstance of royalty. And I thought about all of the queens and kings that had passed through here. Look at the beauty of the changing of the guards and all of the guards with their beautiful horses. It's a beautiful sight. Move on from there and go over to Parliament. Move into the House of Lords and the House of Commons. There with all of its beauty standing up before the world is one of the most beautiful sights in the world.

Then I remember, we went on over to Westminster Abbey. And I thought about several things when we went in this great church, this great cathedral, the centre of the Church of England. We walked around and went to the tombs of the kings and queens buried there. Most of the kings and queens of England are buried right there in the Westminster Abbey. And I walked around. On the one hand I enjoyed and appreciated the great gothic architecture of that massive cathedral. I stood there in awe thinking about the greatness of God and man's feeble attempt to reach up for God. And I thought something else - I thought about the Church of England.

My mind went back to Buckingham Palace, and I said that this is the symbol of a dying system. There was a day that the queens and kings of England could boast that the sun never sets on the British Empire, a day when she occupied the greater portion of Australia, the greater portion of Canada. There was a day when she ruled most of China, most of Africa, and all of India. I started thinking about this empire. I started thinking about the fact that she ruled over India one day. Mahatma Gandhi stood there at every hand, trying to get the freedom of his people, and they never bowed to it. They never, they decided that they were going to stand up and hold India in humiliation and in colonialism many, many years. I remember we passed by Ten Downing Street. That's the place where the prime minister of England lives. And I remember that a few years ago a man lived there by the name of Winston Churchill. One day he stood up before the world and said, "I did not become his Majesty's First Minister to preside over the liquidation of the British Empire." And I thought about the fact that a few weeks ago a man by the name of Anthony Eden lived there. And out of all of his knowledge of the Middle East, he decided to rise up and march his armies with the forces of Israel and France into Egypt, and there they confronted their doom, because they were revolting against world opinion. Egypt, a little country; Egypt, a country with no military power. They could have easily defeated Egypt, but they did not realize that they were fighting more than Egypt. They were attacking world opinion; they were fighting the whole Asian-African bloc, which is the bloc that now thinks and moves and determines the course of the history of the world.

I thought of many things. I thought of the fact that the British Empire exploited India. Think about it! A nation with four hundred million people and the British exploited them so much that out of a population of four hundred million, three hundred and fifty million made an annual income of less than fifty dollars a year. Twenty-five of that had to be used for taxes and the other things of life. I thought about dark Africa, and how the people there, if they can make a hundred dollars a year they are living very well, they think. Two shillings a day - one shilling is fourteen cents, two shillings, twenty-eight cents - that's a good wage. That's because of the domination of the British Empire.

All of these things came to my mind, and when I stood there in Westminster Abbey with all of its beauty, and I thought about all of the beautiful hymns and anthems that the people would go in there to sing. And yet the Church of England never took a stand against this system. The Church of England sanctioned it The Church of England gave it moral stature. All of the exploitation perpetuated by the British Empire was sanctioned by the Church of England.

But something else came to my mind: God comes in the picture even when the Church won't take a stand. God has injected a principle in this universe. God has said that all men must respect the dignity and worth of all human personality, "And if you don't do that, I will take charge." It seems this morning that I can hear God speaking. I can hear him speaking throughout the universe, saying, "Be still and know that I am God. And if you don't stop, if you don't straighten up, if you don't stop exploiting people, I'm going to rise up and break the backbone of your power. And your power will be no more!"

And the power of Great Britain is no more. I looked at France. I looked at Britain. And I thought about the Britain that could boast, "The sun never sets on our great Empire." And I said now she had gone to the level that the sun hardly rises on the British Empire -

because it was based on exploitation, because the God of the universe eventually takes a stand.

And I say to you this morning, my friends, rise up and know that, as you struggle for justice, you do not struggle alone, but God struggles with you. And He is working every day. Somehow I can look out, I can look out across the seas and across the universe, and cry out, "Mine eyes have seen the glory of the coming of the Lord. He is trampling out the vintage where the grapes of wrath are stored." Then I think about it, because His truth is marching on, and I can sing another chorus: "Hallelujah, glory hallelujah! His truth is marching on." Then I can hear Isaiah again, because it has profound meaning to me, that somehow, "Every valley shall be exalted, and every hill shall be made low; the crooked places shall be made straight, and the rough places plain; and the glory of the Lord shall be revealed, and all flesh shall see it together."

That's the beauty of this thing: all flesh shall see it together. Not some from the heights of Park Street and others from the dungeons of slum areas. Not some from the pinnacles of the British Empire and some from the dark deserts of Africa. Not some from inordinate, superfluous wealth and others from abject, deadening poverty. Not some white and not some black, not some yellow and not some brown, but all flesh shall see it together. They shall see it from Montgomery. They shall see it from New York. They shall see it from Ghana. They shall see it from China.

For I can look out and see a great number, as John saw, marching into the great eternity, because God is working in this world, and at this hour, and at this moment. And God grants that we will get on board and start marching with God, because we got orders now to break down the bondage and the walls of colonialism, exploitation, and imperialism, to break them down to the point that no man will trample over another man, but that all men will respect the dignity and worth of all human personality. And then we will be in Canaan's freedom land.

Moses might not get to see Canaan, but his children will see it. He even got to the mountaintop enough to see it and that assured him that it was coming. But the beauty of the thing is that there's always a Joshua to take up his work and take the children on in. And it's there waiting with its milk and honey, and with all of the bountiful beauty that God has in store for His children. Oh, what exceedingly marvellous things God has in store for us. Grant that we will follow Him enough to gain them.

O God, our gracious Heavenly Father, help us to see the insights that come from this new nation. Help us to follow Thee and all of Thy creative works in this world, and that somehow we will discover that we are made to live together as brothers And that it will come in this generation: the day when all men will recognize the fatherhood of God and the brotherhood of man. Amen.

A Time to Break Silence speech
August 28th 1963

I come to this magnificent house of worship tonight because my conscience leaves me no other choice. I join you in this meeting because I am in deepest agreement with the aims and work of the organization which has brought us together: Clergy and Laymen Concerned about Vietnam. The recent statements of your executive committee are the sentiments of my own heart, and I found myself in full accord when I read its opening lines: "A time comes when silence is betrayal." And that time has come for us in relation to Vietnam.

The truth of these words is beyond doubt, but the mission to which they call us is a most difficult one. Even when pressed by the demands of inner truth, men do not easily assume the task of opposing their government's policy, especially in time of war. Nor does the human spirit move without great difficulty against all the apathy of conformist thought within one's own bosom and in the surrounding world. Moreover, when the issues at hand seem as perplexed as they often do in the case of this dreadful conflict, we are always on the verge of being mesmerized by uncertainty; but we must move on.

And some of us who have already begun to break the silence of the night have found that the calling to speak is often a vocation of agony, but we must speak. We must speak with all the humility that is appropriate to our limited vision, but we must speak. And we must rejoice as well, for surely this is the first time in our nation's history that a significant number of its religious leaders have chosen to move beyond the prophesying of smooth patriotism to the high grounds of a firm dissent based upon the mandates of conscience and the reading of history. Perhaps a new spirit is rising among us. If it is, let us trace its movements and pray that our own inner being may be sensitive to its guidance, for we are deeply in need of a new way beyond the darkness that seems so close around us.

Over the past two years, as I have moved to break the betrayal of my own silences and to speak from the burnings of my own heart, as I have called for radical departures from the destruction of Vietnam, many persons have questioned me about the wisdom of my path. At the heart of their concerns this query has often loomed large and loud: "Why are you speaking about the war, Dr. King?" "Why are you joining the voices of dissent?" "Peace and civil rights don't mix," they say. "Aren't you hurting the cause of your people," they ask? And when I hear them, though I often understand the source of their concern, I am nevertheless greatly saddened, for such questions mean that the inquirers have not really known me, my commitment or my calling. Indeed, their questions suggest that they do not know the world in which they live.

In the light of such tragic misunderstanding, I deem it of signal importance to try to state clearly, and I trust concisely, why I believe that the path from Dexter Avenue Baptist Church - the church in Montgomery, Alabama, where I began my pastorate - leads clearly to this sanctuary tonight.

I come to this platform tonight to make a passionate plea to my beloved nation. This speech is not addressed to Hanoi or to the National Liberation Front. It is not addressed to China or to Russia.. Nor is it an attempt to overlook the ambiguity of the total situation and the need for a collective solution to the tragedy of Vietnam. Neither is it an attempt to make North Vietnam or the National Liberation Front paragons of virtue, nor to overlook the role they must play in the successful resolution of the problem. While they both may have justifiable reasons to be suspicious of the good faith of the United States, life and history give eloquent testimony to the fact that conflicts are never resolved without trustful give and take on both sides.

Tonight, however, I wish not to speak with Hanoi and the National Liberation Front, but rather to my fellow Americans, who, with me, bear the greatest responsibility in ending a conflict that has exacted a heavy price on both continents.

Since I am a preacher by trade, I suppose it is not surprising that I have seven major reasons for bringing Vietnam into the field of my moral vision. There is at the outset a very obvious and almost facile connection between the war in Vietnam and the struggle I, and others, have been waging in America. A few years ago there was a shining moment in that struggle. It seemed as if there was a real promise of hope for the poor - both black and white - through the poverty program. There were experiments, hopes, new beginnings. Then came the buildup in Vietnam, and I watched this program broken and eviscerated, as if it were some idle political plaything of a society gone mad on war, and I knew that America would never invest the necessary funds or energies in rehabilitation of its poor so long as adventures like Vietnam continued to draw men and skills and money like some demonic destructive suction tube. So, I was increasingly compelled to see the war as an enemy of the poor and to attack it as such. Perhaps the more tragic recognition of reality took place when it became clear to me that the war was doing far more than devastating the hopes of the poor at home. It was sending their sons and their brothers and their husbands to fight and to die in extraordinarily high proportions relative to the rest of the population. We were taking the black young men who had been crippled by our society and sending them eight thousand miles away to guarantee liberties in Southeast Asia which they had not found in southwest Georgia and East Harlem. And so we have been repeatedly faced with the cruel irony of watching Negro and white boys on TV screens as they kill and die together for a nation that has been unable to seat them together in the same schools. And so we watch them in brutal solidarity burning the huts of a poor village, but we realize that they would hardly live on the same block in Chicago. I could not be silent in the face of such cruel manipulation of the poor.

My third reason moves to an even deeper level of awareness, for it grows out of my experience in the ghettoes of the North over the last three years - especially the last three summers. As I have walked among the desperate, rejected, and angry young men,

I have told them that Molotov cocktails and rifles would not solve their problems. I have tried to offer them my deepest compassion while maintaining my conviction that social change comes most meaningfully through nonviolent action. But they ask - and rightly so - what about Vietnam? They ask if our own nation wasn't using massive doses of violence to solve its problems, to bring about the changes it wanted. Their questions hit home, and I knew that I could never again raise my voice against the violence of the oppressed in the ghettos without having first spoken clearly to the greatest purveyor of violence in the world today - my own government. For the sake of those boys, for the sake of this government, for the sake of the hundreds of thousands trembling under our violence, I cannot be silent.

For those who ask the question, "Aren't you a civil rights leader?" and thereby mean to exclude me from the movement for peace, I have this further answer. In 1957 when a group of us formed the Southern Christian Leadership Conference, we chose as our motto: "To save the soul of America." We were convinced that we could not limit our vision to certain rights for black people, but instead affirmed the conviction that America would never be free or saved from itself until the descendants of its slaves were loosed completely from the shackles they still wear. In a way we were agreeing with Langston Hughes, that black bard of Harlem, who had written earlier:

O, yes, I say it plain, America never was America to me, And yet I swear this oath - America will be!

Now, it should be incandescently clear that no one who has any concern for the integrity and life of America today can ignore the present war. If America's soul becomes totally poisoned, part of the autopsy must read: Vietnam. It can never be saved so long as it destroys the deepest hopes of men the world over. So it is that those of us who are yet determined that

America will be are led down the path of protest and dissent, working for the health of our land.

As if the weight of such a commitment to the life and health of America were not enough, another burden of responsibility was placed upon me in 1954 [sic]; and I cannot forget that the Nobel Prize for Peace was also a commission - a commission to work harder than I had ever worked before for "the brotherhood of man." This is a calling that takes me beyond national allegiances, but even if it were not present I would yet have to live with the meaning of my commitment to the ministry of Jesus Christ. To me the relationship of this ministry to the making of peace is so obvious that I sometimes marvel at those who ask me why I'm speaking against the war. Could it be that they do not know that the good news was meant for all men - for Communist and capitalist, for their children and ours, for black and for white, for revolutionary and conservative? Have they forgotten that my ministry is in obedience to the One who loved his enemies so fully that he died for them? What then can I say to the Vietcong or to Castro or to Mao as a faithful minister of this One? Can I threaten them with death or must I not share with them my life?

And finally, as I try to explain for you and for myself the road that leads from Montgomery to this place I would have offered all that was most valid if I simply said that I must be true to my conviction that I share with all men the calling to be a son of the living God. Beyond the calling of race or nation or creed is this vocation of sonship and brotherhood, and because I believe that the Father is deeply concerned especially for his suffering and helpless and outcast children, I come tonight to speak for them.

This I believe to be the privilege and the burden of all of us who deem ourselves bound by allegiances and loyalties which are broader and deeper than nationalism and which go beyond our nation's self-defined goals and positions. We are called to speak for the weak, for the voiceless, for the victims of our nation and for those it calls "enemy," for no document from human hands can make these humans any less our brothers.

And as I ponder the madness of Vietnam and search within myself for ways to understand and respond in compassion, my mind goes constantly to the people of that peninsula. I speak now not of the soldiers of each side, not of the ideologies of the Liberation Front, not of the junta in Saigon, but simply of the people who have been living under the curse of war for almost three continuous decades now. I think of them, too, because it is clear to me that there will be no meaningful solution there until some attempt is made to know them and hear their broken cries.

They must see Americans as strange liberators. The Vietnamese people proclaimed their own independence in 1954 - in 1945 rather - after a combined French and Japanese occupation and before the communist revolution in China. They were led by Ho Chi Minh. Even though they quoted the American Declaration of Independence in their own document of freedom, we refused to recognize them. Instead, we decided to support France in its re-conquest of her former colony. Our government felt then that the Vietnamese people were not ready for independence, and we again fell victim to the deadly Western arrogance that has poisoned the international atmosphere for so long. With that tragic decision we rejected a revolutionary government seeking self-determination and a government that had been established not by China - for whom the Vietnamese have no great love - but by clearly indigenous forces that included some communists. For the peasants this new government meant real land reform, one of the most important needs in their lives.

For nine years following 1945 we denied the people of

Vietnam the right of independence. For nine years we vigorously supported the French in their abortive effort to re-colonize Vietnam. Before the end of the war we were meeting eighty percent of the French war costs. Even before the French were defeated at Dien Bien Phu, they began to despair of their reckless action, but we did not. We encouraged them with our huge financial and military supplies to continue the war even after they had lost the will. Soon we would be paying almost the full costs of this tragic attempt at re-colonization.

After the French were defeated, it looked as if independence and land reform would come again through the Geneva Agreement. But instead there came the United States, determined that Ho should not unify the temporarily divided nation, and the peasants watched again as we supported one of the most vicious modern dictators, our chosen man, Premier Diem. The peasants watched and cringed as Diem ruthlessly rooted out all opposition, supported their extortionist landlords, and refused even to discuss reunification with the North. The peasants watched as all this was presided over by United States' influence and then by increasing numbers of United States troops who came to help quell the insurgency that Diem's methods had aroused. When Diem was overthrown they may have been happy, but the long line of military dictators seemed to offer no real change, especially in terms of their need for land and peace.

The only change came from America, as we increased our troop commitments in support of governments which were singularly corrupt, inept, and without popular support. All the while the people read our leaflets and received the regular promises of peace and democracy and land reform. Now they languish under our bombs and consider us, not their fellow Vietnamese, the real enemy. They move sadly and apathetically as we herd them off the land of their fathers into concentration camps where minimal social needs are rarely met. They know they must move on or be destroyed by our bombs.

So they go, primarily women and children and the aged. They watch as we poison their water, as we kill a million acres of their crops. They must weep as the bulldozers roar through their areas preparing to destroy the precious trees. They wander into the hospitals with at least twenty casualties from American firepower for one Vietcong-inflicted injury. So far we may have killed a million of them, mostly children. They wander into the towns and see thousands of the children, homeless, without clothes, running in packs on the streets like animals. They see the children degraded by our soldiers as they beg for food. They see the children selling their sisters to our soldiers, soliciting for their mothers.

What do the peasants think as we ally ourselves with the landlords and as we refuse to put any action into our many words concerning land reform? What do they think as we test out our latest weapons on them, just as the Germans tested out new medicine and new tortures in the concentration camps of Europe? Where are the roots of the independent Vietnam we claim to be building? Is it among these voiceless ones?

We have destroyed their two most cherished institutions: the family and the village. We have destroyed their land and their crops. We have cooperated in the crushing of the nation's only non-communist revolutionary political force, the unified Buddhist Church. We have supported the enemies of the peasants of Saigon. We have corrupted their women and children and killed their men.

Now there is little left to build on, save bitterness. Soon the only solid physical foundations remaining will be found at our military bases and in the concrete of the concentration camps we call "fortified hamlets." The peasants may well wonder if we plan to build our new Vietnam on such grounds as these. Could we blame them for such thoughts? We must speak for them and raise the questions they cannot raise. These, too, are our brothers.

Perhaps a more difficult but no less necessary task is to speak for those who have been designated as our enemies. What of the National Liberation Front, that strangely anonymous group we call "VC" or "communists"? What must they think of the United States of America when they realize that we permitted the repression and cruelty of Diem, which helped to bring them into being as a resistance group in the South? What do they think of our condoning the violence which led to their own taking up of arms? How can they believe in our integrity when now we speak of "aggression from the North" as if there were nothing more essential to the war? How can they trust us when now we charge them with violence after the murderous reign of Diem and charge them with violence while we pour every new weapon of death into their land? Surely we must understand their feelings, even if we do not condone their actions. Surely we must see that the men we supported pressed them to their violence. Surely we must see that our own computerized plans of destruction simply dwarf their greatest acts.

How do they judge us when our officials know that their membership is less than twenty-five percent communist, and yet insist on giving them the blanket name? What must they be thinking when they know that we are aware of their control of major sections of Vietnam, and yet we appear ready to allow national elections in which this highly organized political parallel government will not have a part? They ask how we can speak of free elections when the Saigon press is censored and controlled by the military junta. And they are surely right to wonder what kind of new government we plan to help form without them, the only party in real touch with the peasants. They question our political goals and they deny the reality of a peace settlement from which they will be excluded. Their questions are frighteningly relevant. Is our nation planning to build on political myth again, and then shore it up upon the power of new violence?

Here is the true meaning and value of compassion and non-violence, when it helps us to see the enemy's point of view, to hear his questions, to know his assessment of ourselves. For from his view we may indeed see the basic weaknesses of our own condition, and if we are mature, we may learn and grow and profit from the wisdom of the brothers who are called the opposition.

So, too, with Hanoi. In the North, where our bombs now pummel the land, and our mines endanger the waterways, we are met by a deep but understandable mistrust. To speak for them is to explain this lack of confidence in Western words, and especially their distrust of American intentions now. In Hanoi are the men who led the nation to independence against the Japanese and the French, the men who sought membership in the French Commonwealth and were betrayed by the weakness of Paris and the wilfulness of the colonial armies. It was they who led a second struggle against French domination at tremendous costs, and then were persuaded to give up the land they controlled between the thirteenth and seventeenth parallel as a temporary measure at Geneva. After 1954 they watched us conspire with Diem to prevent elections which could have surely brought Ho Chi Minh to power over a united Vietnam, and they realized they had been betrayed again. When we ask why they do not leap to negotiate, these things must be remembered.

Also, it must be clear that the leaders of Hanoi considered the presence of American troops in support of the Diem regime to have been the initial military breach of the Geneva Agreement concerning foreign troops. They remind us that they did not begin to send troops in large numbers and even supplies into the

South until American forces had moved into the tens of thousands.

Hanoi remembers how our leaders refused to tell us the truth about the earlier North Vietnamese overtures for peace, how the president claimed that none existed when they had clearly been made. Ho Chi Minh has watched as America has spoken of peace and built up its forces, and now he has surely heard the increasing international rumours of American plans for an invasion of the North. He knows the bombing and shelling and mining we are doing are part of traditional pre-invasion strategy. Perhaps only his sense of humour and of irony can save him when he hears the most powerful nation of the world speaking of aggression as it drops thousands of bombs on a poor, weak nation more than eight hundred, or rather, eight thousand miles away from its shores.

At this point I should make it clear that while I have tried in these last few minutes to give a voice to the voiceless in Vietnam and to understand the arguments of those who are called "enemy," I am as deeply concerned about our own troops there as anything else. For it occurs to me that what we are submitting them to in Vietnam is not simply the brutalizing process that goes on in any war where armies face each other and seek to destroy. We are adding cynicism to the process of death, for they must know after a short period there that none of the things we claim to be fighting for are really involved. Before long they must know that their government has sent them into a struggle among Vietnamese, and the more sophisticated surely realize that we are on the side of the wealthy, and the secure, while we create a hell for the poor.

Somehow this madness must cease. We must stop now. I speak as a child of God and brother to the suffering poor of Vietnam. I speak for those whose land is being laid waste, whose homes are being destroyed, whose culture is being subverted. I speak for the poor of

America who are paying the double price of smashed hopes at home, and death and corruption in Vietnam. I speak as a citizen of the world, for the world as it stands aghast at the path we have taken. I speak as one who loves America, to the leaders of our own nation: The great initiative in this war is ours; the initiative to stop it must be ours.

This is the message of the great Buddhist leaders of Vietnam. Recently one of them wrote these words, and I quote:

Each day the war goes on the hatred increases in the heart of the Vietnamese and in the hearts of those of humanitarian instinct. The Americans are forcing even their friends into becoming their enemies. It is curious that the Americans, who calculate so carefully on the possibilities of military victory, do not realize that in the process they are incurring deep psychological and political defeat. The image of America will never again be the image of revolution, freedom, and democracy, but the image of violence and militarism.

If we continue, there will be no doubt in my mind and in the mind of the world that we have no honourable intentions in Vietnam. If we do not stop our war against the people of Vietnam immediately, the world will be left with no other alternative than to see this as some horrible, clumsy, and deadly game we have decided to play. The world now demands a maturity of America that we may not be able to achieve. It demands that we admit that we have been wrong from the beginning of our adventure in Vietnam, that we have been detrimental to the life of the Vietnamese people. The situation is one in which we must be ready to turn sharply from our present ways. In order to atone for our sins and errors in Vietnam, we should take the initiative in bringing a halt to this tragic war.

I would like to suggest five concrete things that our government should do immediately to begin the long and difficult process of extricating ourselves from this nightmarish conflict:

Number one: End all bombing in North and South Vietnam.

Number two: Declare a unilateral cease-fire in the hope that such action will create the atmosphere for negotiation.

Three: Take immediate steps to prevent other battlegrounds in Southeast Asia by curtailing our military build-up in Thailand and our interference in Laos.

Four: Realistically accept the fact that the National Liberation Front has substantial support in South Vietnam and must thereby play a role in any meaningful negotiations and any future Vietnam government.

Five: Set a date that we will remove all foreign troops from Vietnam in accordance with the 1954 Geneva Agreement. Part of our ongoing part of our ongoing commitment might well express itself in an offer to grant asylum to any Vietnamese who fears for his life under a new regime which included the Liberation Front. Then we must make what reparations we can for the damage we have done. We must provide the medical aid that is badly needed, making it available in this country, if necessary. Meanwhile... meanwhile, we in the churches and synagogues have a continuing task while we urge our government to disengage itself from a disgraceful commitment. We must continue to raise our voices and our lives if our nation persists in its perverse ways in Vietnam. We must be prepared to match actions with words by seeking out every creative method of protest possible.

As we counsel young men concerning military service, we must clarify for them our nation's role in Vietnam and challenge them with the alternative of conscientious objection. I am pleased to say that this is a path now chosen by more than seventy students at my own alma mater, Morehouse College, and I recommend it to all who find the American course in Vietnam a dishonourable and unjust one. Moreover, I would encourage all ministers of draft age to give up their ministerial exemptions and seek status as conscientious objectors. These are the times for real choices and not false ones. We are at the moment when our lives must be placed on the line if our nation is to survive its own folly. Every man of humane convictions must decide on the protest that best suits his convictions, but we must all protest.

Now there is something seductively tempting about stopping there and sending us all off on what in some circles has become a popular crusade against the war in Vietnam. I say we must enter that struggle, but I wish to go on now to say something even more disturbing.

The war in Vietnam is but a symptom of a far deeper malady within the American spirit, and if we ignore this sobering reality and if we ignore this sobering reality, we will find ourselves organizing "clergy and laymen concerned" committees for the next generation. They will be concerned about Guatemala and Peru. They will be concerned about Thailand and Cambodia. They will be concerned about Mozambique and South Africa. We will be marching for these and a dozen other names and attending rallies without end, unless there is a significant and profound change in American life and policy.

And so, such thoughts take us beyond Vietnam, but not beyond our calling as sons of the living God.

In 1957, a sensitive American official overseas said that it seemed to him that our nation was on the wrong side of a world revolution. During the past ten years, we have seen emerge a pattern of suppression which has now justified the presence of U.S. military advisors in Venezuela. This need to maintain social stability for our investments accounts for the counter revolutionary action of American forces in Guatemala. It tells why American helicopters are being used against guerrillas in Cambodia and why American napalm and Green Beret forces have already been active against rebels in Peru.

It is with such activity in mind that the words of the late John F. Kennedy come back to haunt us. Five years ago he said, "Those who make peaceful revolution impossible will make violent revolution inevitable." Increasingly, by choice or by accident, this is the role our nation has taken, the role of those who make peaceful revolution impossible by refusing to give up the privileges and the pleasures that come from the immense profits of overseas investments. I am convinced that if we are to get on the right side of the world revolution, we as a nation must undergo a radical revolution of values. We must rapidly begin...we must rapidly begin the shift from a thing-oriented society to a person-oriented society. When machines and computers, profit motives and property rights, are considered more important than people, the giant triplets of racism, extreme materialism, and militarism are incapable of being conquered.

A true revolution of values will soon cause us to question the fairness and justice of many of our past and present policies. On the one hand, we are called to play the Good Samaritan on life's roadside, but that will be only an initial act. One day we must come to see that the whole Jericho Road must be transformed so that men and women will not be constantly beaten and robbed as they make their journey on life's highway. True compassion is more than flinging a coin to a beggar. It comes to see that an edifice which produces beggars needs restructuring.

A true revolution of values will soon look uneasily on the glaring contrast of poverty and wealth. With righteous indignation, it will look across the seas and see individual capitalists of the West investing huge sums of money in Asia, Africa, and South America, only to take the profits out with no concern for the social betterment of the countries, and say, "This is not just." It will look at our alliance with the landed gentry of South America and say, "This is not just." The Western arrogance of feeling that it has everything to teach others and nothing to learn from them is not just.

A true revolution of values will lay hand on the world order and say of war, "This way of settling differences is not just." This business of burning human beings with napalm, of filling our nation's homes with orphans and widows, of injecting poisonous drugs of hate into the veins of peoples normally humane, of sending men home from dark and bloody battlefields physically handicapped and psychologically deranged, cannot be reconciled with wisdom, justice, and love. A nation that continues year after year to spend more money on military defence than on programs of social uplift is approaching spiritual death.

America, the richest and most powerful nation in the world, can well lead the way in this revolution of values. There is nothing except a tragic death wish to prevent us from reordering our priorities so that the pursuit of peace will take precedence over the pursuit of war. There is nothing to keep us from molding a recalcitrant status quo with bruised hands until we have fashioned it into a brotherhood.

This kind of positive revolution of values is our best defence against communism. War is not the answer. Communism will never be defeated by the use of atomic bombs or nuclear weapons. Let us not join those who shout war and, through their misguided passions, urge the United States to relinquish its participation in the United Nations. These are days which demand wise restraint and calm reasonableness. We must not engage in a negative anticommunism, but rather in a positive thrust for democracy, realizing that our greatest defence against communism is to take offensive action in behalf of justice. We must with positive action seek to remove those conditions of poverty, insecurity, and injustice, which are the fertile soil in which the seed of communism grows and develops.

These are revolutionary times. All over the globe men are revolting against old systems of exploitation and oppression, and out of the wounds of a frail world, new systems of justice and equality are being born. The shirtless and barefoot people of the land are rising up as never before. The people who sat in darkness have seen a great light. We in the West must support these revolutions. It is a sad fact that because of comfort, complacency, a morbid fear of communism, and our proneness to adjust to injustice, the Western nations that initiated so much of the revolutionary spirit of the modern world have now become the arch anti-revolutionaries. This has driven many to feel that only Marxism has a revolutionary spirit. Therefore, communism is a judgment against our failure to make democracy real and follow through on the revolutions that we initiated. Our only hope today lies in our ability to recapture the revolutionary spirit and go out into a sometimes hostile world declaring eternal hostility to poverty, racism, and militarism. With this powerful commitment we shall boldly challenge the status quo and unjust mores, and thereby speed the day when "every valley shall be exalted, and every mountain and hill shall be made low, and the crooked shall be made straight, and the rough places plain."

A genuine revolution of values means in the final analysis that our loyalties must become ecumenical rather than sectional. Every nation must now develop an overriding loyalty to mankind as a whole in order to preserve the best in their individual societies.

This call for a worldwide fellowship that lifts neighbourly concern beyond one's tribe, race, class, and nation is in reality a call for an all-embracing and unconditional love for all mankind. This oft misunderstood, this oft misinterpreted concept, so readily dismissed by the Nietzsches of the world as a weak and cowardly force, has now become an absolute necessity for the survival of man. When I speak of love I am not speaking of some sentimental and weak response. I am not speaking of that force which is just emotional bosh. I am speaking of that force which all of the great religions have seen as the supreme unifying principle of life. Love is somehow the key that unlocks the door which leads to ultimate reality. This Hindu-Muslim-Christian-Jewish-Buddhist belief about ultimate reality is beautifully summed up in the first epistle of Saint John: "Let us love one another, for love is God. And every one that loveth is born of God and knoweth God. He that loveth not knoweth not God, for God is love." "If we love one another, God dwelleth in us and his love is perfected in us." Let us hope that this spirit will become the order of the day.

We can no longer afford to worship the god of hate or bow before the altar of retaliation. The oceans of history are made turbulent by the ever-rising tides of hate. And history is cluttered with the wreckage of nations and individuals that pursued this self-defeating path of hate. As Arnold Toynbee says: "Love is the ultimate force that makes for the saving choice of life and good against the damning choice of death and evil. Therefore the first hope in our inventory must be the hope that love is going to have the last word."

We are now faced with the fact, my friends, that tomorrow is today. We are confronted with the fierce urgency of now. In this unfolding conundrum of life and history, there is such a thing as being too late. Procrastination is still the thief of time. Life often leaves us standing bare, naked, and dejected with a lost opportunity. The tide in the affairs of men does not remain at flood - it ebbs. We may cry out desperately for time to pause in her passage, but time is adamant to every plea and rushes on. Over the bleached bones and jumbled residues of numerous civilizations are written the pathetic words, "Too late." There is an invisible book of life that faithfully records our vigilance or our neglect. Omar Khayyam is right: "The moving finger writes, and having writ moves on."

We still have a choice today: non-violent coexistence or violent co-annihilation. We must move past indecision to action. We must find new ways to speak for peace in Vietnam and justice throughout the developing world, a world that borders on our doors. If we do not act, we shall surely be dragged down the long, dark, and shameful corridors of time reserved for those who possess power without compassion, might without morality, and strength without sight.

Now let us begin. Now let us rededicate ourselves to the long and bitter, but beautiful, struggle for a new world. This is the calling of the sons of God, and our brothers wait eagerly for our response. Shall we say the odds are too great? Shall we tell them the struggle is too hard? Will our message be that the forces of American life militate against their arrival as full men, and we send our deepest regrets? Or will there be another message - of longing, of hope, of solidarity with their yearnings, of commitment to their cause, whatever the cost? The choice is ours, and though we might prefer it otherwise, we must choose in this crucial moment of human history.

As that noble bard of yesterday, James Russell Lowell, eloquently stated: Once to every man and nation comes a moment to decide, In the strife of Truth and Falsehood, for the good or evil side; Some great cause, God's new Messiah offering each the bloom or blight, And the choice goes by forever 'twixt that darkness and that light. Though the cause of evil prosper, yet 'tis truth alone is strong Though her portions be the scaffold, and upon the throne be wrong Yet that scaffold sways the future, and behind the dim unknown Standeth God within the shadow, keeping watch above his own.

And if we will only make the right choice, we will be

able to transform this pending cosmic elegy into a creative psalm of peace.

If we will make the right choice, we will be able to transform the jangling discords of our world into a beautiful symphony of brotherhood.

If we will but make the right choice, we will be able to speed up the day, all over America and all over the world, when justice will roll down like waters, and righteousness like a mighty stream.

Nobel Peace Prize Acceptance Speech
December 10th 1964

I accept the Nobel Prize for Peace at a moment when twenty-two million Negroes of the United States of America are engaged in a creative battle to end the long night of racial injustice. I accept this award in behalf of a civil rights movement which is moving with determination and a majestic scorn for risk and danger to establish a reign of freedom and a rule of justice.

I am mindful that only yesterday in Birmingham, Alabama, our children, crying out for brotherhood, were answered with fire hoses, snarling dogs and even death. I am mindful that only yesterday in Philadelphia, Mississippi, young people seeing to secure the right to vote were brutalized and murdered. And only yesterday more than 40 houses of worship in the State of Mississippi alone were bombed or burned because they offered a sanctuary to those who would not accept segregation.

I am mindful that debilitating and grinding poverty afflicts my people and chains them to the lowest rung of the economic ladder.

Therefore, I must ask why this prize is awarded to a movement which is beleaguered and committed to unrelenting struggle; to a movement which has not won the very peace and brotherhood which is the essence of the Nobel Prize.

After contemplation, I conclude that this award which I receive on behalf of that movement is profound recognition that non-violence is the answer to the crucial political and moral question of our time, the need for man to overcome oppression and violence without resorting to violence and oppression.

Civilization and violence are antithetical concepts. Negroes of the United States, following the people of India, have demonstrated that non-violence is not sterile passivity, but a powerful moral force which makes for social transformation. Sooner or later all the people of the world will have to discover a way to live together in peace, and thereby transform this pending cosmic elegy into a creative psalm of brotherhood.

If this is to be achieved, man must evolve for all human conflict a method which rejects revenge, aggression and retaliation. The foundation of such a method is love. The tortuous road which has led from Montgomery, Alabama, to Oslo bears witness to this truth. This is a road over which millions of Negroes are travelling to find a new sense of dignity.

This same road has opened for all Americans a new ear of progress and hope. It has led to a new Civil Rights bill, and it will, I am convinced, be widened and lengthened into a superhighway of justice as Negro and white men in increasing numbers create alliances to overcome their common problems.

I accept this award today with an abiding faith in America and an audacious faith in the future of mankind. I refuse to accept despair as the final response to the ambiguities of history. I refuse to accept the idea that the "isness" of man's present nature makes him morally incapable of reaching up for the eternal "oughtness" that forever confronts him.

I refuse to accept the idea that man is mere flotsam and jetsam in the river of life unable to influence the unfolding events which surround him. I refuse to accept the view that mankind is so tragically bound to the starless midnight of racism and war that the bright daybreak of peace and brotherhood can never become a reality.

I refuse to accept the cynical notion that nation after nation must spiral down a militaristic stairway into the hell of thermonuclear destruction. I believe that unarmed truth and unconditional love will have the final word in reality. This is why right temporarily defeated is stronger than evil triumphant.

I believe that even amid today's motor bursts and whining bullets, there is still hope for a brighter tomorrow. I believe that wounded justice, lying prostrate on the blood-flowing streets of our nations, can be lifted from this dust of shame to reign supreme among the children of men.

I have the audacity to believe that peoples everywhere can have three meals a day for their bodies, education and culture for their minds, and dignity, equality and freedom for their spirits. I believe that what self-centred men have torn down, men other-centred can build up. I still believe that one day mankind will bow before the altars of God and be crowned triumphant over war and bloodshed, and non-violent redemptive goodwill will proclaim the rule of the land.

"And the lion and the lamb shall lie down together and every man shall sit under his own vine and fig tree and none shall be afraid."

I still believe that we shall overcome.

This faith can give us courage to face the uncertainties of the future. It will give our tired feet new strength as we continue our forward stride toward the city of freedom. When our days become dreary with low-hovering clouds and our nights become darker than a thousand midnights, we will know that we are living in the creative turmoil of a genuine civilization struggling to be born.

Today I come to Oslo as a trustee, inspired and with renewed dedication to humanity. I accept this prize on behalf of all men who love peace and brotherhood. I say I come as a trustee, for in the depths of my heart I am aware that this prize is much more than an honour to me personally.

Every time I take a flight I am always mindful of the man people who make a successful journey possible, the known pilots and the unknown ground crew.

So you honour the dedicated pilots of our struggle who have sat at the controls as the freedom movement soared into orbit. You honour, once again, Chief (Albert) Luthuli of South Africa, whose struggles with and for his people, are still met with the most brutal expression of man's inhumanity to man.

You honour the ground crew without whose labour and sacrifices the jet flights to freedom could never have left the earth. Most of these people will never make the headlines and their names will not appear in Who's Who. Yet when years have rolled past and when the blazing light of truth is focused on this marvellous age in which we live, men and women will know and children will be taught that we have a finer land, a better people, a more noble civilization, because these humble children of God were willing to suffer for righteousness' sake.

I think Alfred Nobel would know what I mean when I say that I accept this award in the spirit of a curator of some precious heirloom which he holds in trust for its true owners, all those to whom beauty is truth and truth beauty, and in whose eyes the beauty of genuine brotherhood and peace is more precious than diamonds or silver or gold.

MOHANDAS KARAMCHAND GANDHI

INTRODUCTION

Mohandas Karamchand Gandhi was born on 2nd October, 1869 in Porbandar, Gujrat and was murded in 1948 by Nathuram Godsey.

His family belonged to the the Hindu religion and practiced the ahimsa principle of never injuring a living thing. Mohandas Gandhi was one of the most significant persons in the 20th century. He was the one who proved that it is possible to fight very successfully without violence.

When in South Africa (1873 to 1914) he fought legal battle with the White Minority government and secured several civil rights for Asians living there. On return to India, he led the freedom movement against the British rule until the country secured Independence in August 1947.

The Quit India speech
August 8th 1942

BEFORE you discuss the resolution, let me place before you one or two things, I want you to understand two things very clearly and to consider them from the same point of view from which I am placing them before you. I ask you to consider it from my point of view, because if you approve of it, you will be enjoined to carry out all I say. It will be a great responsibility. There are people who ask me whether I am the same man that I was in 1920, or whether there has been any change in me. You are right in asking that question. Let me, however, hasten to assure that I am the same Gandhi as I was in 1920. I have not changed in any fundamental respect. I attach the same importance to non-violence that I did then. If at all, my emphasis on it has grown stronger. There is no real contradiction between the present resolution and my previous writings and utterances.

Occasions like the present do not occur in everybody's and but rarely in anybody's life. I want you to know and feel that there is nothing but purest Ahimsa1 in all that I am saying and doing today. The draft resolution of the Working Committee is based on Ahimsa, the contemplated struggle similarly has its roots in Ahimsa. If, therefore, there is any among you who has lost faith in Ahimsa or is wearied of it, let him not vote for this resolution. Let me explain my position clearly. God has vouchsafed to me a priceless gift in the weapon of Ahimsa. I and my Ahimsa are on our trail today. If in the present crisis, when the earth is being scorched by the flames of Himsa2 and crying for deliverance, I failed to make use of the God given talent, God will not forgive me and I shall be judged un-wrongly of the great gift. I must act now. I may not hesitate and merely look on, when Russia and China are threatened.

Ours is not a drive for power, but purely a non-violent fight for India's independence. In a violent struggle, a successful general has been often known to effect a military coup and to set up a dictatorship. But under the Congress scheme of things, essentially non-violent as it is, there can be no room for dictatorship. A non-violent soldier of freedom will covet nothing for himself, he fights only for the freedom of his country. The Congress is unconcerned as to who will rule, when freedom is attained. The power, when it comes, will belong to the people of India, and it will be for them to decide to whom it placed in the entrusted. May be that the reins will be placed in the hands of the Parsis, for instance-as I would love to see happen-or they may be handed to some others whose names are not heard in the Congress today. It will not be for you then to object saying, "This community is microscopic. That party did not play its due part in the freedom's struggle; why should it have all the power?" Ever since its inception the Congress has kept itself meticulously free of the communal taint. It has thought always in terms of the whole nation and has acted accordingly.

I know how imperfect our Ahimsa is and how far away we are still from the ideal, but in Ahimsa there is no final failure or defeat. I have faith, therefore, that if, in spite of our shortcomings, the big thing does happen, it will be because God wanted to help us by crowning with success our silent, unremitting Sadhana1 for the last twenty-two years.

I believe that in the history of the world, there has not been a more genuinely democratic struggle for freedom than ours. I read Carlyle's French Resolution while I was in prison, and Pandit Jawaharlal has told me something about the Russian revolution. But it is my conviction that inasmuch as these struggles were fought with the weapon of violence they failed to realize the democratic ideal. In the democracy which I have envisaged, a democracy established by non-violence, there will be equal freedom for all. Everybody will be his own master. It is to join a struggle for such democracy that I invite you today. Once you realize this you will forget the differences between the Hindus and Muslims, and think of yourselves as Indians only, engaged in the common struggle for independence.

Then, there is the question of your attitude towards the British. I have noticed that there is hatred towards the British among the people. The people say they are disgusted with their behaviour. The people make no distinction between British imperialism and the British people. To them, the two are one This hatred would even make them welcome the Japanese. It is most dangerous. It means that they will exchange one slavery for another. We must get rid of this feeling. Our quarrel is not with the British people, we fight their imperialism. The proposal for the withdrawal of British power did not come out of anger. It came to enable India to play its due part at the present critical juncture It is not a happy position for a big country like India to be merely helping with money and material obtained willy-nilly from her while the United Nations are conducting the war. We cannot evoke the true spirit of sacrifice and velour, so long as we are not free. I know the British Government will not be able to withhold freedom from us, when we have made enough self-sacrifice. We must, therefore, purge ourselves of hatred. Speaking for myself, I can say that I have never felt any hatred. As a matter of fact, I feel myself to be a greater friend of the British now than ever before. One reason is that they are today in distress. My very friendship, therefore, demands that I should try to save them from their mistakes. As I view the situation, they are on the brink of an abyss. It, therefore, becomes my duty to warn them of their danger even though it may, for the time being, anger them to the point of cutting off the friendly hand that is stretched out to help them. People may laugh, nevertheless that is my claim. At a time when I may have to launch the biggest struggle of my life, I may not harbour hatred against anybody.

MOTHER TERESA

INTRODUCTION

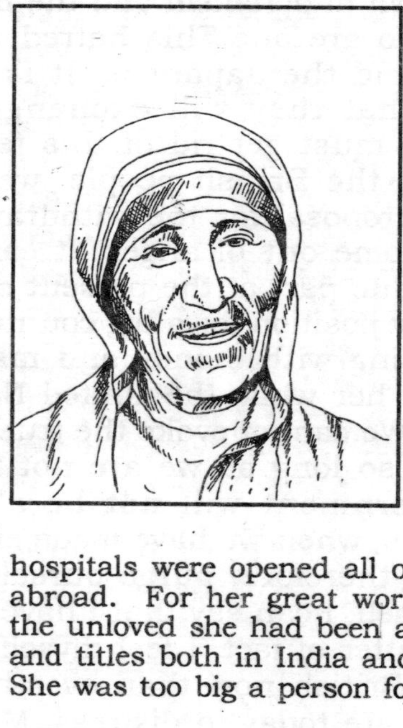

Mother Teresa was born in Yugoslavia on 26th August 1910. She became a nun at the age of 18. She came to India as a Loretto sister to teach in Loretto convents in Kolkata.

In 1950 she started the famous order of the 'Missionaries of Charity'. Soon many homes for the homeless, schools and hospitals were opened all over the country and abroad. For her great work of selfless love for the unloved she had been awarded many prizes and titles both in India and in other countries. She was too big a person for these awards.

The holy work she did could never be made small by being paid for. She worked untiringly till the day she passed away. She died on the 5th of September, 1997 in Kolkata. She was a real saint and both Kolkata and India are proud that she died as an Indian. In her death India lost an angel of mercy that day. It was indeed a black Friday for the whole world. The work she started carries on without any lack of love by her followers all over the world.

Nobel Lecture Speech - December 11, 1979

AS we have gathered here together to thank God for the Nobel Peace Prize I think it will be beautiful that we pray the prayer of St. Francis of Assisi which always surprises me very much- we pray this prayer every day after Holy Communion, because it is very fitting for each one of us, and I always wonder that 4-500 years ago as St. Francis of Assisi composed this prayer that they had the same difficulties that we have today, as we compose this prayer that fits very nicely for us also. I think some of you already have got it- so we will pray together.

Let us thank God for the opportunity that we all have together today, for this gift of peace that reminds us that we have been created to live that peace, and Jesus became man to bring that good news to the poor. He being God became man in all things like us except sin, and he proclaimed very clearly that he had come to give the good news. The news was peace to all of good will and this is something that we all want- the peace of heart- and God loved the world so much that he gave his son - it was a giving - it is as much as if to say it hurt God to give, because he loved the world so much that he gave his son, and he gave him to Virgin Mary, and what did she do with him?

As soon as he came in her life - immediately she went in haste to give that good news, and as she came into the house of her cousin, the child- the unborn child- the child in the womb of Elizabeth, leapt with joy. He was that little unborn child, was the first messenger of peace. He recognised the Prince of Peace, he recognised that Christ has come to bring the good news for you and for me. And as if that was not enough- it was not enough to become a man - he died on the cross to show that greater love, and he died for you and for me and for that leper and for that man dying of hunger and that naked person lying in the street not only of Calcutta, but of Africa, and New York, and London, and Oslo- and insisted that we love one another as he loves each one of us. And we read that in the Gospel very clearly- love as I have loved you- as I love you- as the Father has loved me, I love you- and the harder the Father loved him, he gave him to us, and how much we love one another, we, too, must give each other until it hurts. It is not enough for us to say: I love God, but I do not love my neighbour. St. John says you are a liar if you say you love God, and you don't love your neighbour. How can you love God whom you do not see, if you do not love your neighbour whom you see, whom you touch, with whom you live. And so this is very important for us to realise that love, to be true, has to hurt. It hurt Jesus to love us, it hurt him. And to make sure we remember his great love he made himself the bread of life to satisfy our hunger for his love. Our hunger for God, because we have been created for that love. We have been created in his image. We have been created to love and be loved, and then he has become man to make it possible for us to love as he loved us. He makes himself the hungry one- the naked one - the homeless one- the sick one- the one in prison- the lonely one - the unwanted one- and he says: You did it to me. Hungry for our love, and this is the hunger of our poor people. This is the hunger that you and I must find, it may be in our own home.

I never forget an opportunity I had in visiting a home where they had all these old parents of sons and daughters who had just put them in an institution and forgotten maybe. And I went there, and I saw in that home they had everything, beautiful things, but everybody was looking towards the door. And I did not see a single one with their smile on their face. And I turned to the Sister and I asked: How is that? How is it that the people they have everything here, why are they all looking towards the door, why are they not smiling? I am so used to see the smile on our people, even the dying one smile, and she said: This is nearly every day, they are expecting, they are hoping that a son or daughter will come to visit them. They are hurt because they are forgotten, and see- this is where love comes. That poverty comes right there in our own home, even neglect of love. Maybe in our own family we have somebody who is feeling lonely, who is feeling sick, who is feeling worried, and these are difficult days for everybody. Are we there, are we there to receive them, is the mother there to receive the child?

I was surprised in the West to see so many young boys and girls given into drugs, and I tried to find out why- why it is like that, and the answer was: Because there is no one in the family to receive them. Father and mother are so busy they have no time. Young parents are in some institution and the child takes back to the street and gets involved in something. We are talking of peace. These are things that break peace, but I feel the greatest destroyer of peace today is abortion, because it is a direct war, a direct killing- direct murder by the mother herself. And we read in the Scripture, for God says very clearly: Even if a mother could forget her child- I will not forget you - I have carved you in the palm of my hand. We are carved in the palm of His hand, so close to Him that unborn child has been carved in the hand of God. And that is what strikes me most, the beginning of that sentence, that even if a mother could forget something impossible - but even if she could forget - I will not forget you. And today the greatest means - the greatest destroyer of peace is abortion. And we who are standing here - our parents wanted us. We would not be here if our parents would do that to us. Our children, we want them, we love them, but what of the millions. Many people are very,

very concerned with the children in India, with the children in Africa where quite a number die, maybe of malnutrition, of hunger and so on, but millions are dying deliberately by the will of the mother. And this is what is the greatest destroyer of peace today. Because if a mother can kill her own child- what is left for me to kill you and you kill me- there is nothing between. And this I appeal in India, I appeal everywhere: Let us bring the child back, and this year being the child's year: What have we done for the child? At the beginning of the year I told, I spoke everywhere and I said: Let us make this year that we make every single child born, and unborn, wanted. And today is the end of the year, have we really made the children wanted? I will give you something terrifying. We are fighting abortion by adoption, we have saved thousands of lives, we have sent words to all the clinics, to the hospitals, police stations - please don't destroy the child, we will take the child. So every hour of the day and night it is always somebody, we have quite a number of unwedded mothers- tell them come, we will take care of you, we will take the child from you, and we will get a home for the child. And we have a tremendous demand from families who have no children, that is the blessing of God for us. And also, we are doing another thing which is very beautiful- we are teaching our beggars, our leprosy patients, our slum dwellers, our people of the street, natural family planning.

And in Calcutta alone in six years- it is all in Calcutta- we have had 61,273 babies less from the families who would have had, but because they practise this natural way of abstaining, of self-control, out of love for each other. We teach them the temperature meter which is very beautiful, very simple, and our poor people understand. And you know what they have told me? Our family is healthy, our family is united, and we can have a baby whenever we want. So clear- those people in the street, those beggars- and I think that if our people can do like that how much more you and all the others who can know the ways and means without destroying the life that God has created in us.

The poor people are very great people. They can teach us so many beautiful things. The other day one of them came to thank and said: You people who have vowed chastity you are the best people to teach us family planning. Because it is nothing more than self-control out of love for each other. And I think they said a beautiful sentence. And these are people who maybe have nothing to eat, maybe they have not a home where to live, but they are great people. The poor are very wonderful people. One evening we went out and we picked up four people from the street. And one of them was in a most terrible condition- and I told the Sisters: You take care of the other three, I take of this one that looked worse. So I did for her all that my love can do. I put her in bed, and there was such a beautiful smile on her face. She took hold of my hand, as she said one word only: Thank you - and she died.

I could not help but examine my conscience before her, and I asked what would I say if I was in her place. And my answer was very simple. I would have tried to draw a little attention to myself, I would have said I am hungry, that I am dying, I am cold, I am in pain, or something, but she gave me much more - she gave me her grateful love. And she died with a smile on her face. As that man whom we picked up from the drain, half eaten with worms, and we brought him to the home. I have lived like an animal in the street, but I am going to die like an angel, loved and cared for. And it was so wonderful to see the greatness of that man who could speak like that, who could die like that without blaming anybody, without cursing anybody, without comparing anything. Like an angel- this is the greatness of our people. And that is why we believe what Jesus had said: I was hungry- I was naked- I was homeless - I was unwanted, unloved, uncared for - and you did it to me.

I believe that we are not real social workers. We may be doing social work in the eyes of the people, but we are really contemplatives in the heart of the world. For we are touching the Body Of Christ 24 hours. We have 24 hours in this presence, and so you and I. You too try to bring that presence of God in your family, for the family that prays together stays together. And I think that we in our family don't need bombs and guns, to destroy to bring peace - just get together, love one another, bring that peace, that joy, that strength of presence of each other in the home. And we will be able to overcome all the evil that is in the world.

There is so much suffering, so much hatred, so much misery, and we with our prayer, with our sacrifice are beginning at home. Love begins at home, and it is not how much we do, but how much love we put in the action that we do. It is to God Almighty- how much we do it does not matter, because He is infinite, but how much love we put in that action. How much we do to Him in the person that we are serving.

Some time ago in Calcutta we had great difficulty in getting sugar, and I don't know how the word got around to the children, and a little boy of four years old, Hindu boy, went home and told his parents: I will not eat sugar for three days, I will give my sugar to Mother Teresa for her children. After three days his father and mother brought him to our home. I had never met them before, and this little one could scarcely pronounce my name, but he knew exactly what he had come to do. He knew that he wanted to share his love.

And that is why I have received such a lot of love from you all. From the time that I have come here I have simply been surrounded with love, and with real, real understanding love. It could feel as if everyone in India, everyone in Africa is somebody very special to you. And I felt quite at home I was telling Sister today. I feel in the Convent with the Sisters as if I am in Calcutta with my own Sisters. So completely at home here, right here.

And so here I am talking with you- I want you to find the poor here, right in your own home first. And begin love there. Be that good news to your own people. And find out about your next-door-neighbor - do you know who they are? I had the most extraordinary experience with a Hindu family who had eight children. A gentleman came to our house and said: Mother Teresa, there is a family with eight children, they had not eaten for so long- do something. So I took some rice and I went there immediately. And I saw the children- their eyes shining with hunger - I don't know if you have ever seen hunger. But I have seen it very often. And she took the rice, she divided the rice, and she went out. When she came back I asked her - where did you go, what did you do? And she gave me a very simple answer: They are hungry also. What struck me most was that she knew- and who are they, a Muslim family - and she knew. I didn't bring more rice that evening because I wanted them to enjoy the joy of sharing. But there were those children, radiating joy, sharing the joy with their mother because she had the love to give. And you see this is where love begins- at home. And I want you- and I am very grateful for what I have received. It has been a tremendous experience and I go back to India- I will be back by next week, the 15th I hope - and I will be able to bring your love.

And I know well that you have not given from your abundance, but you have given until it has hurt you. Today the little children they have- I was so surprised - there is so much joy for the children that are hungry. That the children like themselves will need love and care and tenderness, like they get so much from their parents. So let us thank God that we have had this opportunity to come to know each other, and this knowledge of each other has brought us very close. And we will be able to help not only the children of India and Africa, but will be able to help the children of the whole world, because as you know our Sisters are all over the world. And with this prize that I have received as a prize of peace, I am going to try to make the home for many people that have no home. Because I believe that love begins at home, and if we can create a home for the poor- I think that more and more love will spread. And we will be able through this understanding love to bring peace, be good news to the poor. The poor in our own family first, in our country and in the world.

To be able to do this, our Sisters, our lives have to be woven with prayer. They have to be woven with Christ to be able to understand, to be able to share. Because today there is so much suffering - and I feel that the passion of Christ is being relived all over again - are we there to share that passion, to share that suffering of people. Around the world, not only in the poor countries, but I found the poverty of the West so much more difficult to remove. When I pick up a person from the street, hungry, I give him a plate of rice, a piece of bread, I have satisfied. I have removed that hunger. But a person that is shut out, that feels unwanted, unloved, terrified, the person that has been thrown out from society - that poverty is so hurtable and so much, and I find that very difficult. Our Sisters are working amongst that kind of people in the West. So you must pray for us that we may be able to be that good news, but we cannot do that without you, you have to do that here in your country. You must come to know the poor, maybe our people here have material things, everything, but I think that if we all look into our own homes, how difficult we find it sometimes to smile at each other, and that the smile is the beginning of love.

And so let us always meet each other with a smile, for the smile is the beginning of love, and once we begin to love each other naturally we want to do something. So you pray for our Sisters and for me and for our Brothers, and for our Co-Workers that are around the world. That we may remain faithful to the gift of God, to love Him and serve Him in the poor together with you. What we have done we should not have been able to do if you did not share with your prayers, with your gifts, this continual giving. But I don't want you to give me from your abundance, I want that you give me until it hurts.

The other day I received 15 dollars from a man who has been on his back for twenty years, and the only part that he can move is his right hand. And the only companion that he enjoys is smoking. And he said to me: I do not smoke for one week, and I send you this money. It must have been a terrible sacrifice for him, but see how beautiful, how he shared, and with that money I bought bread and I gave to those who are hungry with a joy on both sides, he was giving and the poor were receiving. This is something that you and I- it is a gift of God to us to be able to share our love with others. And let it be as it was for Jesus. Let us love one another as he loved us. Let us love Him with undivided love. And the joy of loving Him and each other- let us give now - that Christmas is coming so close. Let us keep that joy of loving Jesus in our hearts. And share that joy with all that we come in touch with. And that radiating joy is real, for we have no reason not to be happy because we have no Christ with us. Christ in our hearts, Christ in the poor that we meet, Christ in the smile that we give and the smile that we receive. Let us make that one point: That no child will be unwanted, and also that we meet each other always with a smile, especially when it is difficult to smile.

I never forget some time ago about fourteen professors came from the United States from different universities. And they came to Calcutta to our house. Then we were talking about that they had been to the home for the dying. We have a home for the dying in Calcutta, where we have picked up more than 36,000 people only from the streets of Calcutta, and out of that big number more than 18,000 have died a beautiful death. They have just gone home to God; and they came to our house and we talked of love, of compassion, and then one of them asked me: Say, Mother, please tell us something that we will remember, and I said to them: Smile at each other, make time for each other in your family. Smile at each other. And then another one asked me: Are you married, and I said: Yes, and I find it sometimes very difficult to smile at Jesus because he can be very demanding sometimes. This is really something true, and there is where love comes - when it is demanding, and yet we can give it to Him with joy. Just as I have said today, I have said that if I don't go to Heaven for anything else I will be going to Heaven for all the publicity because it has purified me and sacrificed me and made me really ready to go to Heaven. I think that this is something, that we must live life beautifully, we have Jesus with us and He loves us. If we could only remember that God loves me, and I have an opportunity to love others as he loves me, not in big things, but in small things with great love, then Norway becomes a nest of love. And how beautiful it will be that from here a centre for peace has been given. That from here the joy of life of the unborn child comes out. If you become a burning light in the world of peace, then really the Nobel Peace Prize is a gift of the Norwegian people. God bless you!

The National Prayer Breakfast Famous Speech
Washington, D.C. - February 4, 1994

ON the last day, Jesus will say to those at his right hand,

"Come, enter the Kingdom. For I was hungry and you gave me food, I was thirsty and you gave me drink, I was sick and you visited me."

Then Jesus will turn to those on his left hand and say,

"Depart from me because I was hungry and you did not feed me, I was thirsty and you did not give me drink, I was sick and you did not visit me."

These will ask him,

"When did we see you hungry, or thirsty, or sick, and did not come to your help?"

And Jesus will answer them,

"Whatever you neglected to do unto one of the least of these, you neglected to do unto me!"

As we have gathered here to pray together, I think it will be beautiful if we begin with a prayer that expresses very well what Jesus wants us to do for the least. St. Francis of Assisi understood very well these words of Jesus and his life is very well expressed by a prayer. And this prayer, which we say every day after Holy Communion, always surprises me very much, because it is very fitting for each one of us. And I always wonder whether eight hundred years ago when St. Francis lived, they had the same difficulties that we have today. I think that some of you already have this prayer of peace, so we will pray it together.

Let us thank God for the opportunity he has given us today to have come here to pray together. We have come here especially to pray for peace, joy, and love. We are reminded that Jesus came to bring the good news to the poor. He had told us what that good news is when he said,

"My peace I leave with you, my peace I give unto you."

He came not to give the peace of the world, which is only that we don't bother each other. He came to give peace of heart which comes from loving - from doing good to others.

And God loved the world so much that he gave his son. God gave his son to the Virgin Mary, and what did she do with him? As soon as Jesus came into Mary's life, immediately she went in haste to give that good news. And as she came into the house of her cousin, Elizabeth, Scripture tells us that the unborn child - the child in the womb of Elizabeth - leapt with joy. While still in the womb of Mary, Jesus brought peace to John the Baptist, who leapt for joy in the womb of Elizabeth.

And as if that were not enough - as if it were not enough that God the Son should become one of us and bring peace and joy while still in the womb, Jesus also died on the Cross to show that greater love. He died for you and for me, and for that leper and for that man dying of hunger and that naked person lying in the street - not only of Calcutta, but of Africa, of everywhere. Our Sisters serve these poor people in 105 countries throughout the world. Jesus insisted that we love one another as he loves each one of us. Jesus gave his life to love us, and he tells us that he loves each one of us. Jesus gave his life to love us, and he tells us that we also have to give whatever it takes to do good to one another. And in the Gospel Jesus says very clearly, " Love as I have loved you."

Jesus died on the Cross because that is what it took for him to do good for us - to save us from our selfishness and sin. He gave up everything to do the Father's will, to show us that we too must be willing to give everything to do God's will, to love one another as he loves each of us. If we are not willing to give whatever it takes to do good for one another, sin is still in us. That is why we too must give to each other until it hurts.

Love always hurts

It is not enough for us to say, "I love God." But I also have to love my neighbor. St. John says that you are a liar if you say you love God and you don't love your neighbor. How can you love God whom you do not see, if you do not love your neighbor whom you see, whom you touch, with whom you live? And so it is very important for us to realize that love, to be true, has to hurt. I must be willing to give whatever it takes not to harm other people and, in fact, to do good to them. This requires that I be willing to give until it hurts. Otherwise, there is no true love in me and I bring injustice, not peace, to those around me.

It hurt Jesus to love us. We have been created in his image for greater things, to love and to be loved. We must "put on Christ," as Scripture tells us. And so we have been created to love as he loves us. Jesus makes himself the hungry one, the naked one, the homeless one, the unwanted one, and he says, "You did it to me." On the last day he will say to those on his right, "whatever you did to the least of these, you did to me," and he will also say to those on his left, "whatever you neglected to do for the least of these, you neglected to do it for me."

When he was dying on the Cross, Jesus said, "I thirst." Jesus is thirsting for our love, and this is the thirst for everyone, poor and rich alike. We all thirst for the love of others, that they go out of their way to avoid harming us and to do good to us. This is the meaning of true love, to give until it hurts.

I can never forget the experience I had in visiting a home where they kept all these old parents of sons and daughters who had just put them into an institution and, maybe, forgotten them. I saw that in that home these old people had everything: good food, comfortable place, television - everything. But everyone was looking toward the door. And I did not see a single one with a smile on his face.

I turned to Sister and I asked, "Why do these people, who have every comfort here - why are they all looking toward the door? Why are they not smiling?" (I am so used to seeing the smiles on our people." Even the dying ones smile.) And Sister said, "This is the way it is, nearly everyday. They are expecting - they are hoping - that a son or daughter will come to visit them.

They are hurt because they are forgotten."

See, this neglect to love brings spiritual poverty. Maybe in our family we have somebody who is feeling lonely, who is feeling sick, who is feeling worried. Are we there? Are we willing to give until it hurts, in order to be with our families? Or do we put our own interests first? These are the questions we must ask ourselves, especially as we begin this Year of the Family. We must remember that love begins at home, and we must also remember that "the future of humanity passes through the family.

I was surprised in the West to see so many young boys and girls given to drugs. And I tried to find out why. Why is it like that, when those in the West have so many more things than those in the East? And the answer was, "Because there is no one in the family to receive them." Our children depend on us for everything: their health, their nutrition, their security, their coming to know and love God. For all of this, they look to us with trust, hope, and expectation. But often father and mother are so busy that they have no time for their children, or perhaps they are not even married, or have given up on their marriage. So the children go to the streets, and get involved in drugs, or other things. We are talking of love of the child, which is where love and peace must begin. These are the things that break peace.

But I feel that the greatest destroyer of peace today is abortion, because it is a war against the child - a direct killing of the innocent child - murder by the mother herself. And if we accept that a mother can kill even her own child, how can we tell other people not to kill one another? How do we persuade a woman not to have an abortion? As always, we must persuade her with love, and we remind ourselves that love means to be willing to give until it hurts. Jesus gave even his life to love us. So the mother who is thinking of abortion, should be helped to love - that is, to give until it hurts her plans, or her free time, to respect the life of her child. The father of that child, whoever he is, must also give until it hurts. By abortion, the mother does not learn to love, but kills even her own child to solve her problems. And by abortion, the father is told that he does not have to take any responsibility at all for the child he has brought into the world. That father is likely to put other women into the same trouble. So abortion just leads to more abortion. Any country that accepts abortion is not teaching the people to love, but to use any violence to get what they want. That is why the greatest destroyer of love and peace is abortion.

Many people are very, very concerned with the children of India, with the children of Africa, where quite a few die of hunger, and so on. Many people are also concerned about all the violence in this great country of the United States. These concerns are very good. But often these same people are not concerned with the millions who are being killed by the deliberate decision of their own mothers. And this is what is the greatest destroyer of peace today: abortion, which brings people to such blindness.

"I want this child!"

And for this I appeal in India and I appeal everywhere: "Let us bring the child back." The child is God's gift to the family. Each child is created in the special image and likeness of God for greater things - to love and to be loved. In this Year of the Family we must bring the child back to the center of our care and concern. This is the only way that our world can survive, because our children are the only hope for the future. As other people are called to God, only their children can take their places.

But what does God say to us? He says, "Even if a mother could forget her child, I will not forget you. I have carved you in the palm of my hand." We are carved in the palm of his hand; that unborn child has been carved in the hand of God from conception, and is called by God to love and to be loved, not only now in this life, out forever. God can never forget us.

I will tell you something beautiful. We are fighting abortion by adoption - by care of the mother and adoption for her baby. We have saved thousands of lives. We have sent word to the clinics, to the hospitals, and police stations: Please don't destroy the child; we will take the child." So we always have someone tell the mothers in trouble: "Come, we will take care of you, we will get a home for your child."

And we have a tremendous demand from couples who cannot have a child. But I never give a child to a couple who has done something not to have a child. Jesus said, "Anyone who receives a child in my name, receives me." By adopting a child, these couples receive Jesus, but by aborting a child, a couple refuses to receive Jesus.

Please don't kill the child. I want the child. Please give me the child. I am willing to accept any child who would be aborted, and to give that child to a married couple who will love the child, and be loved by the child. From our children's home in Calcutta alone, we have saved over 3,000 children from abortions. These children have brought such love and joy to their adopting parents, and have grown up so full of love and joy! I know that couples have to plan their family, and for that there is natural family planning. The way to plan the family is natural family planning, not contraception. In destroying the power of giving life, through contraception, a husband or wife is doing something to self. This turns the attention to self, and so it destroys the gift of love in him or her. In loving, the husband and wife must turn the attention to each other, as happens in natural family planning, and not to self, as happens in contraception. Once that living love is destroyed by contraception, abortion follows very easily.

The greatness of the poor

I also know that there are great problems in the world

- that many spouses do not love each other enough to practice natural family planning. We cannot solve all the problems in the world, but let us never bring in the worst problem of all, and that is to destroy love. This is what happens when we tell people to practice contraception and abortion.

The poor are very great people. They can teach us so many beautiful things. Once one of them came to thank us for teaching them natural family planning, and said: "You people - who have practiced chastity - you are the best people to teach us natural family planning, because it is nothing more than self-control out of love for each other." And what this poor person said is very true. These poor people maybe have nothing to eat, maybe they have not a home to live in, but they can still be great people when they are spiritually rich. Those who are materially poor can be wonderful people. One evening we went out and we picked up four people from the street. And one of them was in a most terrible condition. I told the Sisters: "You take care of the other three; I will take care of the one who looks worse." So I did for her all that my love can do. I put her in bed, and there was a beautiful smile on her face. She took hold of my hand, and she said one thing only: "Thank you." Then she died.

I could not help but examine my conscience before her. I asked, "What would I say if I were in her place?" And my answer was very simple. I would have tried to draw a little attention to myself. I would have said, "I am hungry, I am dying, I am cold, I am in pain," or something like that. But she gave me much more - she gave me her grateful love. And she died with a smile on her face.

Then there was the man we picked up from the drain, half-eaten by worms. And after we had brought him to the home, he only said, "I have lived like an animal in the street, but am going to die as an angel, loved and cared for." Then, after we had removed all the worms from this body, all he said - with a big smile - was: "Sister, I am going home to God." And he died. It was so wonderful to see the greatness of that man, who could speak like that without blaming anybody, without comparing anything. Like an angel - this is the greatness of people who are spiritually rich, even when they are materially poor.

A sign of care

We are not social workers. We may be doing social work in the eyes of some people, but we must be contemplatives in the heart of the world. For we must bring that presence of God into your family, for the family that prays together, stays together. There is so much hatred, so much misery, and we with our prayer, with our sacrifice, are beginning at home. Love begins at home, and it is not how much we do, but how much love we put into what we do.

If we are contemplatives in the heart of the world with all its problems, these problems can never discourage us. We must always remember what God tells us in the Scripture: Even if the mother could forget the child in her womb - something that is impossible, but even if she could forget - I will never forget you. And so here I am talking with you. I want you to find the poor here, right in your own home first. And begin love there. Bear the good news to your own people first. And find out about your next-door neighbors. Do you know who they are?

I had the most extraordinary experience of love of a neighbor from a Hindu family. A gentleman came to our house and said, "Mother Teresa, there is a family who have not eaten for so long. Do something." So I took some rice and went there immediately. And I saw the children, their eyes shining with hunger. (I don't know if you have ever seen hunger, but I have seen it very often.) And the mother of the family took the rice I gave her, and went out. When she came back, I asked her, "Where did you go? What did you do?" And she gave me a very simple answer: "They are hungry also." What struck me was that she knew. And who were "they?" A Muslim family. And she knew. I didn't bring any more rice that evening, because I wanted them - Hindus and Muslims - to enjoy the joy of sharing.

But there were those children, radiating joy, sharing the joy and peace with their mother because she had the love to give until it hurts. And you see this is where love begins: at home in the family. God will never forget us, and there is something you and I can always do. We can keep the joy of loving Jesus in our hearts, and share that joy with all we come in contact with. Let us make that one point: that no child will be unwanted, unloved, uncared for, or killed and thrown away. And give until it hurts - with a smile.

Because I talk so much of giving with a smile, once a professor from the United States asked me, "Are you married?" And I said, "Yes, and I find it sometimes very difficult to smile at my spouse - Jesus - because he can be very demanding - sometimes this is really something true. And there is where love comes in - when it is demanding, and yet we can give it with joy.

One of the most demanding things for me is traveling everywhere, and with publicity. I have said to Jesus that if I don't go to heaven for anything else, I will be going to heaven for all the traveling with all the publicity, because it has purified me and sacrificed me and made me really ready to go to heaven. If we remember that God loves us, and that we can love others as he loves us, then America can become a sign of peace for the world. From here, a sign of care for the weakest of the weak - the unborn child - must go out to the world. If you become a burning light of justice and peace in the world, then really you will be true to what the founders of this country stood for. God bless you!

NELSON MANDELA

INTRODUCTION

Nelson Rolihlahla Mandela was born in 1918. He earned (1942) a law degree from the University of South Africa.

In 1952 he became ANC deputy national president, advocating nonviolent resistance to apartheid. However, after a group of peaceful demonstrators were massacred (1960) in Sharpeville, Mandela organized a paramilitary branch of the ANC to carry out guerrilla warfare against the white government. After being acquitted (1962) on charges of treason, he was arrested (1964) and convicted of sabotage and sentenced to life in prison, where he became the leading symbol of South Africa's oppressed black majority. Mandela and de Klerk were jointly awarded the Nobel peace prize in 1993. In South Africa's first multiracial elections (1994), Mandela was elected president, and served until 1999, when Thabo Mbeki succeeded him, after Mandela decided not to contest.

No Easy Road to Freedom speech
September 21st 1953

SINCE 1912 and year after year thereafter, in their homes and local areas, in provincial and national gatherings, on trains and buses, in the factories and on the farms, in cities, villages, shanty towns, schools and prisons, the African people have discussed the shameful misdeeds of those who rule the country. Year after year, they have raised their voices in condemnation of the grinding poverty of the people, the low wages, the acute shortage of land, the inhuman exploitation and the whole policy of white domination. But instead of more freedom repression began to grow in volume and intensity and it seemed that all their sacrifices would end up in smoke and dust. Today the entire country knows that their labours were not in vain for a new spirit and new ideas have gripped our people. Today the people speak the language of action: there is a mighty awakening among the men and women of our country and the year 1952 stands out as the year of this upsurge of national consciousness.

In June, 1952, the AFRICAN NATIONAL CONGRESS and the SOUTH AFRICAN INDIAN CONGRESS, bearing in mind their responsibility as the representatives of the downtrodden and oppressed people of South Africa, took the plunge and launched the Campaign for the Defiance of the Unjust Laws. Starting off in Port Elizabeth in the early hours of June 26 and with only thirty-three defiers in action and then in Johannesburg in the afternoon of the same day with one hundred and six defiers, it spread throughout the country like wild fire. Factory and office workers, doctors, lawyers, teachers, students and the clergy; Africans, Coloureds, Indians and Europeans, old and young, all rallied to the national call and defied the pass laws and the curfew and the railway apartheid regulations. At the end of the year, more than 8,000 people of all races had defied. The Campaign called for immediate and heavy sacrifices. Workers lost their jobs, chiefs and teachers were expelled from the service, doctors, lawyers and businessmen gave up their practices and businesses and elected to go to jail. Defiance was a step of great political significance. It released strong social forces which affected thousands of our countrymen. It was an effective way of getting the masses to function politically; a powerful method of voicing our indignation against the reactionary policies of the Government. It was one of the best ways of exerting pressure on the Government and extremely dangerous to the stability and security of the State. It inspired and aroused our people from a conquered and servile community of yes-men to a militant and uncompromising band of comrades-in-arms. The entire country was transformed into battle zones where the forces of liberation were locked up in immortal conflict against those of reaction and evil. Our flag flew in every battlefield and thousands of our countrymen rallied around it. We held the initiative and the forces of freedom were advancing on all fronts. It was against this background and at the height of this Campaign that we held our last annual provincial Conference in Pretoria from the 10th to the 12th of October last year. In a way, that Conference was a welcome reception for those who had returned from the battlefields and a farewell to those who were still going to action. The spirit of defiance and action dominated the entire conference.

Today we meet under totally different conditions. By

the end of July last year, the Campaign had reached a stage where it had to be suppressed by the Government or it would impose its own policies on the country.

The government launched its reactionary offensive and struck at us. Between July last year and August this year forty-seven leading members from both Congresses in Johannesburg, Port Elizabeth and Kimberley were arrested, tried and convicted for launching the Defiance Campaign and given suspended sentences ranging from three months to two years on condition that they did not again participate in the defiance of the unjust laws. In November last year, a proclamation was passed which prohibited meetings of more than ten Africans and made it an offence for any person to call upon an African to defy. Contravention of this proclamation carried a penalty of three years or of a fine of three hundred pounds. In March this year the Government passed the so-called Public Safety Act which empowered it to declare a state of emergency and to create conditions which would permit of the most ruthless and pitiless methods of suppressing our movement. Almost simultaneously, the Criminal Laws Amendment Act was passed which provided heavy penalties for those convicted of Defiance offences. This Act also made provision for the whipping of defiers including women. It was under this Act that Mr. Arthur Matlala who was the local [leader] of the Central Branch during the Defiance Campaign, was convicted and sentenced to twelve months with hard labour plus eight strokes by the Magistrate of Villa Nora. The Government also made extensive use of the Suppression of Communism Act. You will remember that in May last year the Government ordered Moses Kotane, Yusuf Dadoo, J. B. Marks, David Bopape and Johnson Ngwevela to resign from the Congresses and many other organisations and were also prohibited from attending political gatherings. In consequence of these bans, Moses Kotane, J. B. Marks, and David Bopape did not attend our last provincial Conference. In December last year, the Secretary General, Mr. W. M. Sisulu, and I were banned from attending gatherings and confined to Johannesburg for six months. Early this year, the President-General, Chief Luthuli, whilst in the midst of a national tour which he was prosecuting with remarkable energy and devotion, was prohibited for a period of twelve months from attending public gatherings and from visiting Durban, Johannesburg, Cape Town, Port Elizabeth and many other centres. A few days before the President-General was banned, the President of the SAIC, Dr. G. M. Naicker, had been served with a similar notice. Many other active workers both from the African and Indian Congresses and from trade union organisations were also banned.

The Congresses realised that these measures created a new situation which did not prevail when the Campaign was launched in June 1952. The tide of defiance was bound to recede and we were forced to pause and to take stock of the new situation. We had to analyse the dangers that faced us, formulate plans to overcome them and evolve new plans of political struggle. A political movement must keep in touch with reality and the prevailing conditions. Long speeches, the shaking of fists, the banging of tables and strongly worded resolutions out of touch with the objective conditions do not bring about mass action and can do a great deal of harm to the organisation and the struggle we serve. The masses had to be prepared and made ready for new forms of political struggle. We had to recuperate our strength and muster our forces for another and more powerful offensive against the enemy. To have gone ahead blindly as if nothing had happened would have been suicidal and stupid. The conditions under which we meet today are, therefore, vastly different. The Defiance Campaign together with its thrills and adventures has receded. The old methods of bringing about mass action through public mass meetings, press statements and leaflets calling upon the people to go to action have become extremely dangerous and difficult to use effectively. The authorities will not easily permit a meeting called under the auspices of the ANC, few newspapers will publish statements openly criticising the policies of the Government and there is hardly a single printing press which will agree to print leaflets calling upon workers to embark on industrial action for fear of prosecution under the Suppression of Communism Act and similar measures. These developments require the evolution of new forms of political struggle which will make it reasonable for us to strive for action on a higher level than the Defiance Campaign. The Government, alarmed at the indomitable upsurge of national consciousness, is doing everything in its power to crush our movement by removing the genuine representatives of the people from the organisations. According to a statement made by Swart in Parliament on the 1 8th September, 1953, there are thirty-three trade union officials and eighty-nine other people who have been served with notices in terms of the Suppression of Communism Act. This does not include that formidable array of freedom fighters who have been named and blacklisted under the Suppression of Communism Act and those who have been banned under the Riotous Assemblies Act.

Meanwhile the living conditions of the people, already extremely difficult, are steadily worsening and becoming unbearable. The purchasing power of the masses is progressively declining and the cost of living is rocketing. Bread is now dearer than it was two months ago. The cost of milk, meat and vegetables is beyond the pockets of the average family and many of our people cannot afford them. The people are too poor to have enough food to feed their families and children. They cannot afford sufficient clothing, housing and medical care. They are denied the right to security in the event of unemployment, sickness, disability, old age and where these exist, they are of an extremely inferior and useless nature. Because of lack of proper medical amenities our people are ravaged by such dreaded diseases as tuberculosis, venereal disease, leprosy, pellagra, and infantile mortality is very high. The recent state budget made provision for the increase of the cost-of-living allowances for Europeans and not a word was said about the poorest and most hard-hit section of the population - the African people. The insane policies of the Government which have brought about an explosive situation in the country have definitely scared away foreign capital from South Africa and the financial crisis through which the country is now passing is forcing many industrial and business concerns to close down, to retrench their staffs and unemployment is growing every day. The farm labourers are in a particularly dire plight. You will perhaps recall the investigations and exposures of the semi-slave conditions on the Bethal farms made in 1948 by the Reverend Michael Scott and a Guardian Correspondent; by the Drum last year and the Advance in April this year. You will recall how human beings, wearing only sacks with holes for their heads and arms, never given enough food to eat, slept on cement floors on cold nights with only their sacks to cover their shivering bodies. You will remember how they are woken up as early as 4 a. m. and taken to work on the fields with the indunas sjambokking those who tried to straighten their backs, who felt weak and dropped down because of hunger and sheer exhaustion. You will also recall the story of human beings toiling pathetically from the early hours of the morning till sunset, fed only on mealie meal served on filthy sacks spread on the ground and eating with their dirty hands. People falling ill and never once being given medical attention. You will also recall the revolting story of a farmer who was convicted for tying a labourer by his feet from a tree and had him flogged to death, pouring boiling water into his mouth whenever he cried for water. These things which have long vanished from many parts of the world still flourish in SA today. None will deny that they constitute a serious challenge to Congress and we are in duty bound to find an effective remedy for these obnoxious practices.

The Government has introduced in Parliament the Native Labour (Settlement of Disputes) Bill and the Bantu Education Bill. Speaking on the Labour Bill, the Minister of Labour, Ben Schoeman, openly stated that the aim of this wicked measure is to bleed African trade unions to death. By forbidding strikes and lockouts it deprives Africans of the one weapon the workers have to improve their position. The aim of the measure is to destroy the present African trade unions which are controlled by the workers themselves and which fight for the improvement of their working conditions in return for a Central Native Labour Board controlled by the Government and which will be used to frustrate the legitimate aspirations of the African worker. The Minister of Native Affairs, Verwoerd, has also been brutally clear in explaining the objects of the Bantu Education Bill. According to him the aim of this law is to teach our children that Africans are inferior to Europeans. African education would be taken out of the hands of people who taught equality between black and white. When this Bill becomes law, it will not be the parents but the Department of Native Affairs which will decide whether an African child should receive higher or other education. It might well be that the children of those who criticise the Government and who fight its policies will almost certainly be taught how to drill rocks in the mines and how to plough potatoes on the farms of Bethal. High education might well be the privilege of those children whose families have a tradition of collaboration with the ruling circles.

The attitude of the Congress on these bills is very clear

and unequivocal. Congress totally rejects both bills without reservation. The last provincial Conference strongly condemned the then proposed Labour Bill as a measure designed to rob the African workers of the universal right of free trade unionism and to undermine and destroy the existing African trade unions. Conference further called upon the African workers to boycott and defy the application of this sinister scheme which was calculated to further the exploitation of the African worker. To accept a measure of this nature even in a qualified manner would be a betrayal of the toiling masses. At a time when every genuine Congressite should fight unreservedly for the recognition of African trade unions and the realisation of the principle that everyone has the right to form and to join trade unions for the protection of his interests, we declare our firm belief in the principles enunciated in the Universal Declaration of Human Rights that everyone has the right to education; that education shall be directed to the full development of human personality and to the strengthening of respect for human rights and fundamental freedoms. It shall promote understanding, tolerance and friendship among the nations, racial or religious groups and shall further the activities of the United Nations for the maintenance of peace. That parents have the right to choose the kind of education that shall be given to their children.

The cumulative effect of all these measures is to prop up and perpetuate the artificial and decaying policy of the supremacy of the white men. The attitude of the government to us is that: "Let's beat them down with guns and batons and trample them under our feet. We must be ready to drown the whole country in blood if only there is the slightest chance of preserving white supremacy."

But there is nothing inherently superior about the

herrenvolk idea of the supremacy of the whites. In China, India, Indonesia and Korea, American, British, Dutch and French Imperialism, based on the concept of the supremacy of Europeans over Asians, has been completely and perfectly exploded. In Malaya and Indo-China British and French imperialisms are being shaken to their foundations by powerful and revolutionary national liberation movements. In Africa, there are approximately 190,000,000 Africans as against 4,000,000 Europeans. The entire continent is seething with discontent and already there are powerful revolutionary eruptions in the Gold Coast, Nigeria, Tunisia, Kenya, the Rhodesias and South Africa. The oppressed people and the oppressors are at loggerheads. The day of reckoning between the forces of freedom and those of reaction is not very far off. I have not the slightest doubt that when that day comes truth and justice will prevail.

The intensification of repressions and the extensive use of the bans is designed to immobilise every active worker and to check the national liberation movement. But gone forever are the days when harsh and wicked laws provided the oppressors with years of peace and quiet. The racial policies of the Government have pricked the conscience of all men of good will and have aroused their deepest indignation. The feelings of the oppressed people have never been more bitter. If the ruling circles seek to maintain their position by such inhuman methods then a clash between the forces of freedom and those of reaction is certain. The grave plight of the people compels them to resist to the death the stinking policies of the gangsters that rule our country.

But in spite of all the difficulties outlined above, we have won important victories. The general political level of the people has been considerably raised and they are now more conscious of their strength. Action has become the language of the day. The ties between the working people and the Congress have been greatly strengthened. This is a development of the highest importance because in a country such as ours a political organisation that does not receive the support of the workers is in fact paralysed on the very ground on which it has chosen to wage battle. Leaders of trade union organisations are at the same time important officials of the provincial and local branches of the ANC In the past we talked of the African, Indian and Coloured struggles. Though certain individuals raised the question of a united front of all the oppressed groups, the various non-European organisations stood miles apart from one another and the efforts of those for co-ordination and unity were like a voice crying in the wilderness and it seemed that the day would never dawn when the oppressed people would stand and fight together shoulder to shoulder against a common enemy. Today we talk of the struggle of the oppressed people which, though it is waged through their respective autonomous organisations, is gravitating towards one central command.

Our immediate task is to consolidate these victories, to preserve our organisations and to muster our forces for the resumption of the offensive. To achieve this important task the National Executive of the ANC in consultation with the National Action Committee of the ANC and the SAIC formulated a plan of action popularly known as the "M" Plan and the highest importance is [given] to it by the National Executives. Instructions were given to all provinces to implement the "M" Plan without delay.

The underlying principle of this plan is the understanding that it is no longer possible to wage our struggle mainly on the old methods of public meetings and printed circulars. The aim is: to consolidate the Congress machinery; to enable the transmission of important decisions taken on a national level to every member of the organisation without calling public meetings, issuing press statements and printing circulars; to build up in the local branches themselves local Congresses which will effectively represent the strength and will of the people; to extend and strengthen the ties between Congress and the people and to consolidate Congress leadership.

This plan is being implemented in many branches not only in the Transvaal but also in the other provinces and is producing excellent results. The Regional Conferences held in Sophiatown, Germiston, Kliptown and Benoni on the 28th June, 23rd and 30th August and on the 6th September, 1953, which were attended by large crowds, are a striking demonstration of the effectiveness of this plan, and the National Executives must be complimented for it. I appeal to all members of the Congress to redouble their efforts and play their part truly and well in its implementation. The hard, dirty and strenuous task of recruiting members and strengthening our organisation through a house to house campaign in every locality must be done by you all. From now on the activity of Congressites must not be confined to speeches and resolutions. Their activities must find expression in wide scale work among the masses, work which will enable them to make the greatest possible contact with the working people. You must protect and defend your trade unions. If you are not allowed to have your meetings publicly, then you must hold them over your machines in the factories, on the trains and buses as you travel home. You must have them in your villages and shantytowns. You must make every home, every shack and every mud structure where our people live, a branch of the trade union movement and never surrender.

You must defend the right of African parents to decide the kind of education that shall be given to their children. Teach the children that Africans are not one iota inferior to Europeans. Establish your own community schools where the right kind of education will be given to our children. If it becomes dangerous or impossible to have these alternative schools, then again you must make every home, every shack or rickety structure a centre of learning for our children. Never surrender to the inhuman and barbaric theories of Verwoerd.

The decision to defy the unjust laws enabled Congress to develop considerably wider contacts between itself and the masses and the urge to join Congress grew day by day. But due to the fact that the local branches did not exercise proper control and supervision, the admission of new members was not carried out satisfactorily. No careful examination was made of their past history and political characteristics. As a result of this, there were many shady characters ranging from political clowns, place-seekers, splitters, saboteurs, agents-provocateurs to informers and even policemen, who infiltrated into the ranks of Congress. One need only refer to the Johannesburg trial of Dr. Moroka and nineteen others, where a member of Congress who actually worked at the National Headquarters, turned out to be a detective-sergeant on special duty. Remember the case of Leballo of Brakpan who wormed himself into that Branch by producing faked naming letters from the Liquidator, De Villiers Louw, who had instructions to spy on us. There are many other similar instances that emerged during the Johannesburg, Port Elizabeth and Kimberley trials. Whilst some of these men were discovered there are many who have not been found out. In Congress there are still many shady characters, political clowns, place-seekers, saboteurs, provocateurs, informers and policemen who masquerade as progressives but who are in fact the bitterest enemies of our organisation. Outside appearances are highly deceptive and we cannot classify these men by looking at their faces or by listening to their sweet tongues or their vehement speeches demanding immediate action. The friends of the people are distinguishable by the ready and disciplined manner in which they rally behind their organisation and their readiness to sacrifice when the preservation of the organisation has become a matter of life and death. Similarly, enemies and shady characters are detected by the extent to which they consistently attempt to wreck the organisation by creating fratricidal strife, disseminating confusion and undermining and even opposing important plans of action to vitalise the organisation. In this respect it is interesting to note that almost all the people who oppose the "M" Plan are people who have consistently refused to respond when sacrifices were called for, and whose political background leaves much to be desired. These shady characters by means of flattery, bribes and corruption, win the support of the weak-willed and politically backward individuals, detach them from Congress and use them in their own interests. The presence of such elements in Congress constitutes a serious threat to the struggle, for the capacity for political action of an organisation which is ravaged by such disruptive and splitting elements is considerably undermined. Here in South Africa, as in many parts of the world, a revolution is maturing: it is the profound desire, the determination and the urge of the overwhelming majority of the country to destroy for ever the shackles of oppression that condemn them to servitude and slavery. To overthrow oppression has been sanctioned by humanity and is the highest aspiration of every free man. If elements in our organisation seek to impede the realisation of this lofty purpose then these people have placed themselves outside the organisation and must be put out of action before they do more harm. To do otherwise would be a crime and a serious neglect of duty. We must rid ourselves of such elements and give our organisation the striking power of a real militant mass organisation.

Kotane, Marks, Bopape, Tloome and I have been banned from attending gatherings and we cannot join and counsel with you on the serious problems that are facing our country. We have been banned because we champion the freedom of the oppressed people of our country and because we have consistently fought against the policy of racial discrimination in favour of a policy which accords fundamental human rights to all, irrespective of race, colour, sex or language. We are exiled from our own people for we have uncompromisingly resisted the efforts of imperialist America and her satellites to drag the world into the rule of violence and brutal force, into the rule of the napalm, hydrogen and the cobalt bombs where millions of people will be wiped out to satisfy the criminal and greedy appetites of the imperial powers. We have been gagged because we have emphatically and openly condemned the criminal attacks by the imperialists against the people of Malaya, Vietnam, Indonesia, Tunisia and Tanganyika and called upon our people to identify themselves unreservedly with the cause of world peace and to fight against the war policies of America and her satellites. We are being shadowed, hounded and trailed because we fearlessly voiced our horror and indignation at the slaughter of the people of Korea and Kenya. The massacre of the Kenya people by Britain has aroused world-wide indignation and protest. Children are being burnt alive, women are raped, tortured, whipped and boiling water poured on their breasts to force confessions from them that Jomo Kenyatta had administered the Mau Mau oath to them. Men are being castrated and shot dead. In the Kikuyu country there are some villages in which the population has been completely wiped out. We are prisoners in our own country because we dared to raise our voices against these horrible atrocities and because we expressed our solidarity with the cause of the Kenya people.

You can see that "there is no easy walk to freedom anywhere, and many of us will have to pass through the valley of the shadow (of death) again and again before we reach the mountain tops of our desires.

"Dangers and difficulties have not deterred us in the past, they will not frighten us now. But we must be prepared for them like men in business who do not waste energy in vain talk and idle action. The way of preparation (for action) lies in our rooting out all impurity and indiscipline from our organisation and making it the bright and shining instrument that will cleave its way to freedom."

NETAJI SUBHASH CHANDRA BOSE

INTRODUCTION

Subhash Chandra was born on 23rd January, 1897 in Cuttack as the ninth child among 14, of Janakinath Bose, an advocate, and Prabhavati Devi, a pious and God-fearing lady. A brilliant student, he topped the matriculation examination of Calcutta province and passed his B.A. in Philosophy from the Presidency College in Calcutta. One of the veteran leaders of India's freedom movement, specially known for his forming an Indian National Army In 1943 to fight the British with the help of Japan. Reportedly killed In *an* air crash in 1945. Netaji Subhash Chandra Bose gave many memorable speeches during his lifetime , like the one calling upon the Indians to 'Tum mujhe khoon do, mein tumhe azadi doonga' (You give me blood, and I promise you freedom). Awarded Bharat Ratna (posthumously In 1992).

TO DELHI, TO DELHI Speech at a military review of the Indian National Army, July 5, 1943

SOLDIERS of India's Army of Liberation!

Today is the proudest day of my life. Today it has pleased Providence to give me the unique privilege and honour of announcing to the whole world that India's Army of Liberation has come into being. This army has now been drawn up in military formation on the battlefield of Singapore, which was once the bulwark of the British Empire.

This is not only the Army that will emancipate India from the British yoke, it is also the Army that will hereafter create the future national army of Free India. Every Indian must feel proud that this Army, his own Army, has been organized entirely under Indian leadership and that when the historic moment arrives, under Indian leadership it will go to battle.

There are people who thought at one time that the Empire on which the sun did not set was an everlasting empire. No such thought ever troubled me. History had taught me that every empire has its inevitable decline and collapse. Moreover I had seen with my own eyes, cities and fortresses that were once the bulwarks but which became the graveyards of by-gone empires. Standing today on the graveyard of the British empire, even a child is convinced that the almighty British empire is already a thing of the past.

When France declared war on Germany in 1939 and the campaign began, there was but one cry which rose from the lips of German soldiers—"To Paris, To Paris !" When the Brave soldiers of Nippon set out on their march in December 1941 there was but one cry which rose from their lips-"To Singapore. to Singapore !" Comrades ! Soldiers ! Let your battle-cry be-"To-Delhi To Delhi ! " How many of us will individually survive this war of freedom, I do not know. But I do know this, that we shall ultimately win and our task will not end until our surviving heroes hold the victory parade on another graveyard of the British empire, the Lal Kila or Red Fortress of ancient Delhi.

Throughout my public career, I have always felt that though India is otherwise ripe for independence in every way, she has lacked one thing, namely an army of liberation. George Washington of America could fight and win freedom, because he had his army. Garibaldi could liberate Italy, because he had his armed volunteers behind him. It is your privilege and honour to be the first to come forward and organize India's national army. By doing so, you have removed the last obstacle in our path to freedom. Be happy and proud that you are the pioneers, the vanguard, in such a noble cause.

Let me remind you that you have a two-fold task to perform. With the force of arms and at the cost of your blood you will have to win liberty. Then, when India is free, you will have to organize the permanent army of Free India, whose task it will be to preserve our liberty for all time. We must build up our national defense on such an unshakable foundation that never again in our history shall we lose our freedom.

As soldiers, you will always have to cherish and live up to the three-ideals of faithfulness, duty and sacrifice. Soldiers who always remain faithful to their nation, who are always prepared to sacrifice their lives, are invincible. If you, too, want to be invincible, engrave these three ideals in the innermost core of your hearts.

A true soldier needs both military and spiritual training.

You must, all of you, so train yourselves and your comrades that every soldier will have unbounded confidence in himself, will be conscious of being immensely superior to the enemy, will be fearless of death, and will have sufficient initiative to act on his own in any critical situation should the need arise. During the course of the present war, you have seen with your own eyes what wonders scientific training, coupled with courage, fearlessness and dynamism, can achieve. Learn all that you can from this example, and build up for Mother India an absolutely first-class modern army.

To those of you who are officers, I should like to say that your responsibility is a heavy one. Though the responsibility of an officer in every army in this world is indeed great, it is far greater in your case. Because of our political enslavement, we have no tradition like that of Mukden, Port Arthur or Sedan to inspire us. We have to unlearn some of the things that the British taught us and we have to learn much that they did not teach. Nevertheless. I am confident that you will rise to the occasion and fulfill the task that your countrymen have thrown on your brave soldiers. Remember always that officers can make or unmake an army. Remember, too, that the British have suffered defeats on so many fronts largely because of worthless officers. And remember also that out of your ranks will be born the future General Staff of the Army of Free India.

To all of you I should like to say that in the course of this war you will have to acquire the experience and achieve the success which alone can build up a national tradition for our Army. An army that has no tradition of courage, fearlessness and invincibility cannot hold its own in a struggle with a powerful enemy.

Comrades ! You have voluntarily accepted a mission that is the noblest that the human mind can conceive of. For the fulfillment of such a mission no sacrifice is too great, not even the sacrifice of one's life. You are today the custodians of India's national honour and the embodiment of India's hopes and aspirations. So conduct yourself that your countrymen may bless you and posterity may be proud of you.

I have said that today is the proudest day of my life. For an enslaved people, there can be no greater pride, no higher honour, than to be the first soldier in the army of liberation. But this honour carries with it a corresponding responsibility and I am deeply conscious of it. I assure you that I shall be with you in darkness and in sunshine, in sorrow and in joy, in suffering and in victory. For the present, I can offer you nothing except hunger, thirst, privation, forced marches and death. But if you follow me in life and in death, as I am confident you will, I shall lead you to victory and freedom. It does not matter who among us will live to see India free. It is enough that India shall be free and that we shall give our all to make her free. May God now bless our Army and grant us victory in the coming fight !

Inqualab Zindabad ! Azad Hind Zindabad !

Give Me Blood, and I Promise you Freedom!
At a rally of Indians in Burma, July 4, 1944

FRIENDS! Twelve months ago a new programme of 'total mobilisation' or 'maximum sacrifice' was placed before Indians in East Asia. Today I shall give you an account of our achievements during the past year and shall place before you our demands for the coming year. But, before I do so, I want you to realise once again what a golden opportunity we have for winning freedom. The British are engaged in a worldwide struggle and in the course of this struggle they have suffered defeat after defeat on so many fronts. The enemy having been thus considerably weakened, our fight for liberty has become very much easier than it was five years ago. Such a rare and God-given opportunity comes once in a century. That is why we have sworn to fully utilise this opportunity for liberating our motherland from the British yoke.

I am so very hopeful and optimistic about the outcome of our struggle, because I do not rely merely on the efforts of three million Indians in East Asia. There is a gigantic movement going on inside India and millions of our countrymen are prepared for maximum suffering and sacrifice in order to achieve liberty.

Unfortunately, ever since the great fight of 1857, our countrymen are disarmed, whereas the enemy is armed to the teeth. Without arms and without a modern army, it is impossible for a disarmed people to win freedom in this modern age. Through the grace of Providence and through the help of generous Nippon, it has become possible for Indians in East Asia to get arms to build up a modern army. Moreover, Indians in East Asia are united to a man in the endeavor to win freedom and all the religious and other differences that the British tried to engineer inside India, simply do not exist in East Asia. Consequently, we have now an ideal combination of circumstances favouring the success of our struggle- and all that is wanted is that Indians should themselves come forward to pay the price of liberty. According to the programme of 'total mobilisation', I demanded of you men, money and materials. Regarding men, I am glad to tell you that I have obtained sufficient recruits already. Recruits have come to us from every corner of east Asia- from China, Japan, Indo-China, Philippines, Java, Borneo, Celebes, Sumatra, Malaya, Thailand and Burma.

You must continue the mobilisation of men, money and materials with greater vigour and energy, in particular, the problem of supplies and transport has to be solved satisfactorily.

We require more men and women of all categories for administration and reconstruction in liberated areas. We must be prepared for a situation in which the enemy will ruthlessly apply the scorched earth policy, before withdrawing from a particular area and will also force the civilian population to evacuate as was attempted in Burma.

The most important of all is the problem of sending reinforcements in men and in supplies to the fighting fronts. If we do not do so, we cannot hope to maintain our success at the fronts. Nor can we hope to penetrate deeper into India.

Those of you who will continue to work on the Home Front should never forget that East Asia- and particularly Burma- from our base for the war of liberation. If this base is not strong, our fighting forces can never be victorious. Remember that this is a 'total war'- and not merely a war between two armies. That is why for a full one year I have been laying so much stress on 'total mobilisation' in the East.

There is another reason why I want you to look after the Home Front properly. During the coming months I and my colleagues on the War Committee of the Cabinet desire to devote our whole attention to the fighting front- and also to the task of working up the revolution inside India. Consequently, we want to be fully assured that the work at the base will go on smoothly and uninterruptedly even in our absence.

Friends, one year ago, when I made certain demands of you, I told you that if you give me 'total mobilization', I would give you a 'second front'. I have redeemed that pledge. The first phase of our campaign is over. Our victorious troops, fighting side by side with Nipponese troops, have pushed back the enemy and are now fighting bravely on the sacred soil of our dear motherland.

Gird up your loins for the task that now lies ahead. I had asked you for men, money and materials. I have got them in generous measure. Now I demand more of you. Men, money and materials cannot by themselves bring victory or freedom. We must have the motive-power that will inspire us to brave deeds and heroic exploits.

It will be a fatal mistake for you to wish to live and see India free simply because victory is now within reach. No one here should have the desire to live to enjoy freedom. A long fight is still in front of us.

We should have but one desire today- the desire to die so that India may live- the desire to face a martyr's death, so that the path to freedom may be paved with the martyr's blood.

Friend's! my comrades in the War of Liberation! Today I demand of you one thing, above all. I demand of you blood. It is blood alone that can avenge the blood that the enemy has spilt. It is blood alone that can pay the price of freedom.

Give me blood and I Promise you freedom.

Why INA Withdrew, On August 13, 1944

WHEN the Imphal expedition failed largely because of the failure of the Japanese military supplies to the front and the complete dominations the British and American forces had over the skies of Burma, Netaji had to explain that this was not the end of the war. It was a setback but not the final defeat.

We started the operations too late. The monsoon was disadvantageous to us. Our roads were submerged. River traffic had to be against the current. Against this, the enemy had first-class roads. Our only chance was to take Imphal before the rains started; and we would have succeeded if we had more air support and if the enemy forces in Imphal had not special orders to make a stand to the last man. If we had started in January, we would have succeeded. In all sectors, till the rains began, we either held the enemy or advanced. In the Arakan Sector, the enemy was held; In the Kaladan Sector, we routed the enemy and advanced; In Tiddim, we advanced; In Palel and Kohima also, we advanced; In the Haka Sector, we held them - and all this in spite of the numerical superiority that the enemy had, plus equipment and rations.

When the rains came, we had to postpone the general assault on Imphal. The enemy was able to send mechanized divisions and thus was able to retake the Kohima-Imphal Road. The question then arose: where should we hold the line? There were two courses open: either to hold on to the Bishenpur- Palel Line and not allow the enemy to advance; or to fall back and hold a more advantageous position.

What are the lessons we have learnt from the campaign? We have received our baptism by fire. A body of ex-civilians, who were ordered to withdraw, and with fixed bayonets they charged the enemy. They came back victorious.

Our troops have gained much confidence. We have learnt that the Indian troops with the enemy are willing to come over. We must now make arrangements to take them over. We have learnt the tactics of the enemy. We have captured enemy documents. The experience gained by our Commanders has been invaluable. Before the campaign started, the Japanese had no confidence in our troops and wanted to break them up into batches attached to the Japanese Army. I wanted a front to be given to our men and this was ultimately given.

We have also learnt our defects. Transport and supply were defective owing to the difficult terrain. We had no frontline propaganda. Though we had prepared personnel for this, we could not use them owing to lack of transport. Henceforth, each unit of the INA will have a propaganda unit attached to it. We wanted loudspeakers but the Japanese failed to supply them to us. We are now making our own.

INDIA WILL BE FREE, August 17, 1945

BROTHERS and sisters ! A great chapter in the history of India's freedom struggle has come to a close now. India's sons and daughters living in East Asia have secured a permanent place in this chapter.

By contributing men, money and supplies to the struggle for Idian independence, you have set up a shining example of patriotism and sacrifice. I can never forget your generous and enthusiastic response to my call of Total Mobilization. Like a perennial spring you sent your sons and daughters to the Azad Hind Fanj and Jhansi Rani Regiment. You gave generous donations in cash and kind to the war fund of the Provisional Government of Azad Hind. In short, you have carried out your duty as the real sons and daughters of India. I am more aggrieved than you by the fact that your sufferings and sacrifices have not yielded immediate results.

Neverthless they have not gone waste, because they have paved the path of deliverance of our motherland and will be a perpetual source of inspiration to Indians living all over the world. The future will bless you and will speak with pride of your sacrifices at the altar of Indian independence and of your solid achievements.

At this unprecedented juncture in our history I have a word for you. Do not be disheartened by our temporary defeat ; be cheerful and optimistic. Above all, never lose your faith in the destiny of India. There is no power on earth which can keep India in bondage. India will be free and, that too, soon. JAI-HIND !

RAJENDRA PRASAD

INTRODUCTION

Rajendra Prasad was born in Zeradei, in the Siwan district of Bihar.

Dr. Rajendra Prasad was the first President of India. He was a great freedom fighter, and the architect of the Indian Constitution, having served as President of the Constituent Assembly that drafted the Constitution of the Republic from 1948 to 1950.

He had also served as a Cabinet Minister briefly in the first Government of Independent India. He was a very important leader of the Indian Independence Movement.

Inaugural speech at the Anti-Nuclear Arms Convention, New Delhi, June 16, 1962

THE world is passing through a crucial phase in its history. Science and technology have made such tremendous progress that they have made it possible for mankind to live in comfort and free from poverty and disease if only man knew how to utilize the opportunities offered to him and use them not for the purpose of exploitation or destruction but for the benefit of humanity at large. On the other hand, this advance in science and technology has created a situation which may well lead to the destruction of civilization and the annihilation of mankind, should man be foolish and shortsighted enough to abuse and misuse the opportunities and advantages which science and technology have to offer.

It is only necessary to realize the danger involved in the nuclear race to rouse the conscience of mankind and check this mad competition. If it were only a question affecting two combatants, who could fight it out between themselves and destroy each other, one could sit back complacently and say: "If they are so minded let them do their worst to each other and be banned." But unfortunately much more is at stake. It is the future of humanity. Combatants or opposing nations are as much involved in it as noncombatants and neutrals. The slaughter of the innocent and the guilty alike on a mass scale is bad enough. It becomes infinitely worse if not only the living but also many generations of those yet to be born are doomed to be afflicted with congenital physical and mental defects. The nonaligned and neutral people are as much involved in this as those who are knowingly engaged in the criminal conspiracy of creating weapons and conditions that would spell their own annihilation no less than that of others.

There is no known defense against a nuclear attack once it is launched. The only thing that the target country can do Is to perfect a system of instant retaliation that would be able to function even when the rest of the country has been reduced to an atomic wreckage. It can however be poor consolation to the victim of a nuclear attack to know that after he has been wiped out of existence a similar fate would overtake the adversary.

It has further been said that the only way to prevent a nuclear war is to develop an adequate nuclear deterrent. To buttress this argument it is pointed out that it was only the knowledge that if they used poison gas the allied nations would not hesitate to retaliate in kind, which prevented the Axis powers from employing poison gas in the last World War.

Even if deterrence succeeds, the mounting scale of expenditure on armaments resulting from the nuclear arms race will be such as to impoverish the nations concerned and deprive mankind of much of the fruits of scientific advance. According to a report sponsored by the National Planning Association of America, produced by men who were not concerned in any antinuclear campaign, the United States was in 1958 "spending 45 billion dollars per annum on military preparation. In the United States about 10 per cent of the gross national product is now devoted to military purposes. It is estimated that 15 per cent of the gross national product of the Soviet Union is similarly devoted. If the world goes on as it is, neither better nor worse, it is estimated that from the present time till 1970, from 1.500 to 2,000 billion dollars will have been spent on armaments; but this will certainly prove to be an underestimate, since new inventions will necessitate increasingly expensive weapons."

A race for nuclear weapons, of which the nuclear tests are an index, if it remains unchecked, can thus have only three possible results:

(1) It may lead to a thermonuclear war between East and West which will result in the annihilation of whole populations on either side, destroy civilization and turn the world into a radioactive wasteland-

(2) Or, as Bertrand Russell points out, assaults on heavenly bodies by the competing powers may take the place of exploding nuclear weapons in the attempt by each to demonstrate its superior counterforce capacity to the other side. "It may well happen", says Bertrand Russell, "that means will be found to cause them [the terrestrial bodies] to disintegrate. The moon may split and crumble and melt. Poisonous fragments may fall on Moscow and Washington or more innocent regions. Hate and destructiveness having become cosmic will spread madness beyond its present terrestrial confines."

(3) The insane race for supremacy in thermonuclear weapons may lead to the financial bankruptcy Of the countries concerned and turn the whole world into a vast slum inhabited by fearridden neurotics, like the philosophers of Laputa in Dean Swift's satire.

How is it, one may ask, that with all these disastrous consequences of nuclear warfare staring them in the face, the powers still engage in the nuclear arms race? Why cannot they agree to stop the ruinous competition and dump their armaments into the sea, or where their capacity for damage is destroyed? The reason is that both sides are in the grip of mutual fear, suspicion and distrust, and these do not make for sanity. The only cure for fear, Mahatma Gandhi taught us, is faith; for suspicion sincerity; and for distrust trust.

We have seen disarmament conferences dragging on their weary course endlessly only to bog down in a morass of equivocation and double talk. Diplomats hold forth on disarmament but are not prepared to abjure war. They talk about peace but have a mental reservation about the renunciation of force.

The straightest and the simplest way to break through this vicious circle would be for all powers to abjure the use of force altogether, and this must be reflected in their domestic policies. There may be an agreement to enforce collective sanctions, economic and other, not involving the use of force, against any power that violates the agreed code.

In the alternative if any one country taking courage in both hands unilaterally disarms, It would break this vicious circle of mutual fear and distrust and pave the way for universal disarmament. Such a nation would go down in history as the benefactor of mankind and the world will not allow it to fail a victim to aggression. Mankind has advanced in thought. The conscience of the world has been awakened. We have, of late, witnessed One African country after another achieves independence, not by the use of military force but under pressure of world opinion. It will, however, be said that charity should begin at home. India has had the unique privilege of engaging in a successful nonviolent struggle for independence under the leadership of Mahatma Gandhi. She should set the example if her appeal for unilateral disarmament is to carry any weight. I consider this to be a perfectly legitimate challenge. My appeal is addressed to India no less than to the other countries of the world.

It may be, however, that some other country is better qualified than India to take the lead in this respect and will succeed quicker than we are. Mahatma Gandhi was once asked that since he, after fifty years of striving, had not been able on his own admission to demonstrate the full power of the nonviolence of his conception, what chance was there for others to succeed even in a thousand years? He replied: "It may take some a thousand years, and it may take others only one year. Do not think that, if in spite of my fifty years' practice of it I am still imperfect, it must take you many more years. No, there is no rule of three here. You may succeed quicker than I."

He even envisaged some Western nation, by dint of its training in discipline and organization, and its martial valour, attaining the goal of nonviolence even before India, though he never ceased to hope that India would not allow itself to be beaten in the race.

Nuclear weapons, far from ensuring the triumph of one way of life or the other, only promise the extinction of all life. On the other hand, instances can be multiplied to show that military defeat, occupation and annexation of a country did not result in the disappearance of the nation or its way of life: witness Poland, Ireland, Czechoslovakia, to mention only a few. During the last world war resistance movements sprang up in several countries under German occupation. The victims of Nazi aggression realized that capitulation by the forces of their respective Governments did not necessarily mean the end of popular resistance to occupation. It was further noted that these movements were most successful where they were carried on, largely if not wholly, by moral, i.e. nonviolent, means. An outstanding instance of this is provided by the resistance movement in Norway. Violent resistance, where it was tried, proved efficacious only to the extent to which it was the reflection of moral resistance, or the measure of the will to resist in terms of readiness to suffer, and of the intensity of sympathy and active or passive support of the thousands of nonterrorists.

The employment of nuclear weapons is only part of the technique of frightfulness. The idea behind it is that if the tyrant can demonstrate his undoubted capacity to exterminate the adversary, the latter is bound to submit. But if the adversary learns the art of dying without submission or a sense of defeat, if he develops the awareness that there is in us something which the armaments cannot destroy and which survives even the destruction of our physical body, the power of armaments, nuclear or other, will be sterilized. For it is not the physical destruction of the adversary that the tyrant desires as a rule, but only to bend him to his will. "At the back of the policy of terrorism", observed Mahatma Gandhi, "is the assumption that terrorism, If applied in a sufficient measure, will produce the desired result, namely, bending the adversary to the tyrant's will. But supposing a people make up their mind that they will never do the tyrant's will and not retaliate with the tyrant's own methods, the tyrant will not find It worth his while to go on with his terrorism. If sufficient food is given to the tyrant a time will come when he will have had more than surfeit."

This was what happened in our own case. The British could have tried to put us down in 1930 by methods, which they adopted in 1857 to suppress the Indian Revolt. But we did not give them the chance, because we were, by and large, nonviolent: and even though our nonviolence was not of the purest type, it worked. Lord Irwin had to declare that his Government could not impose "the peace of the grave" on India even though they had the capacity.

Being asked whether the atom bomb had not rendered obsolete the weapon of nonviolence, Gandhi answered: "No". On the contrary, nonviolence was the only thing that was now left in the field, he said. "It is the only thing that the atom bomb cannot destroy. I did not move a muscle when I first heard that the atom bomb had wiped out Hiroshima. On the contrary, I said to myself, 'Unless now the world adopts nonviolence, it will spell certain suicide for mankind'."

To provide the antidote to the atom bomb, however, requires nonviolence of the highest type. It may be asked whether this would not make too heavy a demand on human nature. Answering this question Gandhi said: "The critics gratuitously assume the impossibility of human nature, as it is constituted, responding to the strain involved in nonviolent preparation. But that is begging the question. I say, "You have never tried the method on any scale. In so far as it has been tried, it has shown promising results."

After all, the change in our outlook and way of life demanded by Gandhi, by adopting nonviolence or ahimsa is not more drastic than that resulting from our going in the opposite direction. It only requires foresight, faith and determination to leave the trodden path and chalk out a new one, which would be for the benefit not only of the present generation but also countless generations to come. If we feel ourselves unable to undertake and achieve this at one step, let us at least make a move in the right direction by banning all the nuclear tests as a preliminary step towards the removal of the threat to human survival that confronts us today, and thus give humanity breathing time to think out and adopt further steps to rid the world of fear, distrust and suspicion which lie at the root of violence.

RAJIV GANDHI

INTRODUCTION

Rajiv Gandhi was the sixth prime minister of India. He was born in 1944. He was the youngest man to hold this highest post in country. He became a pilot. He had no interest in politics.

After Indira Gandhi's cold-blooded assassination he was chosen to lead his party. In Dec. 1984 he held eighth general elections to obtain a fresh mandate from the electorate. He was elected the Prime Minister of largest democracy in the world. He gave a new thrust to Indian economy. During his period Indians progress by leaps and pounds. On 21 May 1991 in the course of an election campaign. He died in a blast triggered by human bomb. The nation was shocked and plunged in grief.

Speech at Opening Session of Six-Nation Five Continent Peace Initiative, Stockholm, January 21, 1988

WE have come together in the New Year, a year which begins with a breath of hope for the survival of life upon our planet. We are gathered in a city known for its love of peace and harmony. In this bracing winter afternoon.

Stockholm seems suffused with the freshness of a new stirring in the air. We thank Prime Minister Carlsson and the friendly people of Sweden for giving us an opportunity in this beautiful city to reflect upon the distance we have covered and the horizons that lie ahead. As Dag Hammarskjold said:

"Only he who keeps his eye fixed on the horizon will find his right road."

When Olof Palme, Indira Gandhi and our distinguished colleagues in the Six-Nation Five-Continent Peace Initiative issued their first Appeal in May 1984, the dialogue between the nuclear powers had collapsed into accusations of ill-faith and mutual recrimination. When we met in New Delhi three years ago, the dialogue had just resumed. At Ixtapa, there was a glimmer of hope. Now, we have a treaty on the complete elimination of a category of nuclear missiles.

Something of the credit for this must go to the good sense of ordinary people, whose hopes and aspirations we have sought to articulate. Millions across the globe, including those in the nuclear weapon States and the military alliances, have instinctively perceived the incompatibility between nuclear confrontation and lasting of peace. The Six-Nation Five-Continent Peace initiative has given voice to their perceptions.

We sincerely congratulate General Secretary Gorbachev and President Reagan on their vision and on the sensitivity they have shown to the need to dismantle and destroy nuclear weapon systems. The INF Treaty Is a historic beginning, historic, certainly, but, equally certainly, just a beginning. There can be no relapsing into the comfortable complacency of coexisting with the instruments of our own destruction.

What has been achieved will prove a pyrrhic victory unless it leads irreversibly and without interruption to the complete elimination of nuclear weapons. The process may involve the phased reduction of levels of nuclear weaponry. But the goal must remain the dismantling of all nuclear arsenals, as the precursor to general and complete disarmament.

Warheads have been uncoupled from missiles in one class of nuclear weapons. This is not enough. Warheads must be eliminated. Equally, the pursuit of peace must be uncoupled from strategies of nuclear deterrence, and such strategies must be universally repudiated. The militarization of international relations must end. The international order must be based on peaceful coexistence. We have to have a world free of nuclear weapons. Indeed, eventually, we have to have a world free of all weapons.

It is disturbing that, in certain quarters, there is a strident assertion that disarmament is not only utopian but dangerous. We must change the thinking of establishments reared in the theology of nuclear deterrence. They argue that nuclear weapons keep the peace. This is false. If nuclear weapons exist, they will one day be used, as they were in Hiroshima and Nagasaki, as all weapons have been throughout history. And, on the last day, it will make little difference whether their use was by design or by accident. The nuclear debris will bury all hopes of reprieve. There will be no going back, no survival, none to tell the tale. There will be no lessons to be drawn for the future - or there will be no future.

Therefore, even as we congratulate the United States and the Soviet Union, we seek assurance that the treaty they have signed in Washington constitutes the commencement of a time-bound process of nuclear disarmament. What has been covered so far is just a tiny fraction of the awesome armories of global annihilation- 97% remains. Only the United States and the Soviet Union have initiated this small step.

This small step must lead to many more. The other three nuclear weapon powers must be inducted into the process. The process of global 'nuclear disarmament must be reinforced by those countries which are able to cross the threshold of not doing so. There must be no assistance, surreptitious or overt, to those trying to acquire nuclear weapons.

There must be no adding of new dimensions to nuclear weaponry. The chimera of an impenetrable shield in space must be abandoned. There is no "ultimate defense" that can be devised by technology. The search for technological answers thwarts the real search for durable peace. There is no technological solution to the problems of war and peace. It is in the human mind that the defenses for peace are built. Human destiny cannot be mortgaged to a machine.

All quantitative improvements in nuclear weapons must be foregone so that reductions in stockpiles are not offset by weapons of greater destructive power, more accurate and even more swift. Hence, the ineluctable need for an immediate moratorium on all nuclear tests, to set the stage for a Comprehensive Test Ban Treaty.

Another great danger arises from new weapons systems and subtle refinements in sophisticated armaments. We should cry halt to this arms race in emerging technologies. The race is on in conventional and nuclear weapons. It is also insiduously penetrating totally new areas. We should identify these technological developments, debar their military applications, and prevent the emergence of new ways of dealing death.

What we need to end is the option of unleashing global devastation or holding the survival of humanity to ransom. We must protect humanity as much from the known dangers of extinction as from those that are still unknown.

There must also be radical reductions in conventional armaments. The process of conventional disarmament should begin where the bulk of such arms is concentrated and extends to other regions of the world. The ultimate objective should be general and complete disarmament.

What we seek is not a marginal adjustment in the machinery of nuclear confrontation, nor a partial or temporary scaling down of the arms race. What we seek is an effective structure of international security, a structure that discards obsolete mindsets, dangerous delusions, and destructive strategic doctrines. Distant though the prospect of a nuclear-free world might seem, it is a prospect. We must start giving thought now to the international order we would like to see prevail in a world which is rid of nuclear weapons. We have to revert to first principles of nonviolence and tolerance, of compassion and understanding-of one world for one humanity. Coercion must give way to reason. Spheres of influence and special privileges must yield to a true democracy of nations. The cornering of resources for weaponry must be transmuted into the sharing of resources for global development. The pursuit of dominance must be replaced by coexistence and cooperation.

SMT. PRATIBHA DEVISINGH PATIL

PRESIDENT OF INDIA

INTRODUCTION

Pratibha Patil (Marathi, born Dec. 19, 1934) is the 12th and current President of India. She is India's first female president. She was sworn in as President of India on July 25, 2007 by the Chief Justice of India K. G. Balakrishnan. She succeeded Dr. A.P.J. Abdul Kalam. She received her M.A. from Mooljee Jaitha (M.J.) College, Jalgaon and obtained a law degree from the Government Law College, Mumbai. She married educator Devisingh Ransingh Shekhawat on July 7, 1965. The couple have a son and a daughter. Pratibha Patil began her political career in 1962 at the age of 27. Pratibha Patil resigned as the Governor of Rajasthan on June 21, 2007, due to her presidential candidacy.

SPEECH AT BANQUET IN HONOUR OF THE QUEEN OF THE NETHERLANDS New Delhi, 24th October 2007

YOUR Majesty Queen Beatrix,

Your Royal Highness Willem-Alexander, Crown Prince of Orange,

Princess Maxima,

Ladies and Gentleman,

On behalf of the Government and people of India, it gives me great pleasure to warmly welcome Your Majesty as well as the Crown Prince of Orange, Princess Maxima and your delegation to India.

We appreciate the special affinity and deep affection of the Dutch Royal Family for India. We recall Your Majesty's memorable visit to India twenty-one years ago in January 1986. That was an important milestone in our relations. We also remember the role played by His Royal Highness, Prince Claus in fostering greater engagement between our two countries.

Contacts between India and the Netherlands go back to several centuries and include the first voyage to the Indian Ocean by Cornelius Houtman in 1595 as well as by two Dutch ships reaching India in 1597. In the 17th century, Dutch scholars studied Sanskrit, Tamil and Telugu. There are still remnants of Dutch settlements in Gujarat, Tamil Nadu and West Bengal - where traces of Dutch influence in maps and manuscripts, ornaments and furniture and the famous Delft tiles have been found. Exchanges between historians, economists, sociologists, orientalists constitute a major element in cultural exchanges between our two countries. The Kern Institute in the prestigious University of Leiden and the world famous Tropical Institute are repositories of this interest. It is vital that such interest is nurtured as it fosters greater understanding and mutual goodwill. The cultural agreements concluded today will give impetus to cultural exchanges. I hope the planned Festival of India in the Netherlands in 2008 will give the Dutch people a glimpse of India's diverse cultural tradition.

I am happy that our bilateral relations have begun to recapture the vibrancy of these historic contacts. Our bilateral trade has doubled in the past five years. The Netherlands is now among our top ten trading partners. There has been useful investment in India by Dutch companies spread across telecommunication, financial services, agro processing, chemicals and pharmaceutical sectors. The Netherlands, with its renowned expertise in water management, ports, agro-technologies and energy, has much to offer to India.

Recently, there has been a regular exchange of visits at the highest level. The visit of Prime Minister Jan Peter Balkenende to India in January 2006 and Prime Minister Dr. Manmohan Singh to your country in November 2004, during which the India-EU Strategic Partnership was launched, mark significant steps in further deepening and diversifying our relationship. Your visit represents a new high point in such contacts.

Your Majesty's visit to India comes at an interesting time. I do hope that what you see and experience this time will give you a glimpse of a new and dynamic India, the boundless energy and creativity of our people and their march towards prosperity. As one who has had a long-standing interest in the development of India and knowledge of our efforts, Your Majesty would be interested to see the advances in the knowledge economy and in the progressive development of our human resources.

India attaches importance to its relations with the Netherlands. We are also happy to note that in 2006, Prime Minister Balkenende's government declared India as a priority country in Dutch foreign policy. We have reason to be satisfied with the new momentum in our relations. We take particular note of the expansion in economic and commercial relations and the serious interest on both sides to forge cooperation in the fields of our respective expertise and competence.

India and the Netherlands share a common commitment to democratic governance, the rule of law, respect for human rights and religious freedom. Our two countries have enjoyed a tradition of tolerance and have fostered diversity in their social fabric. In India we have evolved a composite culture that celebrates the unity in our diversity. These shared values provide a strong foundation to our ties.

Your Majesty, we are confident that your visit will contribute to the further development of relations between our two countries and flourishing ties between our peoples.

Excellencies, Ladies and Gentlemen, may I request you to join me in a toast: -

- to the health of Her Majesty Queen of the Netherlands

- to friendship and cooperation between India and the Netherlands.

SWAMI VIVEKANANDA

INTRODUCTION

Swami Vivekananda was was born on 12th January 1863 in Calcutta. His parents called him Narendra.

His father was Vishwanatha Datta and his mother Bhuvaneshwari Devi.

He established Shri Ramakrishan Mission to carry on the propagation of his ideas. He visited many cities in North India in response to public demand. He visited America again at the invitation of his American disciples. He participated in the Conference of Religions in Paris and returned home. On 4th July 1902 he performed his daily routine. He taught his disciples as usual. He rested for a while after food; after some time he had a shock. Swamiji left his body at an young age of 39 on the 4th of July 1902.

The World Parliament of Religions, Chicago
WELCOME ADDRESS - Chicago, Sept 11, 1893

SISTERS and Brothers of America,

It fills my heart with joy unspeakable to rise in response to the warm and cordial welcome which you have given us. I thank you in the name of the most ancient order of monks in the world; I thank you in the name of the mother of religions, and I thank you in the name of millions and millions of Hindu people of all classes and sects.

My thanks, also, to some of the speakers on this platform who, referring to the delegates from the Orient, have told you that these men from far-off nations may well claim the honor of bearing to different lands the idea of toleration. I am proud to belong to a religion which has taught the world both tolerance and universal acceptance. We believe not only in universal toleration, but we accept all religions as true. I am proud to belong to a nation which has sheltered the persecuted and the refugees of all religions and all nations of the earth. I am proud to tell you that we have gathered in our bosom the purest remnant of the Israelites, who came to Southern India and took refuge with us in the very year in which their holy temple was shattered to pieces by Roman tyranny. I am proud to belong to the religion which has sheltered and is still fostering the remnant of the grand Zoroastrian nation. I will quote to you, brethren, a few lines from a hymn which I remember to have repeated from my earliest boyhood, which is every day repeated by millions of human beings: "As the different streams having their sources in different paths which men take through different tendencies, various though they appear, crooked or straight, all lead to Thee."

The present convention, which is one of the most august assemblies ever held, is in itself a vindication, a declaration to the world of the wonderful doctrine preached in the Gita: "Whosoever comes to Me, through whatsoever form, I reach him; all men are struggling through paths which in the end lead to me." Sectarianism, bigotry, and its horrible descendant, fanaticism, have long possessed this beautiful earth. They have filled the earth with violence, drenched it often and often with human blood, destroyed civilization and sent whole nations to despair. Had it not been for these horrible demons, human society would be far more advanced than it is now. But their time is come; and I fervently hope that the bell that tolled this morning in honor of this convention may be the death-knell of all fanaticism, of all persecutions with the sword or with the pen, and of all uncharitable feelings between persons wending their way to the same goal.

The World Parliament of Religions, Chicago
CONCLUDING ADDRESS - Chicago, Sept 27, 1893

THE World's Parliament of Religions has become an accomplished fact, and the merciful Father has helped those who laboured to bring it into existence, and crowned with success their most unselfish labour.My thanks to those noble souls whose large hearts and love of truth first dreamed this wonderful dream and then realized it. My thanks to the shower of liberal sentiments that has overflowed this platform. My thanks to this enlightened audience for their uniform kindness to me and for their appreciation of every thought that tends to smooth the friction of religions. A few jarring notes were heard from time to time in this harmony. My special thanks to them, for they have, by their striking contrast, made general harmony the sweeter.Much has been said of the common ground of religious unity. I am not going just now to venture my own theory. But if any one here hopes that this unity will come by the triumph of any one of the religions and the destruction of the others, to him I say, "Brother, yours is an impossible hope." Do I wish that the Christian would become Hindu? God forbid. Do I wish that the Hindu or Buddhist would become Christian? God forbid.

The seed is put in the ground, and earth and air and water are placed around it. Does the seed become the earth, or the air, or the water? No. It becomes a plant. It develops after the law of its own growth, assimilates the air, the earth, and the water, converts them into plant substance, and grows into a plant.Similar is the case with religion. The Christian is not to become a Hindu or a Buddhist, nor a Hindu or a Buddhist to become a Christian. But each must assimilate the spirit of the others and yet preserve his individuality and grow according to his own law of growth.

If the Parliament of Religions has shown anything to the world, it is this: It has proved to the world that holiness, purity and charity are not the exclusive possessions of any church in the world, and that every system has produced men and women of the most exalted character. In the face of this evidence, if anybody dreams of the exclusive survival of his own religion and the destruction of the others, I pity him from the bottom of my heart, and point out to him that upon the banner of every religion will soon be written in spite of resistance: "Help and not fight," "Assimilation and not Destruction," "Harmony and Peace and not Dissension."

WINSTON CHURCHILL

INTRODUCTION

The Right Honourable Sir Winston Leonard Spencer Churchill (1874-1965), the son of Lord Randolph Churchill and an American mother, was educated at Harrow and Sandhurst. After a brief but eventful career in the army, he became a Conservative Member of Parliament in 1900. He held many high posts in Liberal and Conservative governments during the first three decades of the century. At the outbreak of the Second World War, he was appointed First Lord of the Admiralty - a post which he had earlier held from 1911 to 1915. In May, 1940, he became Prime Minister and Minister of Defence and remained in office until 1945.

Retreat from Flanders speech, June 4th 1940

FROM the moment when the defences at Sedan on the Meuse were broken at the end of the second week in May only a rapid retreat to Amiens and the south could have saved the British-French armies who had entered Belgium at the appeal of the Belgian King. This strategic fact was not immediately realized. The French High Command hoped it would be able to close the gap. the armies of the north were under their orders. Moreover, a retirement of that kind would have involved almost certainly the destruction of a fine Belgian Army of twenty divisions and abandonment of the whole of Belgium.

Therefore, when the force and scope of the German penetration was realized and when the new French Generalissimo, General Weygand, assumed command in place of General Gamelin, an effort was made by the French and British Armies in Belgium to keep holding the right hand of the Belgians and give their own right hand to the newly created French Army which was to advance across the Somme in great strength.

However, the German eruption swept like a sharp scythe south of Amiens to the rear of the armies in the north-eight or nine armoured divisions, each with about 400 armoured vehicles of different kinds divisible into small self-contained units. This forced cut off all communications between us and the main French Army. It severed our communications for food and ammunition. It ran first through Amiens, afterward through Abbeville, and it shore its way up the coast to Boulogne and Calais, almost to Dunkerque.

MASS OF ARMY FOLLOWED

Behind this armored and mechanized onslaught came a number of German divisions in lorries, and behind them, again, plodded comparatively slowly the dull, brute mass of the ordinary German Army and German people, always ready to be led to the trampling down in other lands of liberties and comforts they never have known in their own. I said this armoured scythe stroke almost reached Dunkerque-almost but not quite. Boulogne and Calais were scenes of desperate fighting. The guards defended Boulogne for a while and were then withdrawn by orders from this country.

The rifle brigade of the Sixtieth Rifles (Queen Victoria's Rifles), with a battalion of British tanks and 1,000 Frenchmen, in all about 4,000 strong, defended Calais to the last. The British brigadier was given an hour to surrender. He spurned the offer. Four days of intense street fighting passed before the silence reigned in Calais which marked the end of a memorable resistance.

Only thirty unwounded survivors were brought off by the navy, and we do not know the fate of their comrades. Their sacrifice was not, however, in vain. At least two armoured divisions which otherwise would have been turned against the B. E. F. had to be sent to overcome them. They have added another page to the glories of the light division.The time gained enabled the Gravelines water line to be flooded and held by French troops. Thus the port of Dunkerque was held open. When it was found impossible for the armies of the north to reopen their communications through Amiens with the main French armies, only one choice remained. It seemed, indeed, forlorn hope. The Belgian and French armies were almost surrounded. Their sole line of retreat was to a single port and it neighbouring beaches. They were pressed on every side by heavy attacks and were far outnumbered in the air.

When a week ago today I asked the House to fix this afternoon for the occasion of a statement, I feared it would be my hard lot to announce from this box the greatest military disaster of our long history.

WERE PESSIMISTIC AT FIRST

I thought, and there were good judges who agreed with me, that perhaps 20,000 or 30,000 men might be re-embarked, but it certainly seemed that the whole French First Army and the whole B. E. F., north of the Amiens-Abbeville gap would be broken up in open field or else have to capitulate for lack of food and ammunition.

These were the hard and heavy tidings I called on the House and nation to prepare themselves for. The whole root and core and brain of the British armies of later years, seemed due to perish upon the field. That was the prospect a week ago, gut another blow which might have proved final was still to fall upon us.

The King of Belgians called upon us to come to his aid. Had not this ruler and his government severed themselves from the Allies who rescued their country from extinction in the late ware, and had they not sought refuge in what has been proved to be fatal neutrality, then the French and British armies at the outset might well have saved not only Belgium but perhaps even Holland.At the last moment, when Belgium was already invaded, King Leopold called upon us to come to his aid, and even at the last moment we came. He and his brave and efficient army of nearly half a million strong guarded our eastern flank; this kept open our only retreat to the sea.

Suddenly, without any prior consultation and with the least possible notice, without the advice of his ministers and on his own personal act, he sent a plenipotentiary to the German Command surrendering his army and exposing our flank and the means of retreat.

I asked the House a week ago to suspend its judgment because the facts were not clear. I do not think there is now any reason why we should not form our own opinions upon this pitiful episode. The surrender of the Belgian Army compelled the British Army at the shortest notice to cover a flank to the sea of more than thirty miles' length which otherwise would have been cut off.

TWO FORCES LOST CONTACT

In doing this and closing this flank, contact was lost inevitably between the British and two of three corps forming the First French Army who were then further from the coast than we were. It seemed impossible that large numbers of Allied troops could reach the coast. The enemy attacked on all sides in great strength and fierceness, and their main power, air force, was thrown into the battle.

The enemy began to fire cannon along the beaches by which alone shipping could approach or depart. They sowed magnetic mines in the channels and seas and sent repeated waves of hostile aircraft, sometimes more than 100 strong, to cast bombs on a single pier that remained and on the sand dunes.Their U-boats, one of which was sunk, and motor launches took their toll of the vast traffic which now began. For four or five days the intense struggle raged. All armoured divisions, or what was left of them, together with great masses of German infantry and artillery, hurled themselves on the ever narrowing and contracting appendix within which the British and French armies fought.

Meanwhile the Royal Navy, with the willing help of countless merchant seamen and host of volunteers, strained every nerve and every effort and every craft to embark the British and Allied troops. Over 220 light warships and more than 650 other vessels were engaged. they had to approach this difficult coast, often in adverse weather, under and almost ceaseless hail of bombs and increasing concentration of artillery fire. Nor were the seas themselves free from mines and torpedoes.

It was in conditions such as these that our men carried on with little or not rest for days and nights, moving troops across dangerous waters and bringing with them always the men whom they had rescued. The numbers they brought back are the measure of their devotion and their courage. Hospital ships, which were plainly marked, were the special target for Nazi bombs, but the men women aboard them never faltered in their duty. Meanwhile the R. A. F., who already had been intervening in the battle so far as its range would allow it to go from home bases, now used a part of its main metropolitan fighter strength to strike at German bombers. The struggle was protracted and fierce. Suddenly the scene has cleared. The crash and thunder has momentarily, but only for the moment, died away. The miracle of deliverance achieved by the valour and perseverance, perfect discipline, faultless service, skill and unconquerable vitality is a manifesto to us all.

ENEMY "ROUGHLY HANDLED"

The enemy was hurled back by the British and French troops. He was so roughly handled that he dare not molest their departure seriously. The air force decisively defeated the main strength of the German Air Force and inflicted on them a loss of at least four to one.

The navy, using nearly 1,000 ships of all kinds, carried over 335,000 men, French and British, from the jaws of death back to their native land and to the tasks which lie immediately before them.

We must be very careful not to assign to this deliverance attributes of a victory. Wars are not won by evacuations, but there was a victory inside this deliverance which must be noted.

Many of our soldiers coming back have not seen the air force at work. They only saw the bombers which escaped their protective attack. This was a great trial of strength between the British and German Air Forces.

Can you conceive of a greater objective for the power of Germany in the air than to make all evacuations from these beaches impossible and to sink all of the ships, numbering almost 1,000? Could there have been an incentive of greater military importance and significance to the whole purpose of the war?

They tried hard and were beaten back. They were frustrated in their task; we have got the armies away and they have paid fourfold for any losses sustained. Very large formations of German airplanes were turned on several occasions from the attack by a quarter their number of R. A. F. planes and dispersed in different directions. Twelve airplanes have been hunted by two. One airplane was driven into the water and cast away by the charge of a British airplane which had no more ammunition.

All of our types and our pilots have been vindicated. The Hurricane, Spitfire and Defiance have been vindicated. When I consider how much greater would be our advantage in defending the air above this island against overseas attacks, defending the air above this island against overseas attacks, I find in these facts a sure basis on which practical and reassuring thoughts may rest, and I will pay my tribute to these young airmen.

May it not be that the cause of civilization itself will be defended by the skill and devotion of a few thousand airmen? There never has been, I suppose, in all the history of the world such opportunity for youth.

The Knights of the Round Table and Crusaders have fallen back into distant days, not only distant but prosaic; but these young men are going forth every morning, going forth holding in their hands an instrument of colossal shattering power, of whom it may be said that every morn brought forth a noble chance and every chance brought forth a noble deed. These young men deserve our gratitude, as all brave men who in so many ways and so many occasions are ready and will continue to be ready to give their life and their all to their native land.

MORE THAN 30,000 LOST

I return to the army. In a long series of very fierce battles, now on this front, now on that, fighting on three fronts at once, battles fought by two or three divisions against an equal or sometimes larger number

of the enemy, and fought very fiercely on old ground so many of us knew so well, our losses in men exceed 30,000 in killed, wounded and missing. I take this occasion for expressing the sympathy of the House with those who have suffered bereavement or are still anxious.

The President of the Board of Trade (Sir Andrew Duncan) is not here today. His son has been killed, and many here have felt private affliction of the sharpest form, but I would say about the missing - we have had a large number of wounded come home safely to this country - there may be very many reported missing who will come back home some day.

In the confusion of departure it is inevitable that many should be cut off. Against this loss of over 30,000 men we may set the far heavier loss certainly inflicted on the enemy, but our losses in material are enormous. We have perhaps lost one-third of the men we lost in the opening days of the battle on March 21, 1918, but we have lost nearly as many guns - nearly 1,000 - and all our transport and all the armoured vehicles that were with the army of the north.

These losses will impose further delay on the expansion of our military strength. That expansion has not been proceeding as fast as we had hoped. The best of all we had to give has been given to the B. E. F., and although they had not the number of tanks and some articles of equipment which were desirable they were a very well and finely equipped army. They had the first fruits of all our industry had to give. That has gone and now here is further delay.

How long it will be, how long it will last depends upon the exertions which we make on this island. An effort, the like of which has never been seen in our records, is now being made. Work is proceeding night and day. Sundays and week days. Capital and labor have cast aside their interests, rights and customs and put everything into the common stock. Already the flow of munitions has leaped forward. There is no reason why we should not in a few months overtake the sudden

and serious loss that has come upon us without retarding the development of our general program.

Nevertheless, our thankfulness at the escape of our army with so many men, and the thankfulness of their loved ones, who passed through an agonizing week, must not blind us to the fact that what happened in France and Belgium is a colossal military disaster.

The French Army has been weakened, the Belgian Army has been lost and a large part of those fortified lines upon which so much faith was reposed has gone, and many valuable mining districts and factories have passed into the enemy's possession.

The whole of the Channel ports are in his hands, with all the strategic consequences that follow from that, and we must expect another blow to be struck almost immediately at us or at France. We were told that Hitler has plans for invading the British Isles. This has often been thought of before. When Napoleon lay at Boulogne for a year with his flat-bottomed boats and his Grand Army, some one told him there were bitter weeds in England. There certainly were and a good many more of them have since been returned. The whole question of defence against invasion is powerfully affected by the fact that we have for the time being in this island incomparably more military forces than we had in the last war. But his will not continue. We shall not be content with a defensive war. We have our duty to our Allies.

We have to reconstitute and build up the B. E. F. once again under its gallant Commander in Chief, Lord Gort. All this is en train. But now I feel we must put our defence in this island into such a high state of organization that the fewest possible numbers will be required to give effectual security and that the largest possible potential offensive effort may be released. On this we are now engaged. It would be very convenient to enter upon this subject in secret sessions. The government would not necessarily be able to reveal any great military secrets, but we should like to have our discussions free and without the restraint imposed

by the fact that they would be read the next day by the enemy.

The government would benefit by the views expressed by the House. I understand that some request is to be made on this subject, which will be readily acceded to by the government. We have found it necessary to take measures of increasing stringency, not only against enemy aliens and suspicious characters of other nationalities but also against British subjects who may become a danger or a nuisance should the war be transported to the United Kingdom.

I know there are a great many people affected by the orders which we have made who are people affected by the orders which we have made who are passionate enemies of Nazi Germany. I am very sorry from them, but we cannot, under the present circumstances, draw all the distinctions we should like to do. If parachute landings were attempted and fierce nights followed, those unfortunate people would be far better out of the way for their own sake as well as ours.

There is, however, another class for which I feel not the slightest sympathy. Parliament has given us powers to put down fifth column activities with the strongest hand, and we shall use those powers subject to the supervision and correcting of the House without hesitation until we are satisfied and more than satisfied that this malignancy in our midst has been effectually stamped out.

NO ABSOLUTE GUARANTEE

Turning once again to the question of invasion, there has, I will observe, never been a period in all those long centuries of which we boast when an absolute guarantee against invasion, still less against .serous raids, could have been given to our people. In the days of Napoleon the same wind which might have carried his transports across the Channel might have driven away a blockading fleet. There is always the chance, and it is that chance which has excited and befooled the in.aginations of many continental tyrants.

We are assured that novel methods will be adopted, and when we see the originality, malice and ingenuity of aggression which our enemy displays we may certainly prepare ourselves for every kind of novel stratagem and every kind of brutal and treacherous manoeuvre. I think no idea is so outlandish that it should not be considered and viewed with a watchful, but at the same time steady, eye. We must never forget the solid assurances of sea power and those which belong to air power if they can be locally exercised. I have myself full confidence that if all do their duty and if the best arrangements are made, as they are being made, we shall prove ourselves once again able to defend our island home, ride out the storms of ware outlive the menace of tyranny, if necessary, for years, if necessary, alone.

At any rate, that is what we are going to try to do. that is the resolve of His Majesty's Government, every man of them. that is the will of Parliament and the nation. The British Empire and the French Republic, linked together in their cause and their need, will defend to the death their native soils, aiding each other like good comrades to the utmost of their strength, even though a large tract of Europe and many old and famous States have fallen or may fall into the grip of the Gestapo and all the odious apparatus of Nazi rule.

We shall not flag nor fail. We shall go on to the end. We shall fight in France and on the seas and oceans; we shall fight with growing confidence and growing strength in the air. We shall defend our island whatever the cost may be; we shall fight on beaches, landing grounds, in fields, in streets and on the hills. We shall never surrender and even if, which I do not for the moment believe, this island or a large part of it were subjugated and starving, then our empire beyond the seas, armed and guarded by the British Fleet, will carry on the struggle until in God's good time the New World with all its power and might, sets forth to the liberation and rescue of the Old.